D1643423

THE TRESPASSER

THE PHOENIX EDITION OF D. H. LAWRENCE

D. H. LAWRENCE

The Trespasser

WITH AN INTRODUCTION BY
RICHARD ALDINGTON

THE POLYTECHNIC OF WALES
LIBRARY
TREFOREST

HEINEMANN : LONDON

823.912LAW (AW 820 - 31
LAW
LAW

William Heinemann Ltd.
15 Queen Street, Mayfair, London W1X 8BE

LONDON MELBOURNE TORONTO
JOHANNESBURG AUCKLAND

FIRST PUBLISHED IN THE PHOENIX EDITION 1955
REPRINTED 1961, 1965, 1970, 1976

R   0 434 40707 0

PRINTED IN GREAT BRITAIN BY
REDWOOD BURN LIMITED
TROWBRIDGE AND ESHER

214145

(10.12.91)

THE TRESPASSER

INTRODUCTION BY RICHARD ALDINGTON

D. H. LAWRENCE had an easy start on his literary career, if you
remember that it was achieved by merit alone—one of the least
important factors in immediate success. A rebuff by an un-
named *Daily News* writer had confirmed Lawrence so much in
his own self-mistrust that he had put aside all thought of
publishing. His faith in himself as a writer was slight, and he
had a deep dislike for the literary world, "hateful yet powerful
. . . like a disagreeable substratum under a fair country".
Then, in the summer of 1909, Jessie Chambers, the closest
friend of his youth, sent some of his work to *The English
Review*, which, strange to say, was then the best literary
periodical in England. The editor, F. M. Hueffer, accepted
some poems and a story; and later recommended to William
Heinemann a novel then called *Nethermere* (later *The White
Peacock*) on which Lawrence had worked since he was twenty.

The novel, to Lawrence's surprise, was accepted; and it may
have been—probably was—the stimulus of this unexpected
success which started Lawrence off in the spring of 1910 on the
first draft of his second novel, *The Saga of Siegmund*, changed
to *The Livanters*, and after other forms to *The Trespasser*. Large
portions of this first manuscript draft still exist, and are closer
to the final text than one would expect. Then came a check.
In his pretentious literary-London manner Hueffer pontificated:

"This book is a rotten work of genius. It has no construction
or form—it is execrably bad art, being all variations on a
theme. Also it is erotic—not that I personally mind that, but
an erotic work *must* be good art, which this is not."

Anyone who has read Hueffer's phoney novelistic trash will
appreciate the unconscious humour of that. It is not clear
whether or not it came from his reader's report, but most
unfortunately for Lawrence, Heinemann himself wrote that he
did not much care for the book, but said he would publish it.
Piqued, Lawrence withdrew the novel; and Hueffer then told
him he was quite right not to publish it—"it would damage

v

your reputation, perhaps permanently". Lawrence naïvely accepted this high-hatting, for we find him writing to Martin Secker that he had decided not to publish the book "because it is erotic". The chastity of these Edwardian gentlemen is a bewildering theme for meditation.

Some eighteen months later, after Lawrence had begun to write *Paul Morel*—now known to the world as *Sons and Lovers* —the script of *The Trespasser* was seen by Edward Garnett, then reader to Duckworth's. He saw its high qualities at once, and wrote Lawrence a letter of appreciative comment which the poor author found "very exciting". This was in December 1911, when Lawrence's sufferings over the death of his mother a year earlier had culminated in pneumonia and tuberculosis. He came very near to death, saved, he believed, only by the love of his sister, Ada, as earlier he had been saved from death through double pneumonia by his mother. He was compelled to resign his school-teacher's job (hundred a year) for which he had worked so hard all through his youth; and found himself ill, in debt and penniless, save for fifty pounds which Heinemann promised and later paid him.

Meanwhile Garnett lent Lawrence seven guineas for a month's convalescence in a Bournemouth boarding-house— which period Lawrence devoted to re-writing *The Trespasser*. Within four weeks he had completed over 300 of the 482 manuscript pages, and had the book done in February. Duckworth gladly took the novel, and produced it in May 1912. Mitchell Kennerley, of New York, published a small edition from Duckworth's sheets in the same year. For twelve years the novel remained out of print; then revived with Lawrence's ever-growing fame, and was reprinted at least five times between 1924 and 1939.

The Trespasser has rather been overlooked, coming as it did between *The White Peacock* and *Sons and Lovers*— large-scale novels where Lawrence concentrated the experiences of his youth. But *The Trespasser*, whose main action is included within five or six days, has much interest both biographically and artistically. It is the first example of Lawrence's unique power of crowding an immense series of emotional experiences and sense impressions into a very few days, of remembering them with precise and detailed variety, and of evoking them with a skill which makes the poet's experience his reader's. This is the quality of Lawrence's writing, its being "rooted in life" as Katherine Mansfield said of him, which gives him his unique charm and power. It is not *vérissime;* for what is "rooted in life" is a personality of exceptionally poetic imagination and perception.

Nineteen of *The Trespasser's* thirty-one chapters are occupied with the love experiences and life-and-nature perceptions of a man and a girl during a five days' stay on the Isle of Wight and their return to London. Now, Lawrence had stayed on the island in August of 1909, and its beauties had made so deep an impression on him that you might almost say that the Isle of Wight is the "hero" of the book. It means almost more to him than his characters—that "spirit of place" he has interpreted with such beauty and variety. And remember that all those precise descriptions were not based on careful notes—Lawrence never took notes—but on memory, ten months after for the first draft, thirty months for the second.

This nympholepsis, this ecstasy of sky, sea and earth, is an inseparable part of the ecstatic, if sadly frustrated, loves of Helena and Siegmund. There is more than one obstacle to their sexual happiness. Siegmund is a married man with children. More complex, seemingly, is the fact that Helena's subtle, over-sensitive nature recoils from the natural consummation—"she belonged to that class of 'dreaming women' with whom passion exhausts itself at the mouth. Her desire was accomplished in a real kiss". Perhaps; but Siegmund under his flimsy disguise is obviously Lawrence; and the girl's reluctance to consummate was obviously due to the fact that she had been taught to require first the bureaucratic sanction of legal marriage.

Siegmund's wife and children are a symbol of Lawrence's own inhibition, that mother-love which made it impossible for him during her lifetime to give himself to another woman. The scenes where Beatrice and her children combine to harry with their hatred a supposedly erring husband and father are a transposition from Lawrence's own childhood. He had been used to combining with his mother against an allegedly drunken father; and he used the same memories in the opening of *Aaron's Rod.* The suicide of Siegmund is unconvincing, an unreal tragedy invented perhaps to frighten the girl in real life into consenting. How much Lawrence hated and despised suicide may be seen by his references to the fate of Harry Crosby in *The Letters.*

Helena is almost the most interesting of all Lawrence's

women characters, certainly drawn from life, and from the same person who inspired several of his early poems and who figures in the posthumously published *The Witch "A La Mode"*. Lawrence never understood her, yet she lives clearly in his burning words and was obviously a decisive influence on his development as a man and an artist.

THE TRESPASSER

CHAPTER I

"TAKE off that mute, do!" cried Louisa, snatching her fingers from the piano keys, and turning abruptly to the violinist.

Helena looked slowly from her music.

"My dear Louisa," she replied, "it would be simply unendurable." She stood tapping her white skirt with her bow in a kind of a pathetic forbearance.

"But I can't understand it," cried Louisa, bouncing on her chair with the exaggeration of one who is indignant with a beloved. "It is only lately you would even submit to muting your violin. At one time you would have refused flatly, and no doubt about it."

"I have only lately submitted to many things," replied Helena, who seemed weary and stupefied, but still sententious. Louisa drooped from her bristling defiance.

"At any rate," she said, scolding in tones too naked with love, "I don't like it."

"Go on from *Allegro*," said Helena, pointing with her bow to the place on Louisa's score of the Mozart sonata. Louisa obediently took the chords, and the music continued.

A young man, reclining in one of the wicker arm-chairs by the fire, turned luxuriously from the girls to watch the flames poise and dance with the music. He was evidently at his ease, yet he seemed a stranger in the room.

It was the sitting-room of a mean house standing in line with hundreds of others of the same kind, along a wide road in South London. Now and again the trams hummed by, but the room was foreign to the trams and to the sound of the London traffic. It was Helena's room, for which she was responsible. The walls were of the dead-green colour of August foliage; the green carpet, with its border of polished floor, lay like a square of grass in a setting of black loam. Ceiling and frieze and fireplace were smooth white. There was no other colouring.

The furniture, excepting the piano, had a transitory look;

I

two light wicker arm-chairs by the fire, the two frail stands of
dark, polished wood, the couple of flimsy chairs, and the case
of books in the recess—all seemed uneasy, as if they might be
tossed out to leave the room clear, with its green floor and
walls, and its white rim of skirting-board, serene.

On the mantelpiece were white lustres, and a small soapstone
Buddha from China, grey, impassive, locked in his renuncia-
tion. Besides these, two tablets of translucent stone beautifully
clouded with rose and blood, and carved with Chinese symbols;
then a litter of mementoes, rock-crystals, and shells and scraps
of seaweed.

A stranger, entering, felt at a loss. He looked at the bare
wall-spaces of dark green, at the scanty furniture, and was
assured of his unwelcome. The only objects of sympathy in
the room were the white lamp that glowed on a stand near
the wall, and the large, beautiful fern, with narrow fronds,
which ruffled its cloud of green within the gloom of the
window-bay. These only, with the fire, seemed friendly.

The three candles on the dark piano burned softly, the music
fluttered on, but, like numbed butterflies, stupidly. Helena
played mechanically. She broke the music beneath her bow,
so that it came lifeless, very hurting to hear. The young man
frowned, and pondered. Uneasily, he turned again to the
players.

The violinist was a girl of twenty-eight. Her white dress,
high-waisted, swung as she forced the rhythm, determinedly
swaying to the time as if her body were the white stroke of a
metronome. It made the young man frown as he watched. Yet
he continued to watch. She had a very strong, vigorous body.
Her neck, pure white, arched in strength from the fine hollow
between her shoulders as she held the violin. The long white
lace of her sleeve swung, floated, after the bow.

Byrne could not see her face, more than the full curve of
her cheek. He watched her hair, which at the back was
almost of the colour of the soapstone idol, take the candle-
light into its vigorous freedom in front and glisten over her
forehead.

Suddenly Helena broke off the music, and dropped her arm
in irritable resignation. Louisa looked round from the piano,
surprised.

"Why," she cried, "wasn't it all right?"

Helena laughed wearily.

"It was all wrong," she answered, as she put her violin tenderly to rest.

"Oh, I'm sorry I did so badly," said Louisa in a huff. She loved Helena passionately.

"You didn't do badly at all," replied her friend, in the same tired, apathetic tone. "It was I."

When she had closed the black lid of her violin-case, Helena stood a moment as if at a loss. Louisa looked up with eyes full of affection, like a dog that did not dare to move to her beloved. Getting no response, she drooped over the piano. At length Helena looked at her friend, then slowly closed her eyes. The burden of this excessive affection was too much for her. Smiling faintly, she said, as if she were coaxing a child:

"Play some Chopin, Louisa."

"I shall only do that all wrong, like everything else," said the elder plaintively. Louisa was thirty-five. She had been Helena's friend for years.

"Play the mazurkas," repeated Helena calmly.

Louisa rummaged among the music. Helena blew out her violin-candle, and came to sit down on the side of the fire opposite to Byrne. The music began. Helena pressed her arms with her hands, musing.

"They are inflamed still!" said the young man.

She glanced up suddenly, her blue eyes, usually so heavy and tired, lighting up with a small smile.

"Yes," she answered, and she pushed back her sleeve, revealing a fine, strong arm, which was scarlet on the outer side from shoulder to wrist, like some long, red-burned fruit. The girl laid her cheek on the smarting soft flesh caressively.

"It is quite hot," she smiled, again caressing her sun-scalded arm with peculiar joy.

"Funny to see a sunburn like that in mid-winter," he replied, frowning. "I can't think why it should last all these months. Don't you ever put anything on to heal it?"

She smiled at him again, almost pitying, then put her mouth lovingly on the burn.

"It comes out every evening like this," she said softly, with curious joy.

"And that was August, and now it's February!" he exclaimed. "It must be psychological, you know. You make it come—the smart; you invoke it."

She looked up at him, suddenly cold.

"I! I never think of it," she answered briefly, with a kind of sneer.

The young man's blood ran back from her at her acid tone. But the mortification was physical only. Smiling quickly, gently—

"Never?" he re-echoed.

There was silence between them for some moments, whilst Louisa continued to play the piano for their benefit. At last:

"Drat it;" she exclaimed, flouncing round on the piano-stool. The two looked up at her.

"Ye did run well—what hath hindered you?" laughed Byrne.

"You!" cried Louisa. "Oh, I can't play any more," she added, dropping her arms along her skirt pathetically. Helena laughed quickly.

"Oh I can't, Helen!" pleaded Louisa.

"My dear," said Helena, laughing briefly, "you are really under *no* obligation *whatever*."

With the little groan of one who yields to a desire contrary to her self-respect, Louisa dropped at the feet of Helena, laid her arm and her head languishingly on the knee of her friend. The latter gave no sign, but continued to gaze in the fire. Byrne, on the other side of the hearth, sprawled in his chair, smoking a reflective cigarette.

The room was very quiet, silent even of the tick of a clock. Outside, the traffic swept by, and feet pattered along the pavement. But this vulgar storm of life seemed shut out of Helena's room, that remained indifferent, like a church. Two candles burned dimly as on an altar, glistening yellow on the dark piano. The lamp was blown out, and the flameless fire, a red rubble, dwindled in the grate, so that the yellow glow of the candles seemed to shine even on the embers. Still no one spoke.

At last Helena shivered slightly in her chair, though did not change her position. She sat motionless.

"Will you make coffee, Louisa?" she asked. Louisa lifted herself, looked at her friend, and stretched slightly.

"Oh!" she groaned voluptuously. "This is so comfortable!"

"Don't trouble then, I'll go. No, don't get up," said Helena, trying to disengage herself. Louisa reached and put her hands on Helena's wrists.

"I will go," she drawled, almost groaning with voluptuousness and appealing love.

Then, as Helena still made movements to rise, the elder

woman got up slowly, leaning as she did so all her weight on her friend.

"Where is the coffee?" she asked, affecting the dullness of lethargy. She was full of small affectations, being consumed with uneasy love.

"I think, my dear," replied Helena, "it is in its usual place."

"Oh—o-o-oh!" yawned Louisa, and she dragged herself out.

The two had been intimate friends for years, had slept together, and played together and lived together. Now the friendship was coming to an end.

"After all," said Byrne, when the door was closed, "if you're alive you've got to live."

Helena burst into a titter of amusement at this sudden remark.

"Wherefore?" she asked indulgently.

"Because there's no such thing as passive existence," he replied, grinning.

She curled her lip in amused indulgence of this very young man.

"I don't see it at all," she said.

"You can't," he protested, "any more than a tree can help budding in April—it can't help itself, if it's alive; same with you."

"Well, then"—and again there was the touch of a sneer—"if I can't help myself, why trouble, my friend?"

"Because—because I suppose *I* can't help myself—if it bothers me, it does. You see, I"—he smiled brilliantly—"am April."

She paid very little attention to him, but began in a peculiar reedy, metallic tone, that set his nerves quivering:

"But I am not a bare tree. All my dead leaves, they hang to me—and—and go through a kind of *danse macabre*——"

"But you bud underneath—like beech," he said quickly.

"Really, my friend," she said coldly, "I am too tired to bud."

"No," he pleaded, "no!" With his thick brows knitted, he surveyed her anxiously. She had received a great blow in August, and she still was stunned. Her face, white and heavy, was like a mask, almost sullen. She looked in the fire, forgetting him.

"You want March," he said—he worried endlessly over her—"to rip off your old leaves. I s'll have to be March," he laughed.

She ignored him again because of his presumption. He waited awhile, then broke out once more.

"You must start again—you must. Always you rustle your red leaves of a blasted summer. You are not dead. Even if you want to be, you're not. Even if it's a bitter thing to say, you have to say it: you are not dead. . . ."

Smiling a peculiar, painful smile, as if he hurt her, she turned to gaze at a photograph that hung over the piano. It was the profile of a handsome man in the prime of life. He was leaning slightly forward, as if yielding beneath a burden of life, or to the pull of fate. He looked out musingly, and there was no hint of rebellion in the contours of the regular features. The hair was brushed back, soft and thick, straight from his fine brow. His nose was small and shapely, his chin rounded, cleft, rather beautifully moulded. Byrne gazed also at the photo. His look became distressed and helpless.

"You cannot say you are dead with Siegmund," he cried brutally. She shuddered, clasped her burning arms on her breast, and looked into the fire. "You are not dead with Siegmund," he persisted, "so you can't say you live with him. You may live with his memory. But Siegmund is dead, and his memory is not he—himself." He made a fierce gesture of impatience. "Siegmund now—he is not a memory—he is not your dead red leaves—he is Siegmund Dead! And you do not know him, because you are alive, like me, so Siegmund Dead is a stranger to you."

With her head bowed down, cowering like a sulky animal, she looked at him under her brows. He stared fiercely back at her, but beneath her steady, glowering gaze he shrank, then turned aside.

"You stretch your hands blindly to the dead; you look backwards. No, you never touch the thing," he cried.

"I have the arms of Louisa always round my neck," came her voice, like the cry of a cat. She put her hands on her throat as if she must relieve an ache. He saw her lip raised in a kind of disgust, a revulsion from life. She was very sick after the tragedy.

He frowned, and his eyes dilated.

"Folk are good; they are good for one. You never have looked at them. You would linger hours over a blue weed, and let all the people down the road go by. Folks are better than a garden in full blossom——"

She watched him again. A certain beauty in his speech, and his passionate way, roused her when she did not want to be roused, when moving from her torpor was painful. At last——

"You are merciless, you know, Cecil," she said.

"And I will be," protested Byrne, flinging his hand at her. She laughed softly, wearily.

For some time they were silent. She gazed once more at the photograph over the piano, and forgot all the present. Byrne, spent for the time being, was busy hunting for some life-interest to give her. He ignored the simplest—that of love—because he was even more faithful than she to the memory of Siegmund, and blinder than most to his own heart.

"I do wish I had Siegmund's violin," she said quietly, but with great intensity. Byrne glanced at her, then away. His heart beat sulkily. His sanguine, passionate spirit dropped and slouched under her contempt. He, also, felt the jar, heard the discord. She made him sometimes pant with her own horror. He waited, full of hate and tasting of ashes, for the arrival of Louisa with the coffee.

CHAPTER II

SIEGMUND's violin, desired of Helena, lay in its case beside Siegmund's lean portmanteau in the white dust of the lumber-room in Highgate. It was worth twenty pounds, but Beatrice had not yet roused herself to sell it; she kept the black case out of sight.

Siegmund's violin lay in the dark, folded up, as he had placed it for the last time, with hasty, familiar hands, in its red silk shroud. After two dead months the first string had snapped, sharply striking the sensitive body of the instrument. The second string had broken near Christmas, but no one had heard the faint moan of its going. The violin lay mute in the dark, a faint odour of must creeping over the smooth, soft wood. Its twisted, withered strings lay crisped from the anguish of break-ing, smothered under the silk folds. The fragrance of Siegmund himself, with which the violin was steeped, slowly changed into an odour of must.

Siegmund died out even from his violin. He had infused it
with his life, till its fibres had been as the tissue of his own
flesh. Grasping his violin, he seemed to have his fingers on the
strings of his heart and of the heart of Helena. It was his little
beloved that drank his being and turned it into music. And
now Siegmund was dead; only an odour of must remained of
him in his violin.

It lay folded in silk in the dark, waiting. Six months before
it had longed for rest; during the last nights of the season, when
Siegmund's fingers had pressed too hard, when Siegmund's
passion, and joy, and fear had hurt, too, the soft body of his
little beloved, the violin had sickened for rest. On that last
night of opera, without pity Siegmund had struck the closing
phrases from the fiddle, harsh in his impatience, wild in
anticipation.

The curtain came down, the great singers bowed, and Siegmund felt the spattering roar of applause quicken his pulse. It
was hoarse, and savage, and startling on his inflamed soul,
making him shiver with anticipation, as if something had
brushed his hot nakedness. Quickly, with hands of habitual
tenderness, he put his violin away.

The theatre-goers were tired, and life drained rapidly out of
the opera-house. The members of the orchestra rose, laughing,
mingling their weariness with good wishes for the holiday,
with sly warning and suggestive advice, pressing hands warmly
ere they disbanded. Other years Siegmund had lingered, unwilling to take the long farewell of his associates of the
orchestra. Other years he had left the opera-house with a little
pain of regret. Now he laughed, and took his comrades' hands,
and bade farewells, all distractedly, and with impatience. The
theatre, awesome now in its emptiness, he left gladly, hastening like a flame stretched level on the wind.

With his black violin-case he hurried down the street, then
halted to pity the flowers massed pallid under the gaslight of
the market-hall. For himself, the sea and the sunlight opened
great spaces to-morrow. The moon was full above the river. He
looked at it as a man in abstraction watches some clear thing;
then he came to a standstill. It was useless to hurry to his
train. The traffic swung past, the lamplight shone warm on
all the golden faces; but Siegmund had already left the city.
His face was silver and shadows to the moon; the river, in its
soft grey, shaking golden sequins among the folds of its

shadows, fell open like a garment before him, to reveal the white moon-glitter brilliant as living flesh. Mechanically, overcast with the reality of the moonlight, he took his seat in the train, and watched the moving of things. He was in a kind of trance, his consciousness seeming suspended. The train slid out amongst lights and dark places. Siegmund watched the endless movement, fascinated.

This was one of the crises of his life. For years he had suppressed his soul, in a kind of mechanical despair doing his duty and enduring the rest. Then his soul had been softly enticed from its bondage. Now he was going to break free altogether, to have at least a few days purely for his own joy. This, to a man of his integrity, meant a breaking of bonds, a severing of blood-ties, a sort of new birth. In the excitement of this last night his life passed out of his control, and he sat at the carriage-window, motionless, watching things move.

He felt busy within him a strong activity which he could not help. Slowly the body of his past, the womb which had nourished him in one fashion for so many years, was casting him forth. He was trembling in all his being, though he knew not with what. All he could do now was to watch the lights go by, and to let the translation of himself continue.

When at last the train ran out into the full, luminous night, and Siegmund saw the meadows deep in moonlight, he quivered with a low anticipation. The elms, great grey shadows, seemed to loiter in their cloaks across the pale fields. He had not seen them so before. The world was changing.

The train stopped, and with a little effort he rose to go home. The night air was cool and sweet. He drank it thirstily. In the road again he lifted his face to the moon. It seemed to help him; in its brilliance amid the blonde heavens it seemed to transcend fretfulness. It would front the waves with silver as they slid to the shore, and Helena, looking along the coast, waiting, would lift her white hands with sudden joy. He laughed, and the moon hurried laughing alongside, through the black masses of the trees.

He had forgotten he was going home for this night. The chill wetness of his little white garden-gate reminded him, and a frown came on his face. As he closed the door, and found himself in the darkness of the hall, the sense of his fatigue came fully upon him. It was an effort to go to bed. Nevertheless, he went very quietly into the drawing-room. There the moonlight entered, and he thought the whiteness was Helena. He held his breath and stiffened, then breathed again. "To-morrow," he thought, as he laid his violin-case across the arms of a wicker chair. But he had a physical feeling of the presence of Helena: in his shoulders he seemed to be aware of her. Quickly, half lifting his arms, he turned to the moonshine. "To-morrow!" he exclaimed quietly; and he left the room stealthily, for fear of disturbing the children.

In the darkness of the kitchen burned a blue bud of light. He quickly turned up the gas to a broad yellow flame, and sat down at table. He was tired, excited, and vexed with mis-giving. As he lay in his arm-chair, he looked round with disgust.

The table was spread with a dirty cloth that had great brown stains betokening children. In front of him was a cup and saucer, and a small plate with a knife laid across it. The cheese, on another plate, was wrapped in a red-bordered, fringed cloth, to keep off the flies, which even then were crawling round, on the sugar, on the loaf, on the cocoa-tin. Siegmund looked at his cup. It was chipped, and a stain had gone under the glaze, so that it looked like the mark of a dirty mouth. He fetched a glass of water.

The room was drab and dreary. The oil-cloth was worn into a hole near the door. Boots and shoes of various sizes were scattered over the floor, while the sofa was littered with children's clothing. In the black stove the ash lay dead; on the range were chips of wood, and newspapers, and rubbish of papers, and crusts of bread, and crusts of bread-and-jam. As Siegmund walked across the floor, he crushed two sweets underfoot. He had to grope under sofa and dresser to find his slippers; and he was in evening dress.

It would be the same, while ever Beatrice was Beatrice and Siegmund her husband. He ate his bread and cheese mechanically, wondering why he was miserable, why he was not looking forward with joy to the morrow. As he ate, he closed his eyes, half wishing he had not promised Helena, half wishing he had no to-morrow.

Leaning back in his chair, he felt something in the way. It was a small teddy-bear and half of a strong white comb. He grinned to himself. This was the summary of his domestic life—a broken, coarse comb, a child crying because her hair was lugged, a wife who had let the hair go till now, when she had got into a temper to see the job through; and then the teddy-bear, pathetically cocking a black worsted nose, and lifting absurd arms to him.

He wondered why Gwen had gone to bed without her pet. She would want the silly thing. The strong feeling of affection for his children came over him, battling with something else. He sank in his chair, and gradually his baffled mind went dark. He sat, overcome with weariness and trouble, staring blankly into the space. His own stifling roused him. Straightening his shoulders, he took a deep breath, then relaxed again. After a while he rose, took the teddy-bear, and went slowly to bed.

Gwen and Marjory, aged nine and twelve, slept together in a small room. It was fairly light. He saw his favourite daughter lying quite uncovered, her wilful head thrown back, her mouth half open. Her black hair was tossed across the pillow: he could see the action. Marjory snuggled under the sheet. He placed the teddy-bear between the two girls.

As he watched them, he hated the children for being so dear to him. Either he himself must go under, and drag on an existence he hated, or they must suffer. But he had agreed to spend this holiday with Helena, and meant to do so. As he turned, he saw himself like a ghost cross the mirror. He looked back; he peered at himself. His hair still grew thick and dark from his brow: he could not see the grey at the temples. His eyes were dark and tender, and his mouth, under the black moustache, was full with youth.

He rose, looked at the children, frowned, and went to his own small room. He was glad to be shut alone in the little cubicle of darkness.

Outside the world lay in a glamorous pallor, casting shadows that made the farm, the trees, the bulks of villas, look like live creatures. The same pallor went through all the night, glistening on Helena as she lay curled up asleep at the core of the glamour, like the moon; on the sea rocking backwards and forwards till it rocked her island as she slept. She was so calm and full of her own assurance. It was a great rest to be with her. With her, nothing mattered but love and the beauty of things. He felt parched and starving. She had rest and love, like water and manna for him. She was so strong in her self-possession, in her love of beautiful things and of dreams.

The clock downstairs struck two.

"I must get to sleep," he said.

He dragged his portmanteau from beneath the bed and began to pack it. When at last it was finished, he shut it with a snap. The click sounded final. He stood up, stretched himself, and sighed.

"I am fearfully tired," he said.

But that was persuasive. When he was undressed he sat in his pyjamas for some time, rapidly beating his fingers on his knee.

"Thirty-eight years old," he said to himself, "and disconsolate as a child!" He began to muse of the morrow.

When he seemed to be going to sleep, he woke up to find thoughts labouring over his brain, like bees on a hive. Recollections, swift thoughts, flew in and alighted upon him, as wild geese swing down and take possession of a pond. Phrases from the opera tyrannised over him; he played the rhythm with all his blood. As he turned over in this torture, he sighed, and recognised a movement of the De Beriot concerto which Helena had played for her last lesson. He found himself watching her as he had watched then, felt again the wild impatience when she was wrong, started again as, amid the dipping and sliding of her bow, he realised where his thoughts were going. She was wrong, he was hasty; and he felt her blue eyes looking intently at him.

Both started as his daughter Vera entered suddenly. She was a handsome girl of nineteen. Crossing the room, brushing Helena as if she were a piece of furniture in the way, Vera had asked her father a question, in a hard, insulting tone, then had gone out again, just as if Helena had not been in the room.

Helena stood fingering the score of "Pelléas". When Vera had gone, she asked, in the peculiar tone that made Siegmund shiver:

"Why do you consider the music of 'Pelléas' cold?"

Siegmund had struggled to answer. So they passed everything off, without mention, after Helena's fashion, ignoring all that might be humiliating; and to her much was humiliating.

For years she had come as pupil to Siegmund, first as a friend of the household. Then she and Louisa went occasionally to whatever hall or theatre had Siegmund in the orchestra, so that shortly the three formed the habit of coming home together. Then Helena had invited Siegmund to her home; then the three friends went walks together; then the two went walks together, whilst Louisa sheltered them.

Helena had come to read his loneliness and the humiliation of his lot. He had felt her blue eyes, heavily, steadily gazing into his soul, and he had lost himself to her.

That day, three weeks before the end of the season, when Vera had so insulted Helena, the latter had said, as she put on her coat, looking at him all the while with heavy blue eyes: "I think, Siegmund, I cannot come here any more. Your home is not open to me any longer." He had writhed in confusion and humiliation. As she pressed his hand, closely and for a long time, she said: "I will write to you." Then she left him.

Siegmund had hated his life that day. Soon she wrote. A week later, when he lay resting his head on her lap in Richmond Park, she said:

"You are so tired, Siegmund." She stroked his face, and kissed him softly. Siegmund lay in the molten daze of love. But Helena was, if it is not to debase the word, virtuous: an inconsistent virtue, cruel and ugly for Siegmund.

"You are so tired, dear. You must come away with me and rest, the first week in August."

His blood had leapt, and whatever objections he raised, such as having no money, he allowed to be overridden. He was going to Helena, to the Isle of Wight, to-morrow.

Helena, with her blue eyes so full of storm, like the sea, but, also like the sea, so eternally self-sufficient, solitary; with her thick white throat, the strongest and most wonderful thing on earth, and her small hands, silken and light as wind-flowers, would be his to-morrow, along with the sea and the downs. He clung to the exquisite flame which flooded him. . . .

But it died out, and he thought of the return to London, to Beatrice, and the children. How would it be? Beatrice, with her furious dark eyes, and her black hair loosely knotted back, came to his mind as she had been the previous day, flaring with temper when he said to her:

"I shall be going away to-morrow for a few days' holiday."

She asked for detail, some of which he gave. Then, dissatisfied and inflamed, she broke forth in her suspicion and her abuse, and her contempt, while two large-eyed children stood listening by. Siegmund hated his wife for drawing on him the grave, cold looks of condemnation from his children.

Something he had said touched Beatrice. She came of good family, had been brought up like a lady, educated in a convent school in France. He evoked her old pride. She drew herself up with dignity, and called the children away. He wondered if he could bear a repetition of that degradation. It bled him of his courage and self-respect.

In the morning Beatrice was disturbed by the sharp sneck of the hall door. Immediately awake, she heard his quick, firm step hastening down the gravel path. In her impotence, discarded like a worn out object, she lay for the moment stiff with bitterness.

"I am nothing, I am nothing," she said to herself. She lay quite rigid for a time.

There was no sound anywhere. The morning sunlight pierced vividly through the slits of the blind. Beatrice lay rocking herself, breathing hard, her finger-nails pressing into her palm. Then came the sound of a train slowing down in the station, and directly the quick "chuff-chuff-chuff" of its drawing out. Beatrice imagined the sunlight on the puffs of steam, and the two lovers, her husband and Helena, rushing through the miles of morning sunshine.

"God strike her dead! Mother of God, strike her down!" she said aloud, in a low tone. She hated Helena.

Irene, who lay with her mother, woke up and began to question her.

CHAPTER III

IN the miles of morning sunshine, Siegmund's shadows, his children, Beatrice, his sorrow, dissipated like mist, and he was elated as a young man setting forth to travel. When he had passed Portsmouth Town everything had vanished but the old gay world of romance. He laughed as he looked out at the carriage window.

Below, in the street, a military band passed glittering. A brave sound floated up, and again he laughed, loving the tune, the clash and glitter of the band, the movement of scarlet, blithe soldiers beyond the park. People were drifting brightly from church. How could it be Sunday! It was no time; it was Romance, going back to Tristan.

Women, like crocus flowers, in white and blue and lavender, moved gaily. Everywhere fluttered the small flags of holiday. Every form danced lightly in the sunshine.

And beyond it all were the silent hillsides of the island, with Helena. It was so wonderful, he could bear to be patient. She would be all in white, with her cool, thick throat left bare to the breeze, her face shining, smiling as she dipped her head because of the sun, which glistened on her uncovered hair.

He breathed deeply, stirring at the thought. But he would not grow impatient. The train had halted over the town, where scarlet soldiers, and ludicrous blue sailors, and all the brilliant women from church shook like a kaleidoscope down the street. The train crawled on, drawing near to the sea, for which Sieg-mund waited breathless. It was so like Helena, blue, beautiful, strong in its reserve.

Another moment they were in the dirty station. Then the day flashed out, and Siegmund mated with joy. He felt the sea heaving below him. He looked round, and the sea was blue as a periwinkle flower, while gold and white and blood-red sails lit here and there upon the blueness. Standing on the deck, he gave himself to the breeze and to the sea, feeling like one of the ruddy sails—as if he were part of it all. All his body radiated amid the large, magnificent sea-moon like a piece of colour.

The little ship began to pulse, to tremble. White with the softness of a bosom, the water rose up frothing and swaying gently. Ships drew near like inquisitive birds; the old *Victory* shook her myriad pointed flags of yellow and scarlet; the straight old houses of the quay passed by.

Outside the harbour, like fierce creatures of the sea come wildly up to look, the battleships laid their black snouts on the water. Siegmund laughed at them. He felt the foam on his face like a sparkling, felt the blue sea gathering round.

On the left stood the round fortress, quaintly chequered, and solidly alone in the walk of water, amid the silent flight of the golden- and crimson-winged boats.

Siegmund watched the bluish bulk of the island. Like the beautiful women in the myths, his love hid in its blue haze. It seemed impossible. Behind him, the white wake trailed myriads of daisies. On either hand the grim and wicked battleships watched along their sharp noses. Beneath him the clear green water swung and puckered as if it were laughing. In front,

Sieglinde's island drew near and nearer, creeping towards him, bringing him Helena.

Meadows and woods appeared, houses crowded down to the shore to meet him; he was in the quay, and the ride was over. Siegmund regretted it. But Helena was on the island, which rode like an anchored ship under the fleets of cloud that had launched whilst Siegmund was on water. As he watched the end of the pier loom higher, large ponderous trains of cloud cast over him the shadows of their bulk, and he shivered in the chill wind.

His travelling was very slow. The sky's dark shipping pressed closer and closer, as if all the clouds had come to harbour. Over the flat lands near Newport the wind moaned like the calling of many violon-cellos. All the sky was grey. Siegmund waited drearily on Newport station, where the wind swept coldly. It was Sunday, and the station and the island were desolate, having lost their purposes.

Siegmund put on his overcoat and sat down. All his morning's blaze of elation was gone, though there still glowed a great hope. He had slept only two hours of the night. An empty man, he had drunk joy, and now the intoxication was dying out.

At three o'clock of the afternoon he sat alone in the second-class carriage, looking out. A few raindrops struck the pane, then the blurred dazzle of a shower came in a burst of wind, and hid the downs and the reeds that shivered in the marshy places. Siegmund sat in a chilly torpor. He counted the stations. Beneath his stupor his heart was thudding heavily with excitement, surprising him, for his brain felt dead.

The train slowed down: Yarmouth! One more station, then. Siegmund watched the platform, shiny with rain, slide past. On the dry grey under the shelter, one white passenger was waiting. Suddenly Siegmund's heart leaped up, wrenching wildly. He burst open the door, and caught hold of Helena. She dilated, gave a palpitating cry as he dragged her into the carriage.

"You *here!*" he exclaimed, in a strange tone. She was shivering with cold. Her almost naked arms were blue. She could not answer Siegmund's question, but lay clasped against him, shivering away her last chill as his warmth invaded her. He laughed in his heart as she nestled in to him.

"Is it a dream now, dear?" he whispered. Helena clasped

him tightly, shuddering because of the delicious suffusing of his warmth through her.

Almost immediately they heard the grinding of the brakes. "Here we are, then!" exclaimed Helena, dropping into her conventional, cheerful manner at once. She put straight her hat, while he gathered his luggage.

Until tea-time there was a pause in their progress. Siegmund was tingling with an exquisite vividness, as if he had taken some rare stimulant. He wondered at himself. It seemed that every fibre in his body was surprised with joy, as each tree in a forest at dawn utters astonished cries of delight.

When Helena came back, she sat opposite to him to see him. His naïve look of joy was very sweet to her. His eyes were dark blue, showing the fibrils, like a purple-veined flower at twilight, and somehow, mysteriously, joy seemed to quiver in the iris. Helena appreciated him, feature by feature. She liked his clear forehead, with its thick black hair, and his full mouth, and his chin. She loved his hands, that were small, but strong and nervous, and very white. She liked his breast, that breathed so strong and quietly, and his arms, and his thighs, and his knees.

For him, Helena was a presence. She was ambushed, fused in an aura of his love. He only saw she was white, and strong, and full fruited, he only knew her blue eyes were rather awful to him.

Outside, the sea-mist was travelling thicker and thicker inland. Their lodging was not far from the bay. As they sat together at tea, Siegmund's eyes dilated, and he looked frowning at Helena.

"What is it?" he asked, listening uneasily.

Helena looked up at him, from pouring out the tea. His little anxious look of distress amused her.

"The noise, you mean? Merely the fog-horn, dear—not Wotan's wrath, nor Siegfried's dragon. . . ."

The fog was white at the window. They sat waiting. After a few seconds the sound came low, swelling, like the mooing of some great sea animal, alone, the last of the monsters. The whole fog gave off the sound for a second or two, then it died down into an intense silence. Siegmund and Helena looked at each other. His eyes were full of trouble. To see a big, strong man anxious-eyed as a child because of a strange sound amused her. But he was tired.

"I assure you, it *is* only a fog-horn," she laughed.

"Of course. But it is a depressing sort of sound."

"Is it?" she said curiously. "Why? Well—yes—I think I can understand its being so to some people. It's something like the call of the horn across the sea to Tristan."

She hummed softly, then three times she sang the horn-call. Siegmund, with his face expressionless as a mask, sat staring out at the mist. The boom of the siren broke in upon them. To him, the sound was full of fatality. Helena waited till the noise died down, then she repeated her horn-call.

"Yet it is very much like the fog-horn," she said, curiously interested.

"This time next week, Helena!" he said.

She suddenly went heavy, and stretched across to clasp his hand as it lay upon the table.

"I shall be calling to you from Cornwall," she said.

He did not reply. So often she did not take his meaning, but left him alone with his sense of tragedy. She had no idea how his life was wrenched from its roots, and when he tried to tell her, she balked him, leaving him inwardly quite lonely.

"There is *no* next week," she declared, with great cheerfulness. "There is only the present."

At the same moment she rose and slipped across to him. Putting her arms round his neck, she stood holding his head to her bosom, pressing it close, with her hand among his hair. His nostrils and mouth were crushed against her breast. He smelled the silk of her dress and the faint, intoxicating odour of her person. With shut eyes he owned heavily to himself again that she was blind to him. But some other self urged with gladness, no matter how blind she was, so that she pressed his face upon her.

She stroked and caressed his hair, tremblingly clasped his head against her breast, as if she would never release him; then she bent to kiss his forehead. He took her in his arms, and they were still for awhile.

Now he wanted to blind himself with her, to blaze up all his past and future in a passion worth years of living.

After tea they rested by the fire, while she told him all the delightful things she had found. She had a woman's curious passion for details, a woman's peculiar attachment to certain dear trifles. He listened, smiling, revived by her delight, and forgetful of himself. She soothed him like sunshine, and filled him with pleasure; but he hardly attended to her words.

"Shall we go out, or are you too tired? No, you are tired—you are very tired," said Helena.

She stood by his chair, looking down on him tenderly.

"No," he replied, smiling brilliantly at her, and stretching his handsome limbs in relief—"no, not at all tired now."

Helena continued to look down on him in quiet, covering tenderness. But she quailed before the brilliant, questioning gaze of his eyes.

"You must go to bed early to-night," she said, turning aside her face, ruffling his soft black hair. He stretched slightly, stiffening his arms, and smiled without answering. It was a very keen pleasure to be thus alone with her and in her charge. He rose, bidding her wrap herself up against the fog.

"You are sure you're not too tired?" she reiterated.

He laughed.

Outside, the sea-mist was white and woolly. They went hand in hand. It was cold, so she thrust her hand with his into the pocket of his overcoat, while they walked together.

"I like the mist," he said, pressing her hand in his pocket.

"I don't dislike it," she replied, shrinking nearer to him.

"It puts us together by ourselves," he said. She plodded alongside, bowing her head, not replying. He did not mind her silence.

"It couldn't have happened better for us than this mist," he said.

She laughed curiously, almost with a sound of tears.

"Why?" she asked, half tenderly, half bitterly.

"There is nothing else but you, and for you there is nothing else but me—look!"

He stood still. They were on the downs, so that Helena found herself quite alone with the man in a world of mist. Suddenly she flung herself sobbing against his breast. He held her closely, tenderly, not knowing what it was all about, but happy and unafraid.

In one hollow place the siren from the Needles seemed to bellow full in their ears. Both Siegmund and Helena felt their emotion too intense. They turned from it.

"What is the pitch?" asked Helena.

"Where it is horizontal? It slides up a chromatic scale," said Siegmund.

"Yes, but the settled pitch—is it about E?"

"E!" exclaimed Siegmund. "More like F."

"Nay, listen!" said Helena.

They stood still and waited till there came the long booing of the fog-horn.

"There!" exclaimed Siegmund, imitating the sound. "That is not E." He repeated the sound. "It is F."

"Surely it is E," persisted Helena.

"Even F sharp," he rejoined, humming the note.

She laughed, and told him to climb the chromatic scale.

"But you agree?" he said.

"I do not," she replied.

The fog was cold. It seemed to rob them of their courage to talk.

"What is the note in 'Tristan'?" Helena made an effort to ask.

"That is not the same," he replied.

"No, dear, that is not the same," she said in low, comforting tones. He quivered at the caress. She put her arms round him, reached up her face yearningly for a kiss. He forgot they were standing in the public footpath, in daylight, till she drew hastily away. She heard footsteps down the fog.

As they climbed the path the mist grew thinner, till it was only a grey haze at the top. There they were on the turfy lip of the land. The sky was fairly clear overhead. Below them the sea was singing hoarsely to itself.

Helena drew him to the edge of the cliff. He crushed her hand, drawing slightly back. But it pleased her to feel the grip on her hand becoming unbearable. They stood right on the edge, to see the smooth cliff slope into the mist, under which the sea stirred noisily.

"Shall we walk over, then?" said Siegmund, glancing downwards. Helena's heart stood still a moment at the idea, then beat heavily. How could he play with the idea of death, and the five great days in front? She was afraid of him just then.

"Come away, dear," she pleaded.

He would, then, forgo the few consummate days! It was bitterness to her to think so.

"Come away, dear!" she repeated, drawing him slowly to the path.

"You are not afraid?" he asked.

"Not afraid, no. . . ." Her voice had that peculiar, reedy, harsh quality that made him shiver.

"It is too easy a way," he said satirically.

She did not take in his meaning.

"And five days of our own before us, Siegmund!" she scolded. "The mist is Lethe. It is enough for us if its spell lasts five days."

He laughed, and took her in his arms, kissing her very closely.

They walked on joyfully, locking behind them the doors of forgetfulness.

As the sun set, the fog dispersed a little. Breaking masses of mist went flying from cliff to cliff, and far away beyond the cliffs the western sky stood dimmed with gold. The lovers wandered aimlessly over the golf-links to where green mounds and turfed banks suggested to Helena that she was tired, and would sit down. They faced the lighted chamber of the west, whence, behind the torn, dull-gold curtains of fog, the sun was departing with pomp.

Siegmund sat very still, watching the sunset. It was a splendid, flaming bridal chamber where he had come to Helena. He wondered how to express it; how other men had borne this same glory.

"What is the music of it?" he asked.

She glanced at him. His eyelids were half lowered, his mouth slightly open, as if in ironic rhapsody.

"Of what, dear?"

"What music do you think holds the best interpretation of sunset?"

His skin was gold, his real mood was intense. She revered him for a moment.

"I do not know," she said quietly; and she rested her head against his shoulder, looking out west.

There was a space of silence, while Siegmund dreamed on.

"A Beethoven symphony—the one——" and he explained to her.

She was not satisfied, but leaned against him, making her choice. The sunset hung steady, she could scarcely perceive a change.

"The Grail music in 'Lohengrin'," she decided.

"Yes," said Siegmund. He found it quite otherwise, but did not trouble to dispute. He dreamed by himself. This displeased her. She wanted him for herself. How could he leave her alone while he watched the sky? She almost put her two hands over his eyes.

CHAPTER IV

THE gold march of sunset passed quickly, the ragged curtains of mist closed to Soon Siegmund and Helena were shut alone within the dense wide fog. She shivered with the cold and the damp. Startled, he took her in his arms, where she lay and clung to him. Holding her closely, he bent forward, straight to her lips. His moustache was drenched cold with fog, so that she shuddered slightly after his kiss, and shuddered again. He did not know why the strong tremor passed through her. Thinking it was with fear and with cold, he undid his overcoat, put her close on his breast, and covered her as best he could. That she feared him at that moment was half pleasure, half shame to him. Pleadingly he hid his face on her shoulder, held her very tightly, till his face grew hot, buried against her soft strong throat.

"You are so big I can't hold you," she whispered plaintively, catching her breath with fear. Her small hands grasped at the breadth of his shoulders ineffectually.

"You will be cold. Put your hands under my coat," he whispered.

He put her inside his overcoat and his coat. She came to his warm breast with a sharp intaking of delight and fear; she tried to make her hands meet in the warmth of his shoulders, tried to clasp him.

"See! I can't," she whispered.

He laughed short, and pressed her closer.

Then, tucking her head in his breast, hiding her face, she timidly slid her hands along his sides, pressing softly, to find the contours of his figure. Softly her hands crept over the silky back of his waistcoat, under his coats, and as they stirred, his blood flushed up, and up again, with fire, till all Siegmund was hot blood, and his breast was one great ache.

He crushed her to him—crushed her in upon the ache of his chest. His muscles set hard and unyielding; at that moment he was a tense, vivid body of flesh, without a mind; his blood, alive and conscious, running towards her. He remained perfectly still, locked about Helena, conscious of nothing.

She was hurt and crushed, but it was pain delicious to her. It was marvellous to her how strong he was, to keep up that grip of her like steel. She swooned in a kind of intense bliss.

At length she found herself released, taking a great breath, while Siegmund was moving his mouth over her throat, something like a dog snuffing her, but with his lips. Her heart leaped away in revulsion. His moustache thrilled her strangely. His lips, brushing and pressing her throat beneath the ear, and his warm breath flying rhythmically upon her, made her vibrate through all her body. Like a violin under the bow, she thrilled beneath his mouth, and shuddered from his moustache. Her heart was like fire in her breast.

Suddenly she strained madly to him, and, drawing back her head, placed her lips on his, close, till at the mouth they seemed to melt and fuse together. It was the long, supreme kiss, in which man and woman have one being, Two-in-one, the only Hermaphrodite.

When Helena drew away her lips, she was exhausted. She belonged to that class of 'dreaming women' with whom passion exhausts itself at the mouth. Her desire was accomplished in a real kiss. The fire, in heavy flames, had poured through her to Siegmund, from Siegmund to her. It sank, and she felt herself flagging. She had not the man's brightness and vividness of blood. She lay upon his breast, dreaming how beautiful it would be to go to sleep, to swoon unconscious there, on that rare bed. She lay still on Siegmund's breast, listening to his heavily beating heart.

With her the dream was always more than the actuality. Her dream of Siegmund was more to her than Siegmund himself. He might be less than her dream, which is as it may be. However, to the real man she was very cruel.

He held her close. His dream was melted in his blood, and his blood ran bright for her. His dreams were the flowers of his blood. Hers were more detached and inhuman. For centuries a certain type of woman has been rejecting the 'animal' in humanity, till now her dreams are abstract, and full of fantasy, and her blood runs in bondage, and her kindness is full of cruelty.

Helena lay flagging upon the breast of Siegmund. He folded her closely, and his mouth and his breath were warm on her neck. She sank away from his caresses, passively, subtly drew back from him. He was far too sensitive not to be aware of this, and far too much of a man not to yield to the woman. His heart sank, his blood grew sullen at her withdrawal. Still he held her; the two were motionless and silent for some time.

She became distressedly conscious that her feet, which lay
on the wet grass, were aching with cold. She said softly,
gently, as if he was her child whom she must correct and
lead:

"I think we ought to go home, Siegmund." He made a small
sound, that might mean anything, but did not stir or release
her. His mouth, however, remained motionless on her throat,
and the caress went out of it.

"It is cold and wet, dear; we ought to go," she coaxed
determinedly.

"Soon," he said thickly.

She sighed, waited a moment, then said very gently, as if
she were loath to take him from his pleasure:

"Siegmund, I am cold."

There was a reproach in this which angered him.

"Cold!" he exclaimed. "But you are warm with me——"

"But my feet are out on the grass, dear, and they are like
wet pebbles."

"Oh dear!" he said. "Why didn't you give them me to
warm?" He leaned forward, and put his hand on her shoes.

"They are very cold," he said. "We must hurry and make
them warm."

When they rose, her feet were so numbed she could hardly
stand. She clung to Siegmund, laughing.

"I wish you had told me before," he said. "I ought to have
known. . . ."

Vexed with himself, he put his arm round her, and they set
off home.

CHAPTER V

THEY found the fire burning brightly in their room. The only
other person in the pretty, stiffly-furnished cottage was their
landlady, a charming old lady, who let this sitting-room
more for the change, for the sake of having visitors, than for
gain.

Helena introduced Siegmund as "My friend". The old lady

smiled upon him. He was big, and good-looking, and embarrassed. She had had a son years back. . . . And the two were lovers. She hoped they would come to her house for their honeymoon.

Siegmund sat in his great horse-hair chair by the fire, while Helena attended to the lamp. Glancing at him over the glowing globe, she found him watching her with a small, peculiar smile of irony, and anger, and bewilderment. He was not quite himself. Her hand trembled so, she could scarcely adjust the wicks.

Helena left the room to change her dress.

"I shall be back before Mrs. Curtiss brings in the tray. There is the Nietzsche I brought——"

He did not answer as he watched her go. Left alone, he sat with his arms along his knees, perfectly still. His heart beat heavily, and all his being felt sullen, watchful, aloof, like a balked animal. Thoughts came up in his brain like bubbles—random, hissing out aimlessly. Once, in the startling inflammability of his blood, his veins ran hot, and he smiled.

When Helena entered the room his eyes sought hers swiftly, as sparks lighting on the tinder. But her eyes were only moist with tenderness. His look instantly changed. She wondered at his being so silent, so strange.

Coming to him in her unhesitating, womanly way—she was only twenty-six to his thirty-eight—she stood before him, holding both his hands and looking down on him with almost gloomy tenderness. She wore a white dress that showed her throat gathering like a fountain-jet of solid foam to balance her head. He could see the full white arms passing clear through the dripping spume of lace, towards the rise of her breasts. But her eyes bent down upon him with such gloom of tenderness that he dared not reveal the passion burning in him. He could not look at her. He strove almost pitifully to be with her sad, tender, but he could not put out his fire. She held both his hands firm, pressing them in appeal for her dream love. He glanced at her wistfully, then turned away. She waited for him. She wanted his caresses and tenderness. He would not look at her.

"You would like supper now, dear?" she asked, looking where the dark hair ended, and his neck ran smooth, under his collar, to the strong setting of his shoulders.

"Just as you will," he replied.

Still she waited, and still he would not look at her. Something troubled him, she thought. He was foreign to her.

"I will spread the cloth, then," she said, in deep tones of resignation. She pressed his hands closely, and let them drop. He took no notice, but, still with his arms on his knees, he stared into the fire.

In the golden glow of lamplight she set small bowls of white and lavender sweet-peas, and mignonette, upon the round table. He watched her moving, saw the stir of her white, sloping shoulders under the lace, and the hollow of her shoulders firm as marble, and the slight rise and fall of her loins as she walked. He felt as if his breast were scalded. It was a physical pain to him.

Supper was very quiet. Helena was sad and gentle; he had a peculiar, enigmatic look in his eyes, between suffering and mockery and love. He was quite intractable; he would not soften to her, but remained there aloof. He was tired, and the look of weariness and suffering was evident to her through his strangeness. In her heart she wept.

At last she tinkled the bell for supper to be cleared. Meanwhile, restlessly, she played fragments of Wagner on the piano.

"Will you want anything else?" asked the smiling old landlady.

"Nothing at all, thanks," said Helena, with decision.

"Oh! then I think I will go to bed when I've washed the dishes. You will put the lamp out, dear?"

"I am well used to a lamp," smiled Helena. "We use them always at home."

She had had a day before Siegmund's coming, in which to win Mrs. Curtiss' heart, and she had been successful. The old lady took the tray.

"Good-night, dear—good-night, sir. I will leave you. You will not be long, dear?"

"No, we shall not be long. Mr. MacNair is very evidently tired out."

"Yes—yes. It is very tiring, London."

When the door was closed, Helena stood a moment undecided, looking at Siegmund. He was lying in his arm-chair in a dispirited way, and looking in the fire. As she gazed at him with troubled eyes, he happened to glance to her, with the same dark, curiously searching, disappointed eyes.

"Shall I read to you?" she asked bitterly.

THE POLYTECHNIC OF WALES
LIBRARY
TREFOREST

"If you will," he replied.

He sounded so indifferent, she could scarcely refrain from crying. She went and stood in front of him, looking down on him heavily.

"What is it, dear?" she said.

"You," he replied, smiling with a little grimace.

"Why me?"

He smiled at her ironically, then closed his eyes. She slid into his arms with a little moan. He took her on his knee, where she curled up like a heavy white cat. She let him caress her with his mouth, and did not move, but lay there curled up and quiet and luxuriously warm.

He kissed her hair, which was beautifully fragrant of itself, and time after time drew between his lips one long, keen thread, as if he would ravel out with his mouth her vigorous confusion of hair. His tenderness of love was like a soft flame lapping her voluptuously.

After a while they heard the old lady go upstairs. Helena went very still, and seemed to contract. Siegmund himself hesitated in his love-making. All was very quiet. They could hear a faint breathing of the sea. Presently the cat, which had been sleeping in a chair, rose and went to the door.

"Shall I let her out?" said Siegmund.

"Do!" said Helena, slipping from his knee. "She goes out when the nights are fine."

Siegmund rose to set free the tabby. Hearing the front door open, Mrs. Curtiss called from upstairs: "Is that you, dear?"

"I have just let Kitty out," said Siegmund.

"Ah, thank you. Good-night!" They heard the old lady lock her bedroom door.

Helena was kneeling on the hearth. Siegmund softly closed the door, then waited a moment. His heart was beating fast.

"Shall we sit by firelight?" he asked tentatively.

"Yes—if you wish," she replied, very slowly, as if against her will. He carefully turned down the lamp, then blew out the light. His whole body was burning and surging with desire.

The room was black and red with firelight. Helena shone ruddily as she knelt, a bright, bowed figure, full in the glow. Now and then red stripes of firelight leapt across the walls. Siegmund, his face ruddy, advanced out of the shadows.

He sat in the chair beside her, leaning forward, his hands hanging like two scarlet flowers listless in the fire glow, near

to her, as she knelt on the hearth, with head bowed down. One
of the flowers awoke and spread towards her. It asked for her
mutely. She was fascinated, scarcely able to move.

"Come," he pleaded softly.

She turned, lifted her hands to him. The lace fell back, and
her arms, bare to the shoulder, shone rosily. He saw her breasts
raised towards him. Her face was bent between her arms as
she looked up at him afraid. Lit by the firelight, in her white,
clinging dress, cowering between her uplifted arms, she seemed
to be offering him herself to sacrifice.

In an instant he was kneeling, and she was lying on his
shoulder, abandoned to him. There was a good deal of sorrow
in his joy.

It was eleven o'clock when Helena at last loosened
Siegmund's arms, and rose from the armchair where she lay
beside him. She was very hot, feverish, and restless. For the
last half-hour he had lain absolutely still, with his heavy arms
about her, making her hot. If she had not seen his eyes blue
and dark, she would have thought him asleep. She tossed in
restlessness on his breast.

"Am I not uneasy?" she had said, to make him speak. He
had smiled gently.

"It is wonderful to be as still as this," he said. She had lain
tranquil with him, then, for a few moments. To her there was
something sacred in his stillness and peace. She wondered at
him; he was so different from an hour ago. How could he be
the same! Now he was like the sea, blue and hazy in the
morning, musing by itself. Before, he was burning, volcanic,
as if he would destroy her.

She had given him this new soft beauty. She was the earth
in which his strange flowers grew. But she herself wondered at
the flowers produced of her. He was so strange to her, so
different from herself. What next would he ask of her, what
new blossom would she rear in him then. He seemed to grow
and flower involuntarily. She merely helped to produce him.

Helena could not keep still; her body was full of strange
sensations, of involuntary recoil from shock. She was tired,
but restless. All the time Siegmund lay with his hot arms over
her, himself so incomprehensible in his haze of blue, open-
eyed slumber, she grew more breathless and unbearable to
herself.

At last she lifted his arm, and drew herself out of the chair. Siegmund looked at her from his tranquillity. She put the damp hair from her forehead, breathed deep, almost panting. Then she glanced hauntingly at her flushed face in the mirror. With the same restlessness, she turned to look at the night. The cool, dark, watery sea called to her. She pushed back the curtain.

The moon was wading deliciously through shallows of white cloud. Beyond the trees and the few houses was the great concave of darkness, the sea, and the moonlight. The moon was there to put a cool hand of absolution on her brow.

"Shall we go out a moment, Siegmund?" she asked fretfully.

"Ay, if you wish to," he answered, altogether willing. He was filled with an easiness that would comply with her every wish.

They went out softly, walked in silence to the bay. There they stood at the head of the white, living moonpath, where the water whispered at the casement of the land seductively.

"It's the finest night I have seen," said Siegmund. Helena's eyes suddenly filled with tears, at his simplicity of happiness.

"I like the moon on the water," she said.

"I can hardly tell the one from the other," he replied simply. "The sea seems to be poured out of the moon, and rocking in the hands of the coast. They are all one, just as your eyes and hands and what you say, are all you."

"Yes," she answered, thrilled. This was the Siegmund of her dream, and she had created him. Yet there was a quiver of pain. He was beyond her now, and did not need her.

"I feel at home here," he said; "as if I had come home where I was bred."

She pressed his hand hard, clinging to him.

"We go an awful long way round, Helena," he said, "just to find we're all right." He laughed pleasantly. "I have thought myself such an outcast! How can one be outcast in one's own night, and the moon always naked to us, and the sky half her time in rags? What do we want?"

Helena did not know. Nor did she know what he meant. But she felt something of the harmony.

"Whatever I have or haven't from now," he continued, "the darkness is a sort of mother, and the moon a sister, and the stars children, and sometimes the sea is a brother: and there's a family in one house, you see."

"And I, Siegmund?" she said softly, taking him in all seriousness. She looked up at him piteously. He saw the silver of tears among the moonlit ivory of her face. His heart tightened with tenderness, and he laughed, then bent to kiss her.

"The key of the castle," he said. He put his face against hers, and felt on his cheek the smart of her tears.

"It's all very grandiose," he said comfortably, "but it does for to-night, all this that I say."

"It is true for ever," she declared.

"In so far as to-night is eternal," he said.

He remained, with the wetness of her cheek smarting on his, looking from under his brows at the white transport of the water beneath the moon. They stood folded together, gazing into the white heart of the night.

CHAPTER VI

SIEGMUND woke with wonder in the morning. "It is like the magic tales," he thought, as he realised where he was; "and I am transported to a new life, to realise my dream. Fairy-tales are true, after all."

He had slept very deeply, so that he felt strangely new. He issued with delight from the dark of sleep into the sunshine. Reaching out his hand, he felt for his watch. It was seven o'clock. The dew of a sleep-drenched night glittered before his eyes. Then he laughed and forgot the night.

The creeper was tapping at the window, as a little wind blew up the sunshine. Siegmund put out his hands for the unfolding happiness of the morning. Helena was in the next room, which she kept inviolate. Sparrows in the creeper were shaking shadows of leaves among the sunshine; milk-white shallop of cloud stemmed bravely across the bright sky; the sea would be blossoming with a dewy shimmer of sunshine.

Siegmund rose to look, and it was so. Also the houses, like white, and red, and black cattle, were wandering down the bay, with a mist of sunshine between him and them. He leaned with his hands on the window-ledge looking out of the casement. The breeze ruffled his hair, blew down the neck of his sleeping-jacket upon his chest. He laughed, hastily threw on his clothes, and went out.

There was no sign of Helena. He strode along, singing to himself, and spinning his towel rhythmically. A small path led him across a field and down a zigzag in front of the cliffs. Some nooks, sheltered from the wind, were warm with sunshine, scented of honeysuckle and of thyme. He took a sprig of wood-bine that was coloured of cream and butter. The grass wetted his brown shoes and his flannel trousers. Again, a fresh breeze put the scent of the sea in his uncovered hair. The cliff was a tangle of flowers above and below, with poppies at the lip being blown out like red flame, and scabious leaning inquisitively to look down, and pink and white rest-harrow everywhere, very pretty.

Siegmund stood at a bend where heath blossomed in shaggy lilac, where the sunshine but no wind came. He saw the blue bay curl away to the far-off headland. A few birds, white and small, circled, dipped by the thin foam-edge of the water; a few ships dimmed the sea with silent travelling; a few small people, dark or naked-white, moved below the swinging birds.

He chose his bathing-place where the incoming tide had half covered a stretch of fair, bright sand that was studded with rocks resembling square altars, hollowed on top. He threw his clothes on a high rock. It delighted him to feel the fresh, soft fingers of the wind touching him and wandering timidly over his nakedness. He ran laughing over the sand to the sea, where he waded in, thrusting his legs noisily through the heavy green water.

It was cold, and he shrank. For a moment he found himself thigh-deep, watching the horizontal stealing of a ship through the intolerable glitter, afraid to plunge. Laughing, he went under the clear green water.

He was a poor swimmer. Sometimes a choppy wave swamped him, and he rose gasping, wringing the water from his eyes and nostrils, while he heaved and sank with the rock-ing of the waves that clasped his breast. Then he stooped again to resume his game with the sea. It is splendid to play, even at middle age, and the sea is a fine partner.

With his eyes at the shining level of the water, he liked to peer across, taking a seal's view of the cliffs as they confronted the morning. He liked to see the ships standing up on a bright floor; he liked to see the birds come down.

But in his playing he drifted towards the spur of rock, where, as he swam, he caught his thigh on a sharp, submerged point. He frowned at the pain, at the sudden cruelty of the sea; then he thought no more of it, but ruffled his way back to the clear water, busily continuing his play.

When he ran out on to the fair sand his heart, and brain, and body were in a turmoil. He panted, filling his breast with the air that was sparkled and tasted of the sea. As he shuddered a little, the wilful palpitations of his flesh pleased him, as if birds had fluttered against him. He offered his body to the morning, glowing with the sea's passion. The wind nestled in to him, the sunshine came on his shoulders like warm breath. He delighted in himself.

The rock before him was white and wet, like himself; it had a pool of clear water, with shells and one rose anemone.

"She would make so much of this little pool," he thought. And as he smiled, he saw, very faintly, his own shadow in the water. It made him conscious of himself, seeming to look at him. He glanced at himself, at his handsome, white maturity. As he looked he felt the insidious creeping of blood down his thigh, which was marked with a long red slash. Siegmund watched the blood travel over the bright skin. It wound itself redly round the rise of his knee.

"That is I, that creeping red, and this whiteness I pride myself on is I, and my black hair, and my blue eyes are I. It is a weird thing to be a person. What makes me myself, among all these?"

Feeling chill, he wiped himself quickly.

"I am at my best, at my strongest," he said proudly to himself. "She ought to be rejoiced at me, but she is not; she rejects me as if I were a baboon under my clothing."

He glanced at his whole handsome maturity, the firm plating of his breasts, the full thighs, creatures proud in themselves. Only he was marred by the long raw scratch, which he regretted deeply.

"If I was giving her myself, I wouldn't want that blemish on me," he thought.

He wiped the blood from the wound. It was nothing.

"She thinks ten thousand times more of that little pool, with a bit of pink anemone and some yellow weed, than of me. But, by Jove! I'd rather see her shoulders and breast than all heaven and earth put together could show. . . . Why doesn't she like me?" he thought as he dressed. It was his physical self thinking.

After dabbling his feet in a warm pool, he returned home. Helena was in the dining-room arranging a bowl of purple pansies. She looked up at him rather heavily as he stood radiant on the threshold. He put her at her ease. It was a gay, handsome boy she had to meet, not a man, strange and insistent. She smiled on him with tender dignity.

"You have bathed?" she said, smiling, and looking at his damp, ruffled black hair. She shrank from his eyes, but he was quite unconscious.

"You have not bathed!" he said; then bent to kiss her. She smelt the brine in his hair.

"No; I bathe later," she replied. "But what——"

Hesitating, she touched the towel, then looked up at him anxiously.

"It *is* blood?" she said.

"I grazed my thigh—nothing at all," he replied.

"Are you sure?"

He laughed.

"The towel looks bad enough," she said.

"It's an alarmist," he laughed.

She looked in concern at him, then turned aside.

"Breakfast is quite ready," she said.

"And I for breakfast—but shall I do?"

She glanced at him. He was without a collar, so his throat was bare above the neck-band of his flannel shirt. Altogether she disapproved of his slovenly appearance. He was usually so smart in his dress.

"I would not trouble," she said almost sarcastically.

Whistling, he threw the towel on a chair.

"How did you sleep?" she asked gravely, as she watched him beginning to eat.

"Like the dead—solid," he replied. "And you?"

"Oh, pretty well, thanks," she said, rather piqued that he had slept so deeply, whilst she had tossed, and had called his name in a torture of sleeplessness.

"I haven't slept like that for years," he said enthusiastically. Helena smiled gently on him. The charm of his handsome, healthy zest came over her. She liked his naked throat and his shirt-breast, which suggested the breast of the man beneath it. She was extraordinarily happy, with him so bright. The dark-faced pansies, in a little crowd, seemed gaily winking a golden eye at her.

After breakfast, while Siegmund dressed, she went down to the sea. She dwelled, as she passed, on all tiny, pretty things— on the barbaric yellow ragwort, and pink convolvuli; on all the twinkling of flowers, and dew, and snail-tracks drying in the sun. Her walk was one long lingering. More than the spaces, she loved the nooks, and fancy more than imagination.

She wanted to see just as she pleased, without any of humanity's previous vision for spectacles. So she knew hardly any flower's name, nor perceived any of the relationships, nor cared a jot about an adaptation or a modification. It pleased her that the lowest browny florets of the clover hung down; she cared no more. She clothed everything in fancy.

"That yellow flower hadn't time to be brushed and combed by the fairies before dawn came. It is tousled . . ." so she thought to herself. The pink convolvuli were fairy horns or telephones from the day fairies to the night fairies. The rippling sunlight on the sea was the Rhine maidens spreading their bright hair to the sun. That was her favourite form of thinking. The value of all things was in the fancy they evoked. She did not care for people; they were vulgar, ugly, and stupid, as a rule.

Her sense of satisfaction was complete as she leaned on the low sea-wall, spreading her fingers to warm on the stones, con- cocting magic out of the simple morning. She watched the indolent chasing of wavelets round the small rocks, the curling of the deep blue water round the water-shadowed reefs.

"This is very good," she said to herself. "This is eternally cool, and clean and fresh. It could never be spoiled by satiety."

She tried to wash herself with the white and blue morning, to clear away the soiling of the last night's passion.

The sea played by itself, intent on its own game. Its aloof- ness, its self-sufficiency, are its great charm. The sea does not give and take, like the land and the sky. It has no traffic with the world. It spends its passion upon itself. Helena was something like the sea, self-sufficient and careless of the rest.

Siegmund came bareheaded, his black hair ruffling to the wind, his eyes shining warmer than the sea—like cornflowers rather, his limbs swinging backward and forward like the water. Together they leaned on the wall, warming the four white hands upon the grey bleached stone as they watched the water playing.

When Siegmund had Helena near, he lost the ache, the yearning towards something, which he always felt otherwise. She seemed to connect him with the beauty of things, as if she were the nerve through which he received intelligence of the sun, and wind, and sea, and of the moon and the darkness. Beauty she never felt herself came to him through her. It is that makes love. He could always sympathise with the wistful little flowers, and trees lonely in their crowds, and wild, sad sea-birds. In these things he recognised the great yearning, the ache outwards towards something, with which he was ordinarily burdened. But with Helena, in this large sea-morning, he was whole and perfect as the day.

"Will it be fine all day?" he asked, when a cloud came over.

"I don't know," she replied, in her gentle, inattentive manner, as if she did not care at all. "I think it will be a mixed day—cloud and sun—more sun than cloud."

She looked up gravely to see if he agreed. He turned from frowning at the cloud to smile at her. He seemed so bright, teeming with life.

"I like a bare blue sky," he said; "sunshine that you seem to stir about as you walk."

"It is warm enough here, even for you," she smiled.

"Ah, here!" he answered, putting his face down to receive the radiation from the stone, letting his fingers creep towards Helena's. She laughed, and captured his fingers, pressing them into her hand. For nearly an hour they remained thus in the still sunshine by the sea-wall, till Helena began to sigh, and to lift her face to the little breeze that wandered down from the west. She fled as soon from warmth as from cold. Physically, she was always so; she shrank from anything extreme. But psychically she was an extremist, and a dangerous one.

They climbed the hill to the fresh-breathing west. On the highest point of land stood a tall cross, railed in by a red iron fence. They read the inscription.

"That's all right—but a vilely ugly railing!" exclaimed Siegmund.

"Oh, they'd have to fence in Lord Tennyson's white marble," said Helena, rather indefinitely.

He interpreted her according to his own idea.

"Yes, he did belittle great things, didn't he?" said Siegmund.

"Tennyson!" she exclaimed.

"Not peacocks and princesses, but the bigger things."

"I shouldn't say so," she declared.

He sounded indeterminate, but was not really so.

They wandered over the downs westward, among the wind. As they followed the headland to the Needles, they felt the breeze from the wings of the sea brushing them, and heard restless, poignant voices screaming below the cliffs. Now and again a gull, like a piece of spume flung up, rose over the cliff's edge, and sank again. Now and again, as the path dipped in a hollow, they could see the low, suspended intertwining of the birds passing in and out of the cliff shelter.

These savage birds appealed to all the poetry and yearning in Helena. They fascinated her, they almost voiced her. She crept nearer and nearer the edge, feeling she must watch the gulls thread out in flakes of white above the weed-black rocks. Siegmund stood away back, anxiously. He would not dare to tempt Fate now, having too strong a sense of death to risk it.

"Come back, dear. Don't go so near," he pleaded, following as close as he might. She heard the pain and appeal in his voice. It thrilled her, and she went a little nearer. What was death to her but one of her symbols, the death of which the sagas talk—something grand, and sweeping, and dark.

Leaning forward, she could see the line of grey sand and the line of foam broken by black rocks, and over all the gulls, stirring round like froth on a pot, screaming in chorus.

She watched the beautiful birds, heard the pleading of Siegmund, and she thrilled with pleasure, toying with his keen anguish.

Helena came smiling to Siegmund, saying:

"They look so fine down there."

He fastened his hands upon her, as a relief from his pain. He was filled with a keen, strong anguish of dread, like a presentiment. She laughed as he gripped her.

They went searching for a way of descent. At last Siegmund inquired of the coastguard the nearest way down the cliff. He was pointed to the "Path of the Hundred Steps".

"When is a hundred not a hundred?" he said sceptically, as they descended the dazzling white chalk. There were sixty-eight steps. Helena laughed at his exactitude.

"It must be a love of round numbers," he said.

"No doubt," she laughed. He took the thing so seriously.

"Or of exaggeration," he added.

There was a shelving beach of warm white sand, bleached soft as velvet. A sounding of gulls filled the dark recesses of the headland; a low chatter of shingle came from where the easy water was breaking; the confused, shell-like murmur of the sea between the folded cliffs. Siegmund and Helena lay side by side upon the dry sand, small as two resting birds, while thousands of gulls whirled in a white-flaked storm above them, and the great cliffs towered beyond, and high up over the cliffs the multitudinous clouds were travelling, a vast caravan *en route*. Amidst the journeying of oceans and clouds and the circling flight of heavy spheres, lost to sight in the sky, Siegmund and Helena, two grains of life in the vast movement, were travelling a moment side by side.

They lay on the beach like a grey and a white sea-bird together. The lazy ships that were idling down the Solent observed the cliffs and the boulders, but Siegmund and Helena were too little. They lay ignored and insignificant, watching through half-closed fingers the diverse caravan of Day go past. They lay with their latticed fingers over their eyes, looking out at the sailing of ships across their vision of blue water.

"Now, that one with the greyish sails——" Siegmund was saying.

"Like a housewife of forty going placidly round with the duster—yes?" interrupted Helena.

"That is a schooner. You see her four sails, and——"

He continued to classify the shipping, until he was interrupted by the wicked laughter of Helena.

"That is right, I am sure," he protested.

"I won't contradict you," she laughed, in a tone which showed him he knew even less of the classifying of ships than she did.

"So you have lain there amusing yourself at my expense all the time?" he said, not knowing in the least why she laughed. They turned and looked at one another, blue eyes smiling and wavering as the beach wavers in the heat. Then they closed their eyes with sunshine.

Drowsed by the sun, and the white sand, and the foam, their thoughts slept like butterflies on the flowers of delight. But cold shadows startled them up.

"The clouds are coming," he said regretfully.

"Yes; but the wind is quite strong enough for them," she answered.

"Look at the shadows—like blots floating away. Don't they devour the sunshine?"

"It is quite warm enough here," she said, nestling in to him.

"Yes; but the sting is missing. I like to feel the warmth biting in."

"No, I do not. To be cosy is enough."

"I like the sunshine on me, real, and manifest, and tangible. I feel like a seed that has been frozen for ages. I want to be bitten by the sunshine."

She leaned over and kissed him. The sun came bright-footed over the water, leaving a shining print on Siegmund's face. He lay, with half-closed eyes, sprawled loosely on the sand. Looking at his limbs, she imagined he must be heavy, like the boulders. She sat over him, with her finger stroking his eyebrows, that were broad and rather arched. He lay perfectly still, in a half-dream.

Presently she laid her head on his breast, and remained so, watching the sea, and listening to his heart-beats. The throb was strong and deep. It seemed to go through the whole island and the whole afternoon, and it fascinated her: so deep, unheard, with its great expulsions of life. Had the world a heart? Was there also deep in the world a great God thudding out waves of life, like a great heart, unconscious? It frightened her. This was the God she knew not, as she knew not this Siegmund. It was so different from the half-shut eyes with black lashes, and the winsome, shapely nose. And the heart of the world, as she heard it, could not be the same as the curling splash of retreat of the little sleepy waves. She listened for Siegmund's soul, but his heart overbeat all other sound, thudding powerfully.

CHAPTER VII

SIEGMUND woke to the muffled firing of guns on the sea. He looked across at the shaggy grey water in wonder. Then he turned to Helena.

"I suppose," he said, "they are saluting the Czar. Poor beggar!"

"I was afraid they would wake you," she smiled.

They listened again to the hollow, dull sound of salutes from across the water and the downs.

The day had gone grey. They decided to walk, down below, to the next bay.

"The tide is coming in," said Helena.

"But this broad strip of sand hasn't been wet for months. It's as soft as pepper," he replied.

They laboured along the shore, beside the black, sinuous line of shrivelled fucus. The base of the cliff was piled with chalk debris. On the other side was the level plain of the sea. Hand in hand, alone and overshadowed by huge cliffs, they toiled on. The waves staggered in, and fell, overcome at the end of the race.

Siegmund and Helena neared a headland, sheer as the side of a house, its base weighted with a tremendous white mass of boulders, that the green sea broke amongst with a hollow sound, followed by a sharp hiss of withdrawal. The lovers had to cross this desert of white boulders, that glistened in smooth skins uncannily. But Siegmund saw the waves were almost at the wall of the headland. Glancing back, he saw the other headland white-dashed at the base with foam. He and Helena must hurry, or they would be prisoned on the thin crescent of strand still remaining between the great wall and the water.

The cliffs overhead oppressed him—made him feel trapped and helpless. He was caught by them in a net of great boulders, while the sea fumbled for him. But he and Helena. She laboured strenuously beside him, blinded by the skin-like glisten of the white rock.

"I think I will rest awhile," she said.

"No, come along," he begged.

"My dear," she laughed, "there is tons of this shingle to buttress us from the sea."

He looked at the waves curving and driving maliciously at the boulders. It would be ridiculous to be trapped.

"Look at this black wood," she said. "Does the sea really char it?"

"Let us get round the corner," he begged.

"Really, Siegmund, the sea is not so anxious to take us," she said ironically.

When they rounded the first point, they found themselves in a small bay jutted out to sea; the front of the headland was, as usual, grooved. This bay was pure white at the base, from its great heaped mass of shingle. With the huge concave of the cliff behind, the foothold of massed white boulders, and the immense arc of the sea in front, Helena was delighted.

"This is fine, Siegmund!" she said, halting and facing west.

Smiling ironically, he sat down on a boulder. They were quite alone, in this great white niche thrust out to sea. Here, he could see, the tide would beat the base of the wall. It came plunging not far from their feet.

"Would you really like to travel beyond the end?" he asked.

She looked round quickly, thrilled, then answered as if in rebuke:

"This is a fine place. I should like to stay here an hour."

"And then where?"

"Then? Oh, then, I suppose, it would be tea-time."

"Tea on brine and pink anemones, with Daddy Neptune."

She looked sharply at the outjutting capes. The sea did foam perilously near their bases.

"I suppose it *is* rather risky," she said; and she turned, began silently to clamber forwards.

He followed; she should set the pace.

"I have no doubt there's plenty of room, really," he said. "The sea only looks near."

But she toiled on intently. Now it was a question of danger, not of inconvenience, Siegmund felt elated. The waves foamed up, as it seemed, against the exposed headland, from which the massive shingle had been swept back. Supposing they could not get by? He began to smile curiously. He became aware of the tremendous noise of waters, of the slight shudder of the shingle when a wave struck it, and he always laughed to himself. Helena laboured on in silence; he kept just behind her. The point seemed near, but it took longer than they thought. They had against them the tremendous cliff, the enormous weight of shingle, and the swinging sea. The waves struck louder, booming fearfully; wind, sweeping round the corner, wet their faces. Siegmund hoped they were cut off, and hoped anxiously the way was clear. The smile became set on his face.

Then he saw there was a ledge or platform at the base of the cliff, and it was against this the waves broke. They climbed the side of this ridge, hurried round to the front. There the

wind caught them, wet and furious; the water raged below.
Between the two Helena shrank, wilted. She took hold of
Siegmund. The great, brutal wave flung itself at the rock,
then drew back for another heavy spring. Fume and spray
were spun on the wind like smoke. The roaring thud of the
waves reminded Helena of a beating heart. She clung closer
to him, as her hair was blown out damp, and her white dress
flapped in the wet wind. Always, against the rock, came the
slow thud of the waves, like a great heart beating under the
breast. There was something brutal about it that she could
not bear. She had no weapon against brute force.

She glanced up at Siegmund. Tiny drops of mist greyed his
eyebrows. He was looking out to sea, screwing up his eyes,
and smiling brutally. Her face became heavy and sullen. He
was like the heart and the brute sea, just here; he was not her
Siegmund. She hated the brute in him.

Turning suddenly, she plunged over the shingle towards the
wide, populous bay. He remained alone, grinning at the smash-
ing turmoil, careless of her departure. He would easily catch
her.

When at last he turned from the wrestling water, he had
spent his savagery, and was sad. He could never take part in
the great battle of action. It was beyond him. Many things
he had let slip by. His life was whittled down to only a few
interests, only a few necessities. Even here, he had but Helena,
and through her the rest. After this week—well, that was
vague. He left it in the dark, dreading it.

And Helena was toiling over the rough beach alone. He saw
her small figure bowed as she plunged forward. It smote his
heart with the keenest tenderness. She was so winsome, a playmate with beauty and fancy. Why was he cruel to her because
she had not his own bitter wisdom of experience? She was
young and naïve, and should he be angry with her for that?
His heart was tight at the thought of her. She would have to
suffer also, because of him.

He hurried after her. Not till they had nearly come to a
little green mound, where the downs sloped and the cliffs were
gone, did he catch her up. Then he took her hand as they
walked.

They halted on the green hillock beyond the sand, and, without a word, he folded her in his arms. Both were out of breath.
He clasped her close, seeming to rock her with his strong pant-

ing. She felt his body lifting into her, and sinking away. It seemed to force a rhythm, a new pulse, in her. Gradually, with a fine, keen thrilling, she melted down on him, like metal sinking on a mould. He was sea and sunlight mixed, heaving, warm, deliciously strong.

Siegmund exulted. At last she was moulded to him in pure passion.

They stood folded thus for some time. Then Helena raised her burning face, and relaxed. She was throbbing with strange elation and satisfaction.

"It might as well have been the sea as any other way, dear," she said, startling both of them. The speech went across their thoughtlessness like a star flying into the night, from nowhere. She had no idea why she said it. He pressed his mouth on hers. "Not for you," he thought, by reflex. "You can't go that way yet." But he said nothing, strained her very tightly, and kept her lips.

They were roused by the sound of voices. Unclasping, they went to walk at the fringe of the water. The tide was creeping back. Siegmund stooped, and from among the water's combings picked up an electric-light bulb. It lay in some weed at the base of a rock. He held it in his hand to Helena. Her face lighted with a curious pleasure. She took the thing delicately from his hand, fingered it with her exquisite softness.

"Isn't it remarkable!" she exclaimed joyously. "The sea must be very, very gentle—and very kind."

"Sometimes," smiled Siegmund.

"But I did not think it could be so fine-fingered," she said. She breathed on the glass bulb till it looked like a dim magnolia bud; she inhaled its fine savour.

"It would not have treated *you* so well," he said. She looked at him with heavy eyes. Then she returned to her bulb. Her fingers were very small and very pink. She had the most delicate touch in the world, like a faint feel of silk. As he watched her lifting her fingers from off the glass, then gently stroking it, his blood ran hot. He watched her, waited upon her words and movements attentively.

"It is a graceful act on the sea's part," she said. "Wotan is so clumsy—he knocks over the bowl, and flap-flap-flap go the gasping fishes, *pizzicato!*—but the sea——"

Helena's speech was often difficult to render into plain terms. She was not lucid.

"But life's so full of anti-climax," she concluded. Siegmund smiled softly at her. She had him too much in love to disagree or to examine her words.

"There's no reckoning with life, and no reckoning with the sea. The only way to get on with both is to be as near a vacuum as possible, and float," he jested. It hurt her that he was flippant. She proceeded to forget he had spoken.

There were three children on the beach. Helena had handed him back the senseless bauble, not able to throw it away. Being a father:

"I will give it to the children," he said.

She looked up at him, loved him for the thought.

Wandering hand in hand, for it pleased them both to own each other publicly, after years of conventional distance, they came to a little girl who was bending over a pool. Her black hair hung in long snakes to the water. She stood up, flung back her locks to see them as they approached. In one hand she clasped some pebbles.

"Would you like this? I found it down there," said Siegmund, offering her the bulb.

She looked at him with grave blue eyes and accepted his gift. Evidently she was not going to say anything.

"The sea brought it all the way from the mainland without breaking it," said Helena, with the interesting intonation some folk use to children.

The girl looked at her.

"The waves put it out of their lap on to some seaweed with such careful fingers——"

The child's eyes brightened.

"The tide-line is full of treasures," said Helena, smiling.

The child answered her smile a little.

Siegmund had walked away.

"What beautiful eyes she had!" said Helena.

"Yes," he replied.

She looked up at him. He felt her searching him tenderly with her eyes. But he could not look back at her. She took his hand and kissed it, knowing he was thinking of his own youngest child.

CHAPTER VIII

THE way home lay across country, through deep little lanes
where the late foxgloves sat seriously, like sad hounds; over
open downlands, rough with gorse and ling, and through
pocketed hollows of bracken and trees.

They came to a small Roman Catholic church in the fields.
There the carved Christ looked down on the dead whose sleeping forms made mounds under the coverlet. Helena's heart
was swelling with emotion. All the yearning and pathos of
Christianity filled her again.

The path skirted the churchyard wall, so that she had on the
one hand the sleeping dead, and on the other Siegmund, strong
and vigorous, but walking in the old, dejected fashion. She
felt a rare tenderness and admiration for him. It was unusual
for her to be so humble-minded, but this evening she felt she
must minister to him, and be submissive.

She made him stop to look at the graves. Suddenly, as they
stood, she kissed him, clasped him fervently, roused him till
his passion burned away his heaviness, and he seemed tipped
with life, his face glowing as if soon he would burst alight.
Then she was satisfied, and could laugh.

As they went through the fir copse, listening to the birds
like a family assembled and chattering at home in the evening,
listening to the light swish of the wind, she let Siegmund pre-
dominate; he set the swing of their motion; she rested on him
like a bird on a swaying bough.

They argued concerning the way. Siegmund, as usual, submitted to her. They went quite wrong. As they retraced their
steps, stealthily, through a poultry farm whose fowls were
standing in forlorn groups, once more dismayed by evening,
Helena's pride battled with her new subjugation to Siegmund.
She walked head down, saying nothing. He also was silent,
but his heart was strong in him. Somewhere in the distance a
band was playing "The Watch on the Rhine".

As they passed the beeches and were near home, Helena said,
to try him, and to strike a last blow for her pride:

"I wonder what next Monday will bring us."

"Quick curtain," he answered joyously. He was looking
down and smiling at her with such careless happiness that she
loved him. He was wonderful to her. She loved him, was

jealous of every particle of him that evaded her. She wanted to sacrifice to him, make herself a burning altar to him, and she wanted to possess him.

The hours that would be purely their own came too slowly for her.

That night she met his passion with love. It was not his passion she wanted, actually. But she desired that he should want *her* madly, and that he should have all—everything. It was a wonderful night to him. It restored in him the full "will to live". But she felt it destroyed her. Her soul seemed blasted.

At seven o'clock in the morning Helena lay in the deliciously cool water, while small waves ran up the beach full and clear and foamless, continuing perfectly in their flicker the rhythm of the night's passion. Nothing, she felt, had ever been so delightful as this cool water running over her. She lay and looked out on the shining sea. All things, it seemed, were made of sunshine more or less soiled. The cliffs rose out of the shining waves like clouds of strong, fine texture, and rocks along the shore were the dapplings of a bright dawn. The coarseness was fused out of the world, so that sunlight showed in the veins of the morning cliffs and the rocks. Yea, everything ran with sunshine, as we are full of blood, and plants are tissued from green-gold, glistening sap. Substance and solidity were shadows that the morning cast round itself to make itself tangible: as she herself was a shadow, cast by that fragment of sunshine, her soul, over its inefficiency.

She remembered to have seen the bats flying low over a burnished pool at sunset, and the web of their wings had burned in scarlet flickers, as they stretched across the light. Winged momentarily on bits of tissued flame, threaded with blood, the bats had flickered a secret to her.

Now the cliffs were like wings uplifted, and the morning was coming dimly through them. She felt the wings of all the world upraised against the morning in a flashing, multitudinous flight. The world itself was flying. Sunlight poured on the large round world till she fancied it a heavy bee humming on its iridescent atmosphere across a vast air of sunshine.

She lay and rode the fine journey. Sunlight liquid in the water made the waves heavy, golden, and rich with a velvety coolness like cowslips. Her feet fluttered in the shadowy underwater. Her breast came out bright as the breast of a white bird.

Where was Siegmund? she wondered. He also was somewhere among the sea and the sunshine, white and playing like
a bird, shining like a vivid, restless speck of sunlight. She
struck the water, smiling, feeling alone with him. They two
were the owners of this morning, as a pair of wild, large birds
inhabiting an empty sea.

Siegmund had found a white cave welling with green water,
brilliant and full of life as mounting sap. The white rock
glimmered through the water, and soon Siegmund shimmered
also in the living green of the sea, like pale flowers trembling
upward.

"The water," said Siegmund, "is as full of life as I am," and
he pressed forward his breast against it. He swam very well
that morning; he had more wilful life than the sea, so he
mastered it laughingly with his arms, feeling a delight in his
triumph over the waves. Venturing recklessly in his new pride,
he swam round the corner of the rock, through an archway,
lofty and spacious, into a passage where the water ran like a
flood of green light over the skin-white bottom. Suddenly he
emerged in the brilliant daylight of the next tiny scoop of a
bay.

There he arrived like a pioneer, for the bay was inaccessible
from the land. He waded out of the green, cold water on to
sand that was pure as the shoulders of Helena, out of the
shadow of the archway into the sunlight, on to the glistening
petal of this blossom of a sea-bay.

He did not know till he felt the sunlight how the sea had
drunk with its cold lips deeply of his warmth. Throwing himself down on the sand that was soft and warm as white fur,
he lay glistening wet, panting, swelling with glad pride at
having conquered also this small, inaccessible sea-cave, creeping into it like a white bee into a white virgin blossom that
had waited, how long, for its bee.

The sand was warm to his breast, and his belly, and his
arms. It was like a great body he cleaved to. Almost, he
fancied, he felt it heaving under him in its breathing. Then
he turned his face to the sun, and laughed. All the while, he
hugged the warm body of the sea-bay beneath him. He spread
his hands upon the sand; he took it in handfuls, and let it run
smooth, warm, delightful, through his fingers.

"Surely," he said to himself, "it is like Helena;" and he laid
his hands again on the warm body of the shore, let them

wander, discovering, gathering all the warmth, the softness, the strange wonder of smooth warm pebbles, then shrinking from the deep weight of cold his hand encountered as he burrowed under the surface wrist-deep. In the end he found the cold mystery of the deep sand also thrilling. He pushed in his hands again and deeper, enjoying the almost hurt of the dark, heavy coldness. For the sun and the white flower of the bay were breathing and kissing him dry, were holding him in their warm concave, like a bee in a flower, like himself on the bosom of Helena, and flowing like the warmth of her breath in his hair came the sunshine, breathing near and lovingly; yet, under all, was this deep mass of cold, that the softness and warmth merely floated upon.

Siegmund lay and clasped the sand, and tossed it in handfuls till over him he was all hot and cloyed. Then he rose and looked at himself and laughed. The water was swaying reproachfully against the steep pebbles below, murmuring like a child that it was not fair—it was not fair he should abandon his playmate. Siegmund laughed, and began to rub himself free of the clogging sand. He found himself strangely dry and smooth. He tossed more dry sand, and more, over himself, busy and intent like a child playing some absorbing game with itself. Soon his body was dry and warm and smooth as a camomile flower. He was, however, greyed and smeared with sand-dust. Siegmund looked at himself with disapproval, though his body was full of delight and his hands glad with the touch of himself. He wanted himself clean. He felt the sand thick in his hair, even in his moustache. He went painfully over the pebbles till he found himself on the smooth rock bottom. Then he soused himself, and shook his head in the water, and washed and splashed and rubbed himself with his hands assiduously. He must feel perfectly clean and free— fresh, as if he had washed away all the years of soilure in this morning's sea and sun and sand. It was the purification. Siegmund became again a happy priest of the sun. He felt as if all the dirt of misery were soaked out of him, as he might soak clean a soiled garment in the sea, and bleach it white on the sunny shore. So white and sweet and tissue-clean he felt— full of lightness and grace.

The garden in front of their house, where Helena was waiting for him, was long and crooked, with a sunken flagstone pavement running up to the door by the side of the lawn. On either hand the high fence of the garden was heavy with wild clematis and honeysuckle. Helena sat sideways, with a map spread out on her bench under the bushy little laburnum tree, tracing the course of their wanderings. It was very still. There was just a murmur of bees going in and out the brilliant little porches of nasturtium flowers. The nasturtium leaf-coins stood cool and grey; in their delicate shade, underneath in the green twilight, a few flowers shone their submerged gold and scarlet. There was a faint scent of mignonette. Helena, like a white butterfly in the shade, her two white arms for antennæ stretching firmly to the bench, leaned over her map. She was busy, very busy, out of sheer happiness. She traced word after word, and evoked scene after scene. As she discovered a name, she conjured up the place. As she moved to the next mark she imagined the long path lifting and falling happily.

She was waiting for Siegmund, yet his hand upon the latch startled her. She rose suddenly, in agitation. Siegmund was standing in the sunshine at the gate. They greeted each other across the tall roses.

When Siegmund was holding her hand, he said, softly laughing:

"You have come out of the water very beautiful this morning."

She laughed. She was not beautiful, but she felt so at that moment. She glanced up at him, full of love and gratefulness.

"And you," she murmured, in a still tone, as if it were almost sacrilegiously unnecessary to say it.

Siegmund was glad. He rejoiced to be told he was beautiful. After a few moments of listening to the bees and breathing the mignonette, he said:

"I found a little white bay, just like you—a virgin bay. I had to swim there."

"Oh!" she said, very interested in him, not in the fact.

"It seemed just like you. Many things seem like you," he said.

She laughed again in her joyous fashion, and the reed-like vibration came into her voice.

"I saw the sun through the cliffs, and the sea, and you," she said.

He did not understand. He looked at her searchingly. She was white and still and inscrutable. Then she looked up at him; her earnest eyes, that would not flinch, gazed straight into

him. He trembled, and things all swept into a blur. After she
had taken away her eyes he found himself saying:

"You know, I felt as if I were the first man to discover
things: like Adam when he opened the first eyes in the world."

"I saw the sunshine in you," repeated Helena quietly, looking at him with her eyes heavy with meaning.

He laughed again, not understanding, but feeling she meant
love.

"No, but you have altered everything," he said.

The note of wonder, of joy, in his voice touched her almost
beyond self-control. She caught his hand and pressed it; then
quickly kissed it. He became suddenly grave.

"I feel as if it were right—you and me, Helena—so, even
righteous. It is so, isn't it? And the sea and everything, they
all seem with us. Do you think so?"

Looking at her, he found her eyes full of tears. He bent and
kissed her, and she pressed his head to her bosom. He was very
glad.

CHAPTER IX

THE day waxed hot. A few little silver tortoises of cloud had
crawled across the desert of sky, and hidden themselves. The
chalk roads were white, quivering with heat. Helena and
Siegmund walked eastward bareheaded under the sunshine.
They felt like two insects in the niche of a hot hearth as they
toiled along the deep road. A few poppies here and there
among the wild rye floated scarlet in sunshine like blood-drops
on green water. Helena recalled Francis Thompson's poems,
which Siegmund had never read. She repeated what she knew,
and laughed, thinking what an ineffectual pale shadow of a
person Thompson must have been. She looked at Siegmund,
walking in large easiness beside her.

"Artists are supremely unfortunate persons," she announced.

"Think of Wagner," said Siegmund, lifting his face to the
hot bright heaven, and drinking the heat with his blinded face.
All states seemed meagre, save his own. He recalled people who

had loved, and he pitied them—dimly, drowsily, without pain.

They came to a place where they might gain access to the shore by a path down a landslip. As they descended through the rockery, yellow with ragwort, they felt themselves dip into the inert, hot air of the bay. The living atmosphere of the uplands was left overhead. Among the rocks of the sand, white as if smelted, the heat glowed and quivered. Helena sat down and took off her shoes. She walked on the hot, glistening sand till her feet were delightfully, almost intoxicatingly scorched. Then she ran into the water to cool them. Siegmund and she paddled in the light water, pensively watching the haste of the ripples, like crystal beetles, running over the white outline of their feet; looking out on the sea that rose so near to them, dwarfing them by its far reach.

For a short time they flitted silently in the water's edge. Then there settled down on them a twilight of sleep, the little hush that closes the doors and draws the blinds of the house after a festival. They wandered out across the beach above high-water mark, where they sat down together on the sand, leaning back against a flat brown stone, Siegmund with the sunshine on his forehead, Helena drooping close to him, in his shadow. Then the hours ride by unnoticed, making no sound as they go. The sea creeps nearer, nearer, like a snake which watches two birds asleep. It may not disturb them, but sinks back, ceasing to look at them with its bright eyes.

Meanwhile the flowers of their passion were softly shed, as poppies fall at noon, and the seed of beauty ripened rapidly within them. Dreams came like a wind through their souls, drifting off with the seed-dust of beautiful experience which they had ripened, to fertilise the souls of others withal. In them the sea and the sky and ships had mingled and bred new blossoms of the torrid heat of their love. And the seed of such blossoms was shaken as they slept, into the hand of God, who held it in His palm preciously; then scattered it again, to produce new splendid blooms of beauty.

A little breeze came down the cliffs. Sleep lightened the lovers of their experience; new buds were urged in their souls as they lay in a shadowed twilight, at the porch of death. The breeze fanned the face of Helena; a coolness wafted on her throat. As the afternoon wore on she revived. Quick to flag, she was easy to revive, like a white pansy flung into water. She shivered lightly and rose.

Strange, it seemed to her, to rise from the brown stone into life again. She felt beautifully refreshed. All around was quick as a garden wet in the early morning of June. She took her hair and loosened it, shook it free from sand, spread, and laughed like a fringed poppy that opens itself to the sun. She let the wind comb through its soft fingers the tangles of her hair. Helena loved the wind. She turned to it, and took its kisses on her face and throat.

Siegmund lay still, looking up at her. The changes in him were deeper, like alteration in his tissue. His new buds came slowly, and were of a fresh type. He lay smiling at her. At last he said:

"You look now as if you belonged to the sea."

"I do; and some day I shall go back to it," she replied.

For to her at that moment the sea was a great lover, like Siegmund, but more impersonal, who would receive her when Siegmund could not. She rejoiced momentarily in the fact. Siegmund looked at her and continued smiling. His happiness was budded firm and secure.

"Come!" said Helena, holding out her hand.

He rose somewhat reluctantly from his large, fruitful inertia.

CHAPTER X

SIEGMUND carried the boots and the shoes while they wandered over the sand to the rocks. There was a delightful sense of risk in scrambling with bare feet over the smooth irregular jumble of rocks. Helena laughed suddenly from fear as she felt herself slipping. Siegmund's heart was leaping like a child's with excitement as he stretched forward, himself very insecure, to succour her. Thus they travelled slowly. Often she called to him to come and look in the lovely little rock-pools, dusky with blossoms of red anemones and brown anemones that seemed nothing but shadows, and curtained with green of finest sea-silk. Sigemund loved to poke the white pebbles, and startle the little ghosts of crabs in a shadowy scuttle through the weed. He would tease the expectant anemones, causing them to close suddenly over his finger. But Helena liked to

watch without touching things. Meanwhile the sun was slant-
ing behind the cross far away to the west, and the light was
swimming in silver and gold upon the lacquered water. At
last Siegmund looked doubtfully at two miles more of glistening, gilded boulders. Helena was seated on a stone, dabbling
her feet in a warm pool, delicately feeling the wet sea-velvet
of the weeds.

"Don't you think we had better be mounting the cliffs?"
he said.

She glanced up at him, smiling with irresponsible eyes. Then
she lapped the water with her feet, and surveyed her pink toes.
She was absurdly, childishly happy.

"Why should we?" she asked lightly.

He watched her. Her child-like indifference to consequences
touched him with a sense of the distance between them. He
himself might play with the delicious warm surface of life, but
always he recked of the relentless mass of cold beneath—the
mass of life which has no sympathy with the individual, no
cognizance of him.

She loved the trifles and the toys, the mystery and the magic
of things. She would not own life to be relentless. It was either
beautiful, fantastic, or weird, or inscrutable, or else mean and
vulgar, below consideration. He had to get a sense of the
anemone and a sympathetic knowledge of its experience, into
his blood, before he was satisfied. To Helena an anemone was
one more fantastic pretty figure in her kaleidoscope.

So she sat dabbling her pink feet in the water, quite unconscious of his gravity. He waited on her, since he never
could capture her.

"Come," he said very gently. "You are only six years old
to-day."

She laughed as she let him take her. Then she nestled up to
him, smiling in a brilliant, child-like fashion. He kissed her
with all the father in him sadly alive.

"Now put your stockings on," he said.

"But my feet are wet." She laughed.

He kneeled down and dried her feet on his handkerchief,
while she sat tossing his hair with her finger-tips. The sunlight
grew more and more golden.

"I envy the savages their free feet," she said.

"There is no broken glass in the wilderness—or there used
not to be," he replied.

As they were crossing the sands, a whole family entered by the cliff track. They descended in single file, unequally, like the theatre; two boys, then a little girl, the father, another girl, then the mother. Last of all trotted the dog, warily, suspicious of the descent. The boys emerged into the bay with a shout; the dog rushed, barking, after them. The little one waited for her father, calling shrilly:

"Tiss can't fall now, can she, dadda? Shall I put her down?"

"Ay, let her have a run," said the father.

Very carefully she lowered the kitten which she had carried clasped to her bosom. The mite was bewildered and scared. It turned round pathetically.

"Go on, Tissie; you're all right," said the child. "Go on; have a run on the sand."

The kitten stood dubious and unhappy. Then, perceiving the dog some distance ahead, it scampered after him, a fluffy, scurrying mite. But the dog had already raced into the water. The kitten walked a few steps, turning its small face this way and that, and mewing piteously. It looked extraordinarily tiny as it stood, a fluffy handful, staring away from the noisy water, its thin cry floating over the plash of waves.

Helena glanced at Siegmund, and her eyes were shining with pity. He was watching the kitten and smiling.

"Crying because things are too big, and it can't take them in," he said.

"But look how frightened it is," she said.

"So am I." He laughed. "And if there are any gods looking on and laughing at me, at least they won't be kind enough to put me in their pinafores. . . ."

She laughed very quickly.

"But why?" she exclaimed. "Why should you want putting in a pinafore?"

"I don't," he laughed.

On the top of the cliff they were between two bays, with darkening blue water on the left, and on the right gold water smoothing to the sun. Siegmund seemed to stand waist-deep in shadow, with his face bright and glowing. He was watching earnestly.

"I want to absorb it all," he said.

When at last they turned away:

"Yes," said Helena slowly; "one can recall the details, but never the atmosphere."

He pondered a moment.

"How strange!" he said. "I can recall the atmosphere, but not the detail. It is a moment to me, not a piece of scenery. I should say the picture was in me, not out there."

Without troubling to understand—she was inclined to think it verbiage—she made a small sound of assent.

"That is why you want to go again to a place, and I don't care so much, because I have it with me," he concluded.

CHAPTER XI

THEY decided to find their way through the lanes to Alum Bay, and then, keeping the cross in sight, to return over the downs, with the moon-path broad on the water before them. For the moon was rising late. Twilight, however, rose more rapidly than they had anticipated. The lane twisted among meadows and wild lands and copses—a wilful little lane, quite incomprehensible. So they lost their distant landmark, the white cross.

Darkness filtered through the daylight. When at last they came to a signpost, it was almost too dark to read it. The fingers seemed to withdraw into the dusk the more they looked.

"We must go to the left," said Helena.

To the left rose the downs, smooth and grey near at hand, but higher black with gorse, like a giant lying asleep with a bearskin over his shoulders.

Several pale chalk-tracks ran side by side through the turf. Climbing, they came to a disused chalk-pit, which they circumvented. Having passed a lonely farmhouse, they mounted the side of the open down, where was a sense of space and freedom.

"We can steer by the night," said Siegmund, as they trod upwards pathlessly. Helena did not mind whither they steered. All places in that large fair night were home and welcome to her. They drew nearer to the shaggy cloak of furze.

"There will be a path through it," said Siegmund.

But when they arrived there was no path. They were confronted by a tall, impenetrable growth of gorse, taller than Siegmund.

"Stay here," said he, "while I look for a way through. I am afraid you will be tired."

She stood alone by the walls of gorse. The lights that had flickered into being during the dusk grew stronger, so that a little farmhouse down the hill glowed with great importance on the night, while the far-off invisible sea became like a road-way, large and mysterious, its specks of light moving slowly, and its bigger lamps stationed out amid the darkness. Helena wanted the day-wanness to be quite wiped off the west. She asked for the full black night, that would obliterate everything save Siegmund. Siegmund it was that the whole world meant. The darkness, the gorse, the downs, the specks of light, seemed only to bespeak him. She waited for him to come back. She could hardly endure the condition of intense waiting.

He came, in his grey clothes almost invisible. But she felt him coming.

"No good," he said, "no vestige of a path. Not a rabbit-run."

"Then we will sit down awhile," said she calmly.

" 'Here on this mole-hill,' " he quoted mockingly.

They sat down in a small gap in the gorse, where the turf was very soft, and where the darkness seemed deeper. The night was all fragrance, cool odour of darkness, keen, savoury scent of the downs, touched with honeysuckle and gorse and bracken scent.

Helena turned to him, leaning her hand on his thigh.

"What day is it, Siegmund?" she asked, in a joyous, wonder-ing tone. He laughed, understanding, and kissed her.

"But really," she insisted, "I would not have believed the labels could have fallen off everything like this."

He laughed again. She still leaned towards him, her weight on her hand, stopping the flow in the artery down his thigh.

"The days used to walk in procession like seven marionettes, each in order and costume, going endlessly round." She laughed, amused at the idea.

"It is very strange," she continued, "to have the days and nights smeared into one piece, as if the clock-hand only went round once in a lifetime."

"That is how it is," he admitted, touched by her eloquence. "You have torn the labels off things, and they all are so different. This morning! It does seem absurd to talk about this morning. Why should I be parcelled up into mornings and evenings and nights? *I* am not made up of sections of time. Now, nights and days go racing over us like cloud-shadows and sunshine over the sea, and all the time we take no notice."

She put her arms round his neck. He was reminded by a sudden pain in his leg how much her hand had been pressing on him. He held his breath from pain. She was kissing him softly over the eyes. They lay cheek to cheek, looking at the stars. He felt a peculiar tingling sense of joy, a keenness of perception, a fine, delicate tingling as of music.

"You know," he said, repeating himself, "it is true. You seem to have knit all things in a piece for me. Things are not separate; they are all in a symphony. They go moving on and on. You are the motive in everything."

Helena lay beside him, half upon him, sad with bliss.

"You must write a symphony of this—of us," she said, prompted by a disciple's vanity.

"Some time," he answered. "Later, when I have time."

"Later," she murmured—"later than what?"

"I don't know," he replied. "This is so bright we can't see beyond." He turned his face to hers and through the darkness smiled into her eyes that were so close to his. Then he kissed her long and lovingly. He lay, with her head on his shoulder, looking through her hair at the stars.

"I wonder how it is you have such a fine natural perfume," he said, always in the same abstract, inquiring tone of happiness.

"Haven't all women?" she replied, and the peculiar penetrating twang of a brass reed was again in her voice.

"I don't know," he said, quite untouched. "But you are scented like nuts, new kernels of hazel-nuts, and a touch of opium. . . ." He remained abstractedly breathing her with his open mouth, quite absorbed in her.

"You are so strange," she murmured tenderly, hardly able to control her voice to speak.

"I believe," he said slowly, "I can see the stars moving through your hair. No, keep still, *you* can't see them." Helena lay obediently very still. "I thought I could watch them travelling, crawling like gold flies on the ceiling," he continued in a slow sing-song. "But now you make your hair tremble, and the stars rush about." Then, as a new thought struck him: "Have you noticed that you can't recognise the constellations lying back like this. I can't see one. Where is the north, even?"

She laughed at the idea of his questioning her concerning these things. She refused to learn the names of the stars or of the constellations, as of the wayside plants. "Why should I want to label them?" she would say. "I prefer to look at them, not to hide them under a name." So she laughed when he asked her to find Vega or Arcturus.

"How full the sky is!" Siegmund dreamed on—"like a crowded street. Down here it is vastly lonely in comparison. We've found a place far quieter and more private than the stars, Helena. Isn't it fine to be up here, with the sky for nearest neighbour?"

"I did well to ask you to come?" she inquired wistfully. He turned to her.

"As wise as God for the minute," he replied softly. "I think a few furtive angels brought us here—smuggled us in."

"And you are glad?" she asked. He laughed.

"*Carpe diem*," he said. "We have plucked a beauty, my dear. With this rose in my coat I dare go to hell or anywhere."

"Why hell, Siegmund?" she asked in displeasure.

"I suppose it is the *postero*. In everything else I'm a failure, Helena. But," he laughed, "this day of ours is a rose not many men have plucked."

She kissed him passionately, beginning to cry in a quick, noiseless fashion.

"What does it matter, Helena?" he murmured. "What does it matter? We are here yet."

The quiet tone of Siegmund moved her with a vivid passion of grief. She felt she should lose him. Clasping him very closely, she burst into uncontrollable sobbing. He did not understand, but he did not interrupt her. He merely held her very close, while he looked through her shaking hair at the motionless stars. He bent his head to hers, he sought her face with his lips, heavy with pity. She grew a little quieter. He felt his cheek all wet with her tears, and, between his cheek and hers, the ravelled roughness of her wet hair that chafed and made his face burn.

"What is it, Helena?" he asked at last. "Why should you cry?"

She pressed her face in his breast, and said in a muffled, un-recognisable voice:

"You won't leave me, will you, Siegmund?"

"How could I? How should I?" he murmured soothingly. She lifted her face suddenly and pressed on him a fierce kiss.

"How could I leave you?" he repeated, and she heard his voice waking, the grip coming into his arms, and she was glad.

An intense silence came over everything. Helena almost expected to hear the stars moving, everything below was so still. She had no idea what Siegmund was thinking. He lay with his arms strong around her. Then she heard the beating of his heart, like the muffled sound of salutes, she thought. It gave her the same thrill of dread and excitement, mingled with a sense of triumph. Siegmund had changed again, his mood was gone, so that he was no longer wandering in a night of thoughts, but had become different, incomprehensible to her. She had no idea what she thought or felt. All she knew was that he was strong, and was knocking urgently with his heart on her breast, like a man who wanted something and who dreaded to be sent away. How he came to be so concentratedly urgent she could not understand. It seemed an unreasonable, an incomprehensible obsession to her. Yet she was glad, and she smiled in her heart, feeling triumphant and restored. Yet again, dimly, she wondered where was the Siegmund of ten minutes ago, and her heart lifted slightly with yearning, to sink with a dismay. This Siegmund was so incomprehensible. Then again, when he raised his head and found her mouth, his lips filled her with a hot flush like wine, a sweet, flaming flush of her whole body, most exquisite, as if she were nothing but a soft rosy flame of fire against him for a moment or two. That, she decided, was supreme, transcendental.

The lights of the little farmhouse below had vanished, the yellow specks of ships were gone. Only the pier-light, far away, shone in the black sea like the broken piece of a star. Overhead was a silver-greyness of stars; below was the velvet blackness of the night and the sea. Helena found herself glimmering with fragments of poetry, as she saw the sea, when she looked very closely, glimmered dustily with a reflection of stars.

> "Tiefe Stille herrscht im Wasser
> Ohne Regung ruht das Meer . . ."

She was fond of what scraps of German verse she knew. With

French verse she had no sympathy; but Goethe and Heine and Uhland seemed to speak her language.

> "Die luft ist kühl, und es dunkelt,
> Und ruhig fliesst der Rhein."

She liked Heine best of all:

> "Wie Träume der Kindheit seh'ich es flimmern
> Auf deinen wogenden Wellengebiet,
> Und alte Errinnrung erzählt mir auf's Neue
> Von all dem lieben herrlichen Spielzeug,
> Von all den blinkenden Weihnachtsgaben . . ."

As she lay in Siegmund's arms again, and he was very still, dreaming she knew not what, fragments such as these flickered and were gone, like the gleam of a falling star over water. The night moved on imperceptibly across the sky. Unlike the day, it made no sound and gave no sign, but passed unseen, unfelt, over them. Till the moon was ready to step forth. Then the eastern sky blenched, and there was a small gathering of clouds round the opening gates:

> "Aus alten Märchen winket es
> Hervor mit weisser Hand,
> Da singt es und da klingt es
> Von einem Zauberland."

Helena sang this to herself as the moon lifted herself slowly among the clouds. She found herself repeating them aloud in in a forgetful singsong, as children do.

"What is it?" said Siegmund. They were both of them sunk in their own stillness, therefore it was a moment or two before she repeated her singsong, in a little louder tone. He did not listen to her, having forgotten that he had asked her a question.

"Turn your head," she told him, when she had finished the verse, "and look at the moon."

He pressed back his head, so that there was a gleaming pallor on his chin and his forehead and deep black shadow over his eyes and his nostrils. This thrilled Helena with a sense of mystery and magic.

" 'Die grosse Blumen schmachten,' " she said to herself,

curiously awake and joyous. "The big flowers open with black petals and silvery ones, Siegmund. You are the big flowers, Siegmund; yours is the bridegroom face, Siegmund, like a black and glistening flesh-petalled flower, Siegmund, and it blooms in the Zauberland, Siegmund—this is the magic land."

Between the phrases of this whispered ecstasy she kissed him swiftly on the throat, in the shadow, and on his faintly gleaming cheeks. He lay still, his heart beating heavily; he was almost afraid of the strange ecstasy she concentrated on him. Meanwhile she whispered over him sharp, breathless phrases in German and English, touching him with her mouth and her cheeks and her forehead.

" 'Und Liebesweisen tönen'—not to-night, Siegmund. They are all still—gorse and the stars and the sea and the trees, are all kissing, Siegmund. The sea has its mouth on the earth, and the gorse and the trees press together, and they all look up at the moon, they put up their faces in a kiss, my darling. But they haven't you—and it all centres in you, my dear, all the wonder-love is in you, more than in them all, Siegmund—Siegmund!"

He felt the tears falling on him as he lay with heart beating in slow heavy drops under the ecstasy of her love. Then she sank down and lay prone on him, spent, clinging to him, lifted up and down by the beautiful strong motion of his breathing. Rocked thus on his strength, she swooned lightly into unconsciousness.

When she came to herself she sighed deeply. She woke to the exquisite heaving of his life beneath her.

"I have been beyond life. I have been a little way into death!" she said to her soul, with wide-eyed delight. She lay dazed, wondering upon it. That she should come back into a marvellous, peaceful happiness astonished her.

Suddenly she became aware that she must be slowly weighing down the life of Siegmund. There was a long space between the lift of one breath and the next. Her heart melted with sorrowful pity. Resting herself on her hands, she kissed him—a long, anguished kiss, as if she would fuse her soul into his for ever. Then she rose, sighing, sighing again deeply. She put up her hands to her head and looked at the moon. "No more," said her heart, almost as if it sighed too—"no more!"

She looked down at Siegmund. He was drawing in great heavy breaths. He lay still on his back, gazing up at her, and she stood motionless at his side, looking down at him. He felt stunned, half-conscious. Yet as he lay helplessly looking up at her some other consciousness inside him murmured: "Hawwa —Eve—Mother!" She stood compassionate over him. Without touching him she seemed to be yearning over him like a mother. Her compassion, her benignity, seemed so different from his little Helena. This woman, tall and pale, drooping with the strength of her compassion, seemed stable, immortal, not a fragile human being, but a personification of the great mother-hood of women.

"I am her child, too," he dreamed, as a child murmurs unconscious in sleep. He had never felt her eyes so much as now, in the darkness, when he looked only into deep shadow. She had never before so entered and gathered his plaintive masculine soul to the bosom of her nurture.

"Come," she said gently, when she knew he was restored. "Shall we go?"

He rose, with difficulty gathering his strength.

CHAPTER XII

SIEGMUND made a great effort to keep the control of his body. The hill-side, the gorse, when he stood up, seemed to have fallen back into shadowed vagueness about him. They were meaningless dark heaps at some distance, very great, it seemed.

"I can't get hold of them," he said distractedly to himself. He felt detached from the earth, from all the near, concrete, beloved things; as if these had melted away from him, and left him, sick and unsupported, somewhere alone on the edge of an enormous space. He wanted to lie down again, to relieve himself of the sickening effort of supporting and controlling his body. If he could lie down again perfectly still he need not struggle to animate the cumbersome matter of his body, and then he would not feel thus sick and outside himself.

But Helena was speaking to him, telling him they would see the moon-path. They must set off downhill. He felt her arm

clasped firmly, joyously, round his waist. Therein was his
stability and warm support. Siegmund felt a keen flush of
pitiful tenderness for her as she walked with buoyant feet
beside him, clasping him so happily, all unconscious. This pity
for her drew him nearer to life.

He shuddered lightly now and again, as they stepped lurch-
ing down the hill. He set his jaws hard to suppress this
shuddering. It was not in his limbs, or even on the surface of
his body, for Helena did not notice it. Yet he shuddered almost
in anguish internally.

"What is it?" he asked himself in wonder.

His thought consisted of these detached phrases, which he
spoke verbally to herself. Between-whiles he was conscious
only of an almost insupportable feeling of sickness, as a man
feels who is being brought from under an anæsthetic; also he
was vaguely aware of a teeming stir of activity, such as one
may hear from a closed hive, within him.

They swung rapidly downhill. Siegmund still shuddered, but
not so uncontrollably. They came to a stile which they must
climb. As he stepped over it needed a concentrated effort of
will to place his foot securely on the step. The effort was so
great that he became conscious of it.

"Good Lord!" he said to himself. "I wonder what it is."

He tried to examine himself. He thought of all the organs of
his body—his brain, his heart, his liver. There was no pain, and
nothing wrong with any of them, he was sure. His dim searching resolved itself into another detached phrase. "There is
nothing the matter with me," he said.

Then he continued vaguely wondering, recalling the sensation of wretched sickness which sometimes follows drunken-
ness, thinking of the times when he had fallen ill.

"But I am not like that," he said, "because I don't feel
tremulous. I am sure my hand is steady."

Helena stood still to consider the road. He held out his hand
before him. It was motionless as a dead flower on this silent
night.

"Yes, I think this is the right way," said Helena, and they
set off again, as if gaily.

"It certainly feels rather deathly," said Siegmund to himself. He remembered distinctly, when he was a child and had
diphtheria, he had stretched himself in the horrible sickness,
which he felt was—and here he chose the French word—

'l'agonie'. But his mother had seen and had cried aloud, which suddenly caused him to struggle with all his soul to spare her her suffering.

"Certainly it is like that," he said. "Certainly it is rather deathly. I wonder how it is."

Then he reviewed the last hour.

"I believe we are lost!" Helena interrupted him.

"Lost! What matter!" he answered indifferently, and Helena pressed him tighter, nearer to her in a kind of triumph. "But did we not come this way?" he added.

"No. See"—her voice was reeded with restrained emotion— "we have certainly not been along this bare path which dips up and down."

"Well, then, we must merely keep due eastward, towards the moon pretty well, as much as we can," said Siegmund, looking forward over the down, where the moon was wrestling heroically to win free of the pack of clouds which hung on her like wolves on a white deer. As he looked at the moon he felt a sense of companionship. Helena, not understanding, left him so much alone; the moon was nearer.

Siegmund continued to review the last hours. He had been so wondrously happy. The world had been filled with a new magic, a wonderful, stately beauty which he had perceived for the first time. For long hours he had been wandering in another —a glamorous, primordial world.

"I suppose," he said to himself, "I have lived too intensely. I seem to have had the stars and moon and everything else for guests, and now they've gone my house is weak."

So he struggled to diagnose his case of splendour and sickness. He reviewed his hour of passion with Helena.

"Surely," he told himself, "I have drunk life too hot, and it has hurt my cup. My soul seems to leak out—I am half here, half gone away. That's why I understand the trees and the night so painfully."

Then he came to the hour of Helena's strange ecstasy over him. That, somehow, had filled him with passionate grief. It was happiness concentrated one drop too keen, so that what should have been vivid wine was like a pure poison scathing him. But his consciousness, which had been unnaturally active, now was dulling. He felt the blood flowing vigorously along the limbs again, and stilling his brain, sweeping away his sickness, soothing him.

"I suppose," he said to himself for the last time, "I suppose living too intensely kills you, more or less."

Then Siegmund forgot. He opened his eyes and saw the night about him. The moon had escaped from the cloud-pack, and was radiant behind a fine veil which glistened to her rays, and which was broidered with a lustrous halo, very large indeed, the largest halo Siegmund had ever seen. When the little lane turned full towards the moon, it seemed as if Siegmund and Helena would walk through a large Moorish arch of horse-shoe shape, the enormous white halo opening in front of them. They walked on, keeping their faces to the moon, smiling with wonder and a little rapture, until once more the little lane curved wilfully, and they were walking north. Helena observed three cottages crouching under the hill and under trees to cover themselves from the magic of the moonlight.

"We certainly did not come this way before," she said triumphantly. The idea of being lost delighted her.

Siegmund looked round at the grey hills smeared over with a low, dim glisten of moon-mist. He could not yet fully realise that he was walking along a lane in the Isle of Wight. His surroundings seemed to belong to some state beyond ordinary experience—some place in romance, perhaps, or among the hills where Brünhild lay sleeping in her large bright halo of fire. How could it be that he and Helena were two children of London wandering to find their lodging in Freshwater? He sighed, and looked again over the hills where the moonlight was condensing in mist ethereal, frail, and yet substantial, reminding him of the way the manna must have condensed out of the white moonlit mists of Arabian deserts.

"We may be on the road to Newport," said Helena presently, "and the distance is ten miles."

She laughed, not caring in the least whither they wandered, exulting in this wonderful excursion! She, and Siegmund alone in a glistening wilderness of night at the back of habited days and nights! Siegmund looked at her. He by no means shared her exultation, though he sympathised with it. He walked on alone in his deep seriousness, of which she was not aware. Yet when he noticed her abandon, he drew her nearer, and his heart softened with protecting tenderness towards her, and grew heavy with responsibility.

The fields breathed off a scent as if they were come to life with the night, and were talking with fragrant eagerness. The farms huddled together in sleep, and pulled the dark shadow over them to hide from the supernatural white night; the cottages were locked and darkened. Helena walked on in triumph through this wondrous hinterland of night, actively searching for the spirits, watching the cottages they approached, listening, looking for the dreams of those sleeping inside, in the darkened rooms. She imagined she could see the frail dream-faces at the windows; she fancied they stole out timidly into the gardens, and went running away among the rabbits on the gleamy hill-side. Helena laughed to herself, pleased with her fancy of wayward little dreams playing with weak hands and feet among the large, solemn-sleeping cattle. This was the first time, she told herself, that she had ever been out among the grey-frocked dreams and white-armed fairies. She imagined herself lying asleep in her room, while her own dreams slid out down the moonbeams. She imagined Siegmund sleeping in his room, while his dreams, dark-eyed, their blue eyes very dark and yearning at night-time, came wandering over the grey grass seeking her dreams.

So she wove her fancies as she walked, until for very weariness she was fain to remember that it was a long way—a long way. Siegmund's arm was about her to support her; she rested herself upon it. They crossed a stile and recognised, on the right of the path, the graveyard of the Catholic chapel. The moon, which the days were paring smaller with envious keen knife, shone upon the white stones in the burial-ground. The carved Christ upon His cross hung against a silver-grey sky. Helena looked up wearily, bowing to the tragedy. Siegmund also looked, and bowed his head.

"Thirty years of earnest love; three years' life like a passionate ecstasy—and it was finished. He was very great and very wonderful. I am very insignificant, and shall go out ignobly. But we are the same; love, the brief ecstasy, and the end. But mine is one rose, and His all the white beauty in the world."

Siegmund felt his heart very heavy, sad, and at fault, in presence of the Christ. Yet he derived comfort from the knowledge that life was treating him in the same manner as it had treated the Master, though his compared small and despicable with the Christ-tragedy. Siegmund stepped softly into the shadow of the pine copse.

"Let me get under cover," he thought. "Let me hide in it; it is good, the sudden intense darkness. I am small and futile: my small, futile tragedy!"

Helena shrank in the darkness. It was almost terrrible to her, and the silence was like a deep pit. She shrank to Siegmund. He drew her closer, leaning over her as they walked, trying to assure her. His heart was heavy, and heavy with a tenderness approaching grief, for his small, brave Helena.

"Are you sure this is the right way?" he whispered to her.

"Quite, quite sure," she whispered confidently in reply. And presently they came out into the hazy moonlight, and began stumbling down the steep hill. They were both very tired, both found it difficult to go with ease or surety this sudden way down. Soon they were creeping cautiously across the pasture and the poultry farm. Helena's heart was beating, as she imagined what a merry noise there would be should they wake all the fowls. She dreaded any commotion, any questioning, this night, so she stole carefully along till they issued on the high-road not far from home.

CHAPTER XIII

In in the morning, after bathing, Siegmund leaned upon the sea-wall in a kind of reverie. It was late, towards nine o'clock, yet he lounged, dreamily looking out on the turquoise blue water, and the white haze of morning, and the small, fair shadows of ships slowly realising before him. In the bay were two battle-ships, uncouth monsters, lying as naïve and curious as sea-lions strayed afar.

Siegmund was gazing oversea in a half-stupid way, when he heard a voice beside him say:

"Where have they come from; do you know, sir?"

He turned, saw a fair, slender man of some thirty-five years standing beside him and smiling faintly at the battleships.

"The men-of-war? There are a good many at Spithead," said Siegmund.

The other glanced negligently into his face.

"They look rather incongruous, don't you think? We left the sea empty and shining, and when we come again, behold, these objects keeping their eye on us!"

Siegmund laughed.

"You are not an Anarchist, I hope?" he said jestingly.

"A Nihilist, perhaps," laughed the other. "But I am quite fond of the Czar, if pity is akin to love. No; but you can't turn round without finding some policeman or other at your elbow—look at them, abominable ironmongery!—ready to put his hand on your shoulder."

The speaker's grey-blue eyes, always laughing with mockery, glanced from the battleships and lit on the dark blue eyes of Siegmund. The latter felt his heart lift in a convulsive movement. This stranger ran so quickly to a perturbing intimacy.

"I suppose we are in the hands of—God," something moved Siegmund to say. The stranger contracted his eyes slightly as he gazed deep at the speaker.

"Ah!" he drawled curiously. Then his eyes wandered over the wet hair, the white brow, and the bare throat of Siegmund, after which they returned again to the eyes of his interlocutor. "Does the Czar sail this way?" he asked at last.

"I do not know," replied Siegmund, who, troubled by the other's penetrating gaze, had not expected so trivial a question.

"I suppose the newspaper will tell us?" said the man.

"Sure to," said Siegmund.

"You haven't seen it this morning?"

"Not since Saturday."

The swift blue eyes of the man dilated. He looked curiously at Siegmund.

"You are not alone on your holiday?"

"No." Siegmund did not like this—he gazed over the sea in displeasure.

"I live here—at least for the present—name, Hampson——"

"Why, weren't you one of the first violins at the Savoy fifteen years back?" asked Siegmund.

They chatted awhile about music. They had known each other, had been fairly intimate, and had since become strangers. Hampson excused himself for having addressed Siegmund:

"I saw you with your nose flattened against the window," he said, "and as I had mine in the same position too, I thought we were fit to be re-acquainted."

Siegmund looked at the man in astonishment.

"I only mean you were staring rather hard at nothing. It's a pity to try and stare out of a beautiful blue day like this, don't you think?"

"Stare beyond it, you mean?" asked Siegmund.

"Exactly!" replied the other, with a laugh of intelligence. "I call a day like this 'the blue room'. It's the least draughty apartment in all the confoundedly draughty House of Life."

Siegmund look at him very intently. This Hampson seemed to express something in his own soul.

"I mean," the man explained, "that after all, the great mass of life that washes unidentified, and that we call death, creeps through the blue envelope of the day, and through our white tissue, and we can't stop it, once we've begun to leak."

"What do you mean by 'leak'?" asked Siegmund.

"Goodness knows—I talk through my hat. But once you've got a bit tired of the house, you glue your nose to the window-pane, and stare for the dark—as you were doing."

"But, to use your metaphor, I'm not tired of the House—if you mean Life," said Siegmund.

"Praise God! I've met a poet who's not afraid of having his pocket picked—or his soul, or his brain!" said the stranger, throwing his head back in a brilliant smile, his eyes dilated.

"I don't know what you mean, sir," said Siegmund, very quietly, with a strong fear and a fascination opposing each other in his heart.

"You're not tired of the House, but of your own particular room—say, suite of rooms——"

"To-morrow I am turned out of this 'blue room'," said Siegmund with a wry smile. The other looked at him seriously.

"Dear Lord!" exclaimed Hampson; then: "Do you remember Flaubert's saint, who laid naked against a leper? I could *not* do it."

"Nor I," shuddered Siegmund.

"But you've got to—or something near it!"

Siegmund looked at the other with frightened, horrified eyes.

"What of yourself?" he said, resentfully.

"I've funked—ran away from my leper, and now am eating my heart out, and staring from the window at the dark."

"But can't you *do* something?" said Siegmund.

The other man laughed with amusement, throwing his head back and showing his teeth.

"I won't ask you what *your* intentions are," he said, with

delicate irony in his tone. "You know, I am a tremendously busy man. I earn five hundred a year by hard work; but it's no good. If you have acquired a liking for intensity in life, you can't do without it. I mean vivid soul experience. It takes the place, with us, of the old adventure, and physical excitement."

Siegmund looked at the other man with baffled, anxious eyes.

"Well, and what then?" he said.

"What then? A craving for intense life is nearly as deadly as any other craving. You become a *concentré*; you feed your normal flame with oxygen, and it devours your tissue. The soulful ladies of romance are always semi-transparent."

Siegmund laughed.

"At least, I am quite opaque," he said.

The other glanced over his easy, mature figure and strong throat.

"Not altogether," said Hampson. "And you, I should think, are one whose flame goes nearly out, when the stimulant is lacking."

Siegmund glanced again at him, startled.

"You haven't much reserve. You're like a tree that'll flower till it kills itself," the man continued. "You'll run till you drop, and then you won't get up again. You've no dispassionate intellect to control you and economise."

"You're telling me very plainly what I am and am not," said Siegmund, laughing rather sarcastically. He did not like it.

"Oh, it's only what I think," replied Hampson. "We're a good deal alike, you see, and have gone the same way. You married and I didn't; but women have always done as they liked with me."

"That's hardly so in my case," said Siegmund.

Hampson eyed him critically.

"Say one woman; it's enough," he replied.

Siegmund gazed, musing, over the sea.

"The best sort of women—the most interesting—are the worst for us," Hampson resumed. "By instinct they aim at suppressing the gross and animal in us. Then they are supersensitive—refined a bit beyond humanity. We, who are as little gross as need be, become their instruments. Life is grounded in them, like electricity in the earth; and we take from them their unrealised life, turn it into light or warmth or power for them. The ordinary woman is, alone, a great potential force, an accumulator, if you like, charged from the source of life. In us her force becomes evident.

"She can't live without us, but she destroys us. These deep, interesting women don't want *us*; they want the flowers of the spirit they can gather of us. We, as natural men, are more or less degrading to them and to their love of us; therefore they destroy the natural man in us—that is, us altogether."

"You're a bit downright, are you not?" asked Siegmund, deprecatingly. He did not disagree with what his friend said, nor tell him such statements were arbitrary.

"That's according to my intensity," laughed Hampson. "I can open the blue heaven with looking, and push back the doors of day a little, and see—God knows what! One of these days I shall slip through. Oh, I am perfectly sane; I only strive beyond myself!"

"Don't you think it's wrong to get like it?" asked Siegmund.

"Well, I do, and so does everybody; but the crowd profits by us in the end. When they understand my music, it will be an education to them; and the whole aim of mankind is to render life intelligible."

Siegmund pondered a little.

"You make me feel—as if I were loose, and a long way off from myself," he said slowly.

The young man smiled, then looked down at the wall, where his own hands lay white and fragile, showing the blue veins.

"I can scarcely believe they are me," he said. "If they rose up and refused me, I should not be surprised. But aren't they beautiful?"

He looked, with a faint smile, at Siegmund.

Siegmund glanced from the stranger's to his own hands, which lay curved on the sea-wall as if asleep. They were small for a man of his stature, but, lying warm in the sun, they looked particularly secure in life. Instinctively, with a wave of self-love, he closed his fists over his thumbs.

"I wonder," said Hampson softly, with strange bitterness, "that she can't see it; I wonder she doesn't cherish you. You are full and beautiful enough in the flesh—why will she help to destroy you, when she loved you to such extremity?"

Siegmund looked at him with awe-stricken eyes. The frail, swift man, with his intensely living eyes, laughed suddenly.

"Fools—the fools, these women!" he said. "Either they smash their own crystal, or it revolts, turns opaque, and leaps out of their hands. Look at me, I am whittled down to the quick; but your neck is thick with compressed life; it is a stem so tense with life that it will hold up by itself. I am very sorry."

All at once he stopped. The bitter despair in his tone was the voice of a heavy feeling of which Siegmund had been vaguely aware for some weeks. Siegmund felt a sense of doom. He laughed, trying to shake it off.

"I wish I didn't go on like this," said Hampson piteously. "I wish I could be normal. How hot it is already! You should wear a hat. It is really hot." He pulled open his flannel shirt.

"I like the heat," said Siegmund.

"So do I."

Directly, the young man dashed the long hair on his forehead into some sort of order, bowed, and smiling in his gay fashion, walked leisurely to the village.

Siegmund stood awhile as if stunned. It seemed to him only a painful dream. Sighing deeply to relieve himself of the pain, he set off to find Helena.

CHAPTER XIV

IN the garden of tall rose trees and nasturtiums Helena was again waiting. It was past nine o'clock, so she was growing impatient. To herself, however, she professed a great interest in a little book of verses she had bought in St. Martin's Lane for twopence.

> "A late, harsh blackbird smote him with her wings,
>   As through the glade, dim in the dark, she flew. . . ."

So she read. She made a curious, pleased sound, and remarked to herself that she thought these verses very fine. But she watched the road for Siegmund.

> "And now she takes the scissors on her thumb . . .
>   Oh then, no more unto my lattice come."

"H'm!" she said, "I really don't know whether I like that or not."

Therefore she read the piece again before she looked down the road.

"He really is very late. It is absurd to think he may have got drowned; but if he were washing about at the bottom of the sea, his hair loose on the water!"

Her heart stood still as she imagined this.

"But what nonsense! I like these verses very much. I will read them as I walk along the side path, where I shall hear the bees, and catch the flutter of a butterfly among the words. That will be a very fitting way to read this poet."

So she strolled to the gate, glancing up now and again. There, sure enough, was Siegmund coming, the towel hanging over his shoulder, his throat bare, and his face bright. She stood in the mottled shade.

"I have kept you waiting," said Siegmund.

"Well, I was reading, you see."

She would not admit her impatience.

"I have been talking," he said.

"Talking!" she exclaimed in slight displeasure. "Have you found an acquaintance even here?"

"A fellow who was quite close friends in Savoy days; he made me feel queer—sort of Doppelgänger, he was."

Helena glanced up swiftly and curiously.

"In what way?" she said.

"He talked all the skeletons in the cupboard—such piffle it seems, now! The sea is like a harebell, and there are two battleships lying in the bay. You can hear the voices of the men on deck distinctly. Well, have you made the plans for to-day?"

They went into the house to breakfast. She watched him helping himself to the scarlet and green salad.

"Mrs. Curtiss," she said, in rather reedy tone, "has been very motherly to me this morning; oh, very motherly!"

Siegmund, who was in a warm, gay mood, shrank up.

"What, has she been saying something about last night?" he asked.

"She was very much concerned for me—was afraid something dreadful had happened," continued Helena, in the same keen, sarcastic tone, which showed she was trying to rid herself of her own mortification.

"Because we weren't in till about eleven?" said Siegmund, also with sarcasm.

"I mustn't do it again. Oh no, I mustn't do it again, really."

"For fear of alarming the old lady?" he asked.

" 'You know, dear, it troubles *me* a good deal . . . but if I were your *mother*, I don't know *how* I should feel,' " she quoted.

"When one engages rooms one doesn't usually stipulate for a stepmother to nourish one's conscience," said Siegmund. They laughed, making jest of the affair; but they were both too thin-skinned. Siegmund writhed within himself with mortification, while Helena talked as if her teeth were on edge.

"I don't *mind* in the least," she said. "The poor old woman has her opinions, and I mine."

Siegmund brooded a little.

"I know I'm a moral coward," he said bitterly.

"Nonsense!" she replied. Then, with a little heat: "But you *do* continue to try so hard to justify yourself, as if *you* felt you needed justification."

He laughed bitterly.

"I tell you—a little thing like this—it remains tied tight round something inside me, reminding me for hours—well, what everybody else's opinion of me is."

Helena laughed rather plaintively.

"I thought you were so sure we were right," she said.

He winced again.

"In myself I am. But in the eyes of the world——"

"If you feel so in yourself, is not that enough?" she said brutally.

He hung his head, and slowly turned his serviette-ring.

"What is myself?" he asked.

"Nothing very definite," she said, with a bitter laugh.

They were silent. After a while she rose, went lovingly over to him, and put her arms round his neck.

"This is our last clear day, dear," she said.

A wave of love came over him, sweeping away all the rest. He took her in his arms. . . .

"It will be hot to-day," said Helena, as they prepared to go out.

"I felt the sun steaming in my hair as I came up," he replied.

"I shall wear a hat—you had better do so too."

"No," he said. "I told you I wanted a sun-soaking; now I think I shall get one."

She did not urge or compel him. In these matters he was old enough to choose for himself.

This morning they were rather silent. Each felt the tarnish on their remaining day.

"I think, dear," she said, "we ought to find the little path that escaped us last night."

"We were lucky to miss it," he answered. "You don't get a walk like that twice in a lifetime, in spite of the old ladies."

She glanced up at him with a winsome smile, glad to hear his words.

They set off, Siegmund bare-headed. He was dressed in flannels and a loose canvas shirt, but he looked what he was— a Londoner on holiday. He had the appearance, the diffident bearing, and the well-cut clothes of a gentleman. He had a slight stoop, a strong-shouldered stoop, and as he walked he looked unseeing in front of him.

Helena belonged to the unclassed. She was not ladylike, nor smart, nor assertive. One could not tell whether she were of independent means or a worker. One thing was obvious about her: she was evidently educated.

Rather short, of strong figure, she was much more noticeably a *concentrée* than was Siegmund. Unless definitely looking at something she always seemed coiled within herself.

She wore a white voile dress made with the waist just below her breasts, and the skirt dropping straight and clinging. On her head was a large, simple hat of burnt straw.

Through the open-worked sleeves of her dress she could feel the sun bite vigorously.

"I wish you had put on a hat, Siegmund," she said.

"Why?" he laughed. "My hair is like a hood." He ruffled it back with his hand. The sunlight glistened on his forehead.

On the higher paths a fresh breeze was energetically chasing the butterflies and driving the few small clouds disconsolate out of the sky. The lovers stood for some time watching the people of the farm in the down below dip their sheep on this sunny morning. There was a ragged noise of bleating from the flock penned in a corner of the yard. Two red-armed men seized a sheep, hauled it to a large bath that stood in the middle of the yard, and there held it, more or less in the bath, whilst a third man baled a dirty yellow liquid over its body. The white legs of the sheep twinkled as it butted this way and that to escape the yellow douche, the blue-shirted men ducked and struggled. There was a faint splashing and shouting to be heard even from a distance. The farmer's wife and children stood by ready to rush in with assistance if necessary.

Helena laughed with pleasure.

"That is really a very quaint and primitive proceeding," she said. "It is cruder than Theocritus."

"In an instant it makes me wish I were a farmer," he laughed. "I think every man has a passion for farming at the bottom of his blood. It would be fine to be plain-minded, to see no farther than the end of one's nose, and to own cattle and land."

"Would it?" asked Helena sceptically.

"If I had a red face, and went to sleep as soon as I sat comfortable, I should love it," he said.

"It amuses me to hear you long to be stupid," she replied.

"To have a simple, slow-moving mind and an active life is the desideratum."

"Is it?" she asked ironically.

"I would give anything to be like that," he said.

"That is, not to be yourself," she said pointedly.

He laughed without much heartiness.

"Don't they seem a long way off?" he said, staring at the bucolic scene. "They are farther than Theocritus—down there is farther than Sicily, and more than twenty centuries from us. I wish it weren't."

"Why do you?" she cried, with curious impatience.

He laughed.

Crossing the down, scattered with dark bushes, they came directly opposite the path through the furze.

"There it is!" she cried. "How could we miss it?"

"Ascribe it to the fairies," he replied, whistling the bird music out of *Siegfried*, then pieces of *Tristan*. They talked very little.

She was tired. When they arrived at a green, naked hollow near the cliff's edge, she said:

"This shall be our house to-day."

"Welcome home!" said Siegmund.

He flung himself down on the high, breezy slope of the dip, looking out to sea. Helena sat beside him. It was absolutely still, and the wind was slackening more and more. Though they listened attentively, they could hear only an indistinct breathing sound, quite small, from the water below: no clap-

ping nor hoarse conversation of waves. Siegmund lay with his
hands beneath his head, looking over the sparkling sea. To put
her page in the shadow, Helena propped her book against him
and began to read.

Presently the breeze, and Siegmund, dropped asleep. The sun
was pouring with dreadful persistence. It beat and beat on
Helena, gradually drawing her from her book in a confusion
of thought. She closed her eyes wearily, longing for shade.
Vaguely she felt a sympathy with Adama in "Adam Cast
Forth". Her mind traced again the tumultuous, obscure
strugglings of the two, forth from Eden through the primitive wildernesses, and she felt sorrowful. Thinking of Adam
blackened with struggle, she looked down at Siegmund. The
sun was beating him upon the face and upon his glistening
brow. His two hands, which lay out on the grass, were full
of blood, the veins of his wrists purple and swollen with heat.
Yet he slept on, breathing with a slight, panting motion. Helena
felt deeply moved. She wanted to kiss him as he lay helpless,
abandoned to the charge of the earth and the sky. She wanted
to kiss him, and shed a few tears. She did neither, but instead,
moved her position so that she shaded his head. Cautiously
putting her hand on his hair, she found it warm, quite hot, as
when you put your hand under a sitting hen, and feel the hot-
feathered bosom.

"It will make him ill," she whispered to herself, and she
bent over to smell the hot hair. She noticed where the sun
was scalding his forehead. She felt very pitiful and helpless
when she saw his brow becoming inflamed with the sun-
scalding.

Turning weariedly away, she sought relief in the landscape.
But the sea was glittering unbearably, like a scaled dragon
wreathing. The houses of Freshwater slept, as cattle sleep
motionless in the hollow valley. Green Farringford on the
slope, was drawn over with a shadow of heat and sleep. In
the bay below the hill the sea was hot and restless. Helena was
sick with sunshine and the restless glitter of water.

" 'And there shall be no more sea,' " she quoted to herself,
she knew not wherefrom.

"No more sea, no more anything," she thought dazedly, as
she sat in the midst of this fierce welter of sunshine. It seemed
to her as if all the lightness of her fancy and her hope were
being burned away in this tremendous furnace, leaving her,

Helena, like a heavy piece of slag seamed with metal. She tried
to imagine herself resuming the old activities, the old manner
of living.

"It is impossible," she said; "it is impossible! What shall I
be when I come out of this? I shall not come out, except as
metal to be cast in another shape. No more the same Siegmund,
no more the same life. What will become of us—what will
happen?"

She was roused from these semi-delirious speculations in the
sun furnace by Siegmund's waking. He opened his eyes, took
a deep breath, and looked smiling at Helena.

"It is worth while to sleep," said he, "for the sake of waking
like this. I was dreaming of huge ice-crystals."

She smiled at him. He seemed unconscious of fate, happy
and strong. She smiled upon him almost in condescension.

"I should like to realise your dream," she said. "This is
terrible!"

They went to the cliff's edge, to receive the cool up-flow of
air from the water. She drank the travelling freshness eagerly
with her face, and put forward her sunburnt arms to be refreshed.

"It is really a very fine sun," said Siegmund lightly. "I feel
as if I were almost satisfied with heat."

Helena felt the chagrin of one whose wretchedness must go
unperceived, while she affects a light interest in another's
pleasure. This time, when Siegmund "failed to follow her",
as she put it, she felt she must follow him.

"You are having your satisfaction complete this journey,"
she said, smiling; "even a sufficiency of me."

"Ay!" said Siegmund drowsily. "I think I am. I think this
is about perfect, don't you?"

She laughed.

"I want nothing more and nothing different," he continued;
"and that's the extreme of a decent time, I should think."

"The extreme of a decent time!" she repeated.

But he drawled on lazily:

"I've only rubbed my bread on the cheese-board until now.
Now I've got all the cheese—which is you, my dear."

"I certainly feel eaten up," she laughed, rather bitterly. She
saw him lying in a royal ease, his eyes naïve as a boy's, his
whole being careless. Although very glad to see him thus
happy, for herself she felt very lonely. Being listless with sun-

weariness, and heavy with a sense of impending fate, she felt a great yearning for his sympathy, his fellow-suffering. Instead of receiving this, she had to play to his buoyant happiness, so as not to shrivel one petal of his flower, or spoil one minute of his consummate hour.

From the high point of the cliff where they stood, they could see the path winding down to the beach, and broadening upwards towards them. Slowly approaching up the slight incline came a black invalid's chair, wheeling silently over the short dry grass. The invalid, a young man, was so much deformed that already his soul seemed to be wilting in his pale sharp face, as if there were not enough life-flow in the distorted body to develop the fair bud of the spirit. He turned his pain-sunken eyes towards the sea, whose meaning, like that of all things, was half obscure to him. Siegmund glanced, and glanced quickly away, before he should see. Helena looked intently for two seconds. She thought of the torn, shrivelled seaweed flung above the reach of the tide—"the life tide," she said to herself. The pain of the invalid overshadowed her own distress. She was fretted to her soul.

"Come!" she said quietly to Siegmund, no longer resenting the completeness of his happiness, which left her unnecessary to him.

"We will leave the poor invalid in possession of our green hollow—so quiet," she said to herself.

They sauntered downwards towards the bay. Helena was brooding on her own state, after her own fashion.

"The Mist Spirit," she said to herself. "The Mist Spirit draws a curtain round us—it is very kind. A heavy gold curtain sometimes; a thin, torn curtain sometimes. I want the Mist Spirit to close the curtain again. I do not want to think of the outside. I am afraid of the outside, and I am afraid when the curtain tears open in rags. I want to be in our own fine world inside the heavy gold mist-curtain."

As if in answer or in protest to her thoughts, Siegmund said:

"Do you want anything better than this, dear? Shall we come here next year, and stay for a whole month?"

"If there be any next year," said she.

Siegmund did not reply.

She wondered if he had really spoken in sincerity, or if he, too, were mocking fate. They walked slowly through the broiling sun towards their lodging.

"There will be an end to this," said Helena, communing with herself. "And when we come out of the mist-curtain, what will it be? No matter—let come what will. All along Fate has been resolving, from the very beginning, resolving obvious discords, gradually, by unfamiliar progression; and out of original combinations weaving wondrous harmonies with our lives. Really, the working out has been wondrous, is wondrous now. The Master-Fate is too great an artist to suffer an anti-climax. I am sure the Master-Musician is too great an artist to allow a bathetic anti-climax."

CHAPTER XV

THE afternoon of the blazing day passed drowsily. Lying close together on the beach, Siegmund and Helena let the day exhale its hours like perfume, unperceived. Siegmund slept, a light evanescent sleep irised with dreams and with suffering: nothing definite, the colour of dreams without shape. Helena, as usual, retained her consciousness much more clearly. She watched the far-off floating of ships, and the near wading of children through the surf. Endless trains of thought, like little waves, rippled forward and broke on the shore of her drowsiness. But each thought-ripple, though it ran lightly, was tinged with copper-coloured gleams as from a lurid sunset. Helena felt that the sun was setting on her and Siegmund. The hour was too composed, spell-bound, for grief or anxiety or even for close perception. She was merely aware that the sun was wheeling down, tangling Siegmund and her in the traces, like overthrown charioteers. So the hours passed.

After tea they went eastwards on the downs. Siegmund was animated, so that Helena caught his mood. It was very rare that they spoke of the time preceding their acquaintance. Helena knew little or nothing of Siegmund's life up to the age of thirty, whilst he had never learned anything concerning her childhood. Somehow she did not encourage him to self-discovery. To-day, however, the painful need of lovers for self-revelation took hold on him.

"It is awfully funny," he said. "I was *so* gone on Beatrice when I married her. She had only just come back from Egypt. Her father was an army officer, a very handsome man, and, I believe, a bit of a rake. Beatrice is really well connected, you know. But old FitzHerbert ran through all his money, and through everything else. He was too hot for the rest of the family, so they dropped him altogether.

"He came to live at Peckham when I was sixteen. I had just left school, and was to go into father's business. Mrs. Fitz-Herbert left cards, and very soon we were acquainted. Beatrice had been a good time in a French convent school. She had only knocked about with the army a little while, but it had brought her out. I remember I thought she was miles above me—which she was. She wasn't bad-looking, either, and you know men all like her. I bet she'd marry again, in spite of the children.

"At first I fluttered round her. I remember I'd got a little, silky moustache. They all said I looked older than sixteen. At that time I was mad on the violin, and she played rather well. Then FitzHerbert went off abroad somewhere, so Beatrice and her mother half lived at our house. The mother was an invalid.

"I remember I nearly stood on my head one day. The conservatory opened off the smoking-room, so when I came in the room, I heard my two sisters and Beatrice talking about good-looking men.

" 'I consider Bertram will make a handsome man,' said my younger sister.

" 'He's got beautiful eyes," said my other sister.

" 'And a real darling nose and chin!' cried Beatrice. 'If only he was more *solide*! He is like a windmill, all limbs.'

" 'He will fill out. Remember, he's not quite seventeen,' said my elder sister.

"Ah, he is *doux*—he is *câlin*,' said Beatrice.

" 'I think he is rather *too* spoony for his age,' said my elder sister.

" 'But he's a fine boy for all that. See how thick his knees are,' my younger sister chimed in.

" 'Ah, *si*, *si*!' cried Beatrice.

"I made a row against the door, then walked across.

" 'Hello, is somebody in here?' I said, as I pushed into the little conservatory.

"I looked straight at Beatrice, and she at me. We seemed to

have formed an alliance in that look: she was the other half of my consciousness, I of hers. Ha! Ha! there were a lot of white narcissus, and little white hyacinths, Roman hyacinths, in the conservatory. I can see them now, great white stars, and tangles of little ones, among a bank of green; and I can recall the keen, fresh scent on the warm air; and the look of Beatrice . . . her great dark eyes.

"It's funny, but Beatrice is as dead—ay, far more dead—than Dante's. And I am not that young fool, not a bit.

"I was very romantic, fearfully emotional, and the soul of honour. Beatrice said nobody cared a thing about her. Fitz-Herbert was always jaunting off, the mother was a fretful invalid. So I was seventeen, earning half a guinea a week, and she was eighteen, with no money, when we ran away to Brighton and got married. Poor old Pater, he took it awfully well. I have been a frightful drag on him, you know.

"There's the romance. I wonder how it will all end."

Helena laughed, and he did not detect her extreme bitterness of spirit.

They walked on in silence for some time. He was thinking back, before Helena's day. This left her very much alone, and forced on her the idea that, after all, love, which she chose to consider as single and wonderful a thing in a man's life as birth, or adolescence, or death, was temporary, and formed only an episode. It was her hour of disillusion.

"Come to think of it," Siegmund continued, "I have always shirked. Whenever I've been in a tight corner I've gone to Pater."

"I think," she said, "marriage has been a tight corner you couldn't get out of to go to anybody."

"Yet I'm here," he answered simply.

The blood suffused her face and neck.

"And some men would have made a better job of it. When it's come to sticking out against Beatrice, and sailing the domestic ship in spite of her, I've always funked. I tell you I'm something of a moral coward."

He had her so much on edge she was inclined to answer, "So be it." Instead, she ran back over her own history: it consisted of petty discords in contemptible surroundings, then of her dreams and fancies, finally—Siegmund.

"In my life," she said, with the fine, grating discord in her tones, "I might say *always*, the real life has seemed just outside

—brownies running and fairies peeping—just beyond the common, ugly place where I am. I seem to have been hedged in by vulgar circumstances, able to glimpse outside now and then, and see the reality."

"You are so hard to get at," said Siegmund. "And so scornful of familiar things."

She smiled, knowing he did not understand. The heat had jaded her, so that physically she was full of discord, of dreariness that set her teeth on edge. Body and soul, she was out of tune.

A warm, noiseless twilight was gathering over the downs and rising darkly from the sea. Fate, with wide wings, was hovering just over her. Fate, ashen grey and black, like a carrion crow, had her in its shadow. Yet Siegmund took no notice. He did not understand. He walked beside her whistling to himself, which only distressed her the more.

They were alone on the smooth hills to the east. Helena looked at the day melting out of the sky, leaving the permanent structure of the night. It was her turn to suffer the sickening detachment which comes after moments of intense living.

The rosiness died out of the sunset as embers fade into thick ash. In herself, too, the ruddy glow sank and went out. The earth was a cold dead heap, coloured drearily, the sky was dark with flocculent grey ash, and she herself an upright mass of soft ash.

She shuddered slightly with horror. The whole face of things was to her livid and ghastly. Being a moralist rather than an artist, coming of fervent Wesleyan stock, she began to scourge herself. She had done wrong again. Looking back, no one had she touched without hurting. She had a destructive force; anyone she embraced she injured. Faint voices echoed back from her conscience. The shadows were full of complaint against her. It was all true, she was a harmful force, dragging Fate to petty, mean conclusions.

Life and hope were ash in her mouth. She shuddered with discord. Despair grated between her teeth. This dreariness was worse than any her dreary, lonely life had known. She felt she could bear it no longer.

Siegmund was there. Surely he could help? He would rekindle her. But he was straying ahead, carelessly whistling the Spring Song from *Die Walküre*. She looked at him, and again shuddered with horror. Was that really Siegmund, that stooping, thick-shouldered, indifferent man? Was that the Siegmund who had seemed to radiate joy into his surroundings, the Siegmund whose coming had always changed the whole weather of her soul? Was that the Siegmund whose touch was keen with bliss for her, whose face was a panorama of passing God? She looked at him again. His radiance was gone, his aura had ceased. She saw him a stooping man, past the buoyancy of youth, walking and whistling rather stupidly—in short, something of the "clothed animal on end", like the rest of men.

She suffered an agony of disillusion. Was this the real Siegmund, and her own only a projection of her soul? She took her breath sharply. Was he the real clay, and that other, her beloved, only the breathing of her soul upon this. There was an awful blank before her.

"Siegmund!" she said in despair.

He turned sharply at the sound of her voice. Seeing her face pale and distorted in the twilight, he was filled with dismay. She mutely lifted her arms to him, watching him in despair. Swiftly he took her in his arms, and asked in a troubled voice:

"What is it, dear? Is something wrong?"

His voice was nothing to her—it was stupid. She felt his arms round her, felt her face pressed against the cloth of his coat, against the beating of his heart. What was all this? This was not comfort or love. He was not understanding or helping, only chaining her, hurting. She did not want his brute embrace —she was most utterly alone, gripped so in his arms. If he could not save her from herself, he must leave her free to pant her heart out in free air. The secret thud, thud of his heart, the very self of that animal in him she feared and hated, repulsed her. She struggled to escape.

"What is it? Won't you tell me what is the matter?" he pleaded.

She began to sob, dry wild sobs, feeling as if she would go mad. He tried to look at her face, for which she hated him. And all the time he held her fast, all the time she was imprisoned in the embrace of this brute, blind creature, whose heart confessed itself in thud, thud, thud.

"Have you heard anything against us? Have I done anything? Have I said anything? Tell me—at any rate tell me, Helena."

Her sobbing was like the chattering of dry leaves. She grew frantic to be free. Stifled in that prison any longer, she would choke and go mad. His coat chafed her face; as she struggled she could see the strong working of his throat. She fought against him; she struggled in panic to be free.

"Let me go!" she cried. "Let me go! Let me go!" He held her in bewilderment and terror. She thrust her hands in his chest and pushed him apart. Her face, blind to him, was very much distorted by her suffering. She thrust him furiously away with great strength.

His heart stood still with wonder. She broke from him and dropped down, sobbing wildly, in the shelter of the tumuli. She was bunched in a small, shaken heap. Siegmund could not bear it. He went on one knee beside her, trying to take her hand in his, and pleading:

"Only tell me, Helena, what it is. Tell me what it is. At least tell me, Helena; tell me what it is. Oh, but this is dreadful!"

She had turned convulsively from him. She shook herself, as if beside herself, and at last covered her ears with her hands, to shut out this unreasoning pleading of his voice.

Seeing her like this, Siegmund at last gave in. Quite still, he knelt on one knee beside her, staring at the late twilight. The intense silence was crackling with the sound of Helena's dry, hissing sobs. He remained silenced, stunned by the unnatural conflict. After waiting a while, he put his hand on her. She winced convulsively away.

Then he rose, saying in his heart, "It is enough." He went behind the small hill, and looked at the night. It was all exposed. He wanted to hide, to cover himself from the openness, and there was not even a bush under which he could find cover.

He lay down flat on the ground, pressing his face into the wiry turf, trying to hide. Quite stunned, with a death taking place in his soul, he lay still, pressed against the earth. He held his breath for a long time before letting it go, then again he held it. He could scarcely bear, even by breathing, to betray himself. His consciousness was dark.

Helena had sobbed and struggled the life animation back into herself. At length, weary but comfortable, she lay still to rest. Almost she could have gone to sleep. But she grew chilly, and a ground insect tickled her face. Was somebody coming?

It was dark when she rose. Siegmund was not in sight. She tidied herself, and rather frightened, went to look for him. She saw him like a thick shadow on the earth. Now she was heavy with tears good to shed. She stood in silent sorrow, looking at him.

Suddenly she became aware of someone passing and looking curiously at them.

"Dear!" she said softly, stooping and touching his hair. He began to struggle with himself to respond. At that minute he would rather have died than face anyone. His soul was too much uncovered.

"Dear, someone is looking," she pleaded.

He drew himself up from cover. But he kept his face averted. They walked on.

"Forgive me, dear," she said softly.

"Nay, it's not you," he answered, and she was silenced. They walked on till the night seemed private. She turned to him, and "Siegmund!" she said, in a voice of great sorrow and pleading.

He took her in his arms, but did not kiss her, though she lifted her face. He put his mouth against her throat, below the ear, as she offered it, and stood looking out through the ravel of her hair, dazed, dreamy.

The sea was smoking with darkness under half-luminous heavens. The stars, one after another, were catching alight. Siegmund perceived first one, and then another dimmer one, flicker out in the darkness over the sea. He stood perfectly still, watching them. Gradually he remembered how, in the cathedral, the tapers of the choir-stalls would tremble and set steadily to burn, opening the darkness point after point with yellow drops of flame, as the acolyte touched them, one by one, delicately with his rod. The night was religious, then, with its proper order of service. Day and night had their ritual, and passed in uncouth worship.

Siegmund found himself in an abbey. He looked up the nave of the night, where the sky came down on the sea-like arches, and he watched the stars catch fire. At least it was all sacred, whatever the God might be. Helena herself, the bitter bread, was stuff of the ceremony, which he touched with his lips as part of the service.

He had Helena in his arms, which was sweet company, but in spirit he was quite alone. She would have drawn him back to her, and on her woman's breast have hidden him from Fate, and saved him from searching the unknown. But this night he did not want comfort. If he were "an infant crying in the night", it was crying that a woman could not still. He was abroad seeking courage and faith for his own soul. He, in loneliness, must search the night for faith.

"My fate is finely wrought out," he thought to himself. "Even damnation may be finely imagined for me in the night. I have come so far. Now I must get clarity and courage to follow out the theme. I don't want to botch and bungle even damnation."

But he needed to know what was right, what was the proper sequence of his acts. Staring at the darkness, he seemed to feel his course, though he could not see it. He bowed in obedience. The stars seemed to swing softly in token of submission.

CHAPTER XVI

FEELING him abstract, withdrawn from her, Helena experienced the dread of losing him. She was in his arms, but his spirit ignored her. That was insufferable to her pride. Yet she dared not disturb him—she was afraid. Bitterly she repented her of the giving way to her revulsion a little space before. Why had she not smothered it and pretended? Why had she, a woman, betrayed herself so flagrantly? Now perhaps she had lost him for good. She was consumed with uneasiness.

At last she drew back from him, held him her mouth to kiss. As he gently, sadly kissed her she pressed him to her bosom. She must get him back, whatever else she lost. She put her hand tenderly on his brow.

"What are you thinking of?" she asked.

"I?" he replied. "I really don't know. I suppose I was hardly thinking anything."

She waited a while, clinging to him, then, finding some difficulty in speech, she asked:

"Was I very cruel, dear?"

It was so unusual to hear her grieved and filled with humility that he drew her close into him.

"It was pretty bad, I suppose," he replied. "But I should think neither of us could help it."

She gave a little sob, pressed her face into his chest, wishing she had helped it. Then, with Madonna love, she clasped his head upon her shoulder, covering her hands over his hair. Twice she kissed him softly in the nape of the neck, with fond, re-assuring kisses. All the while, delicately, she fondled and soothed him, till he was child to her Madonna.

They remained standing with his head on her shoulder for some time, till at last he raised himself to lay his lips on hers in a long kiss of healing and renewal—long, pale kisses of after-suffering.

Someone was coming along the path. Helena let him go, shook herself free, turned sharply aside, and said:

"Shall we go down to the water?"

"If you like," he replied, putting out his hand to her. They went thus with clasped hands down the cliff path to the beach.

There they sat in the shadow of the uprising island, facing the restless water. Around them the sand and shingle were grey; there stretched a long pale line of surf, beyond which the sea was black and smeared with star-reflections. The deep, velvety sky shone with lustrous stars.

As yet the moon was not risen. Helena proposed that they should lie on a tuft of sand in a black cleft of the cliff to await its coming. They lay close together without speaking. Each was looking at a low, large star which hung straight in front of them, dripping its brilliance in a thin streamlet of light along the sea almost to their feet. It was a star-path fine and clear, trembling in its brilliance, but certain upon the water. Helena watched it with delight. As Siegmund looked at the star, it seemed to him a lantern hung at the gate to light someone home. He imagined himself following the thread of the star-track. What was behind the gate?

They heard the wash of a steamer crossing the bay. The water seemed populous in the night-time, with dark, uncanny comings and goings.

Siegmund was considering.

"What *was* the matter with you?" he asked.

She leaned over him, took his head in her lap, holding his face between her two hands as she answered in a low, grave voice, very wise and old in experience:

"Why, you see, dear, you won't understand. But there was such a greyish darkness, and through it—the crying of lives I have touched. . . ."

His heart suddenly shrank and sank down. She acknowledged then that she also had helped to injure Beatrice and his children. He coiled with shame.

". . . A crying of lives against me, and I couldn't silence them, nor escape out of the darkness. I wanted you—I saw you in front, whistling the Spring Song, but I couldn't find you—it was not you—I couldn't find you."

She kissed his eyes and his brows.

"No, I don't see it," he said. "You would always be you. I could think of hating you, but you'd still be yourself."

She made a moaning, loving sound. Full of passionate pity, she moved her mouth on his face, as a woman does on her child that has hurt itself.

"Sometimes," she murmured, in a low, grieved confession, "you lose me."

He gave a brief laugh.

"I lose you!" he repeated. "You mean I lose my attraction for you, or my hold over you, and then you——?"

He did not finish. She made the same grievous murmuring noise over him.

"It shall not be any more," she said.

"All right," he replied, "since you decide it."

She clasped him round the chest and fondled him, distracted with pity.

"You mustn't be bitter," she murmured.

"Four days is enough," he said. "In a fortnight I should be intolerable to you. I am not masterful."

"It is not so, Siegmund," she said sharply.

"I give way always," he repeated. "And then—to-night!"

"To-night, to-night!" she cried in wrath. "To-night I have been a fool!"

"And I?" he asked.

"You—what of you?" she cried. Then she became sad. "I have little perverse feelings," she lamented.

"And I can't bear to compel anything, for fear of hurting it. So I'm always pushed this way and that, like a fool."

"You don't know how you hurt me, talking so," she said.

He kissed her. After a moment he said:

"You are not like other folk. 'Ihr Lascheks seid ein anderes Geschlecht.' I thought of you when we read it."

"Would you rather have me more like the rest, or more unlike, Siegmund? Which is it?"

"Neither," he said. "You are *you*."

They were quiet for a space. The only movement in the night was the faint gambolling of starlight on the water. The last person had passed in black silhouette between them and the sea.

He was thinking bitterly. She seemed to goad him deeper and deeper into life. He had a sense of despair, a preference of death. The German she read with him—she loved its loose and violent romance—came back to his mind: "Der Tod geht einem zur Seite, fast sichtbarlich, und jagt einem immer tiefer ins Leben."

Well, the next place he would be hunted to, like a hare run down, was home. It seemed impossible the morrow would take him back to Beatrice.

"This time to-morrow night," he said.

"Siegmund!" she implored.

"Why not?" he laughed.

"Don't, dear," she pleaded.

"All right, I won't."

Some large steamer crossing the mouth of the bay made the water clash a little as it broke in accentuated waves. A warm puff of air wandered in on them now and again.

"You won't be tired when you go back?" Helena asked.

"Tired!" he echoed.

"You know how you were when you came," she reminded him, in tones full of pity. He laughed.

"Oh, that is gone," he said.

With a slow, mechanical rhythm she stroked his cheek.

"And will you be sad?" she said, hesitating.

"Sad!" he repeated.

"But will you be able to take the old life up, happier, when you go back?"

"The old life will take me up, I suppose," he said.

There was a pause.

"I think, dear," she said, "I have done wrong."

"Good Lord—you have not!" he replied sharply, pressing back his head to look at her, for the first time.

"I shall have to send you back to Beatrice and the babies—to-morrow—as you are now. . . ."

" 'Take no thought for the morrow.' Be quiet, Helena!" he exclaimed as the reality bit him. He sat up suddenly.

"Why?" she asked, afraid.

"Why!" he repeated. He remained sitting, leaning forward on the sand, staring intently at Helena. She looked back in fear at him. The moment terrified her, and she lost courage.

With a fluttered motion she put her hand on his, which was pressed hard on the sand as he leaned forward. At once he relaxed his intensity, laughed, then became tender.

Helena yielded herself like a forlorn child to his arms, and there lay, half crying, whilst he smoothed her brow with his fingers, and grains of sand fell from his palm on her cheek. She shook with dry, withered sobs, as a child does when it snatches itself away from the lancet of the doctor and hides in the mother's bosom, refusing to be touched.

But she knew the morrow was coming, whether or not, and she cowered down on his breast. She was wild with fear of the parting and the subsequent days. They must drink, after to-morrow, separate cups. She was filled with vague terror of what it would be. The sense of the oneness and unity of their fates was gone.

Siegmund also was cowed by the threat of separation. He had more definite knowledge of the next move than had Helena. His heart was certain of calamity, which would overtake him directly. He shrank away. Wildly he beat about to find a means of escape from the next day and its consequences. He did not want to go. Anything rather than go back.

In the midst of their passion of fear the moon rose. Siegmund started to see the rim appear ruddily beyond the sea. His struggling suddenly ceased, and he watched, spellbound, the oval horn of fiery gold come up, resolve itself. Some golden liquor dripped and spilled upon the far waves, where it shook in ruddy splashes. The gold-red cup rose higher, looming before him very large, yet still not all discovered. By degrees the horn of gold detached itself from the darkness at back of the waves. It was immense and terrible. When would the tip be placed upon the table of the sea?

It stood at last, whole and calm, before him; then the night took up this drinking-cup of fiery gold, lifting it with majestic movement overhead, letting stream forth the wonderful unwasted liquor of gold over the sea—a libation.

Siegmund looked at the shaking flood of gold and paling gold spread wider as the night upraised the blanching crystal, poured out farther and farther the immense libation from the whitening cup, till at last the moon looked frail and empty.

And there, exhaustless in the night, the white light shook on the floor of the sea. He wondered how it would be gathered up. "I gather it up into myself," he said. And the stars and the cliffs and a few trees were watching, too. "If I have spilled my life," he thought, "the unfamiliar eyes of the land and sky will gather it up again."

Turning to Helena, he found her face white and shining as the empty moon.

CHAPTER XVII

TOWARDS morning, Siegmund went to sleep. For four hours, until seven o'clock, the womb of sleep received him and nourished him again.

"But it is finest of all to wake," he said, as the bright sunshine of the window, and the lumining green sunshine coming through the lifted hands of the leaves, challenged him into the open.

The morning was exceedingly fair, and it looked at him so gently that his blue eyes trembled with self-pity. A fragment of scarlet geranium glanced up at him as he passed, so that amid the vermilion tyranny of the uniform it wore he could see the eyes of the flower, wistful, offering him love, as one sometimes see the eyes of a man beneath the brass helmet of a soldier, and is startled. Everything looked at him with the same eyes of tenderness, offering him, timidly, a little love.

"They are all extraordinarily sweet," said Siegmund to the full-mouthed scabious and the awkward, downcast ragwort. Three or four butterflies fluttered up and down in agitated little leaps, around him. Instinctively Siegmund put his hand forward to touch them.

"The careless little beggars!" he said.

When he came to the cliff tops there was the morning, very bravely dressed, rustling forward with a silken sound and much silken shining to meet him. The battleships had gone; the sea was blue with a *panier* of diamonds; the sky was full with a misty tenderness like love. Siegmund had never recognised

before the affection that existed between him and everything.
We do not realise how tremendously dear and indispensable
to us are the hosts of common things, till we must leave them,
and we break our hearts.

"We have been very happy together," everything seemed to
say.

Siegmund looked up into the eyes of the morning with a
laugh.

"It is very lovely," he said, "whatever happens."

So he went down to the beach; his dark blue eyes, darker
from last night's experience, smiled always with the pride of
love. He undressed by his usual altar-stone.

"How closely familiar everything is," he thought. "It seems
almost as if the curves of this stone were rounded to fit in my
soul."

He touched the smooth white slope of the stone gently with
discovering fingers, in the same way as he touched the cheek
of Helena, or of his own babies. He found great pleasure in
this feeling of intimacy with things. A very soft wind, shy as
a girl, put its arms round him, and seemed to lay its cheek
against his chest. He placed his hands beneath his arms, where
the wind was caressing him, and his eyes opened with wondering pleasure.

"They find no fault with me," he said. "I suppose they are
as fallible as I, and so don't judge," he added, as he waded
thigh-deep into the water, thrusting it to hear the mock-angry
remonstrance.

"Once more," he said, and he took the sea in his arms. He
swam very quietly. The water buoyed him up, holding him
closely clasped. He swam towards the white rocks of the headlands; they rose before him like beautiful buttressed gates, so
glistening that he half expected to see fantail pigeons puffing
like white irises in the niches, and white peacocks with dark
green feet stepping down the terraces, trailing a sheen of silver.

"Helena is right," he said to himself as he swam, scarcely
swimming, but moving upon the bosom of the tide; "she is
right, it is all enchanted. I have got into her magic at last.
Let us see what it is like."

He determined to visit again his little bay. He swam carefully round the terraces, whose pale shadows through the swift-
spinning emerald facets of the water seemed merest fancy.
Siegmund touched them with his foot; they were hard, cold,

dangerous. He swam carefully. As he made for the archway, the shadows of the headland chilled the water. There under water, clamouring in a throng at the base of the submerged walls, were sea-women with dark locks, and young sea-girls, with soft hair, vividly green, striving to climb up out of the darkness into the morning, their hair swirling in abandon. Siegmund was half afraid of their frantic efforts.

But the tide carried him swiftly through the high gate into the porch. There was exultance in this sweeping entry. The skin-white, full-fleshed walls of the archway were dappled with green lights that danced in and out among themselves. Siegmund was carried along in an invisible chariot, beneath the jewel-stained walls. The tide swerved, threw him as he swam against the inward-curving white rock; his elbow met the rock, and he was sick with pain. He held his breath, trying to get back the joy and magic. He could not believe that the lovely, smooth side of the rock, fair as his own side with its ripple of muscles, could have hurt him thus. He let the water carry him till he might climb out on to the shingle. There he sat upon a warm boulder, and twisted to look at his arm. The skin was grazed, not very badly, merely a ragged scarlet patch no bigger than a carnation petal. The bruise, however, was painful, especially when, a minute or two later, he bent his arm.

"No," said he pitiably to himself, "it is impossible it should have hurt me. I suppose I was careless."

Nevertheless, the aspect of the morning changed. He sat on the boulder looking out on the sea. The azure sky and the sea laughed on, holding a bright conversation one with another. The two headlands of the tiny bay gossiped across the street of water. All the boulders and pebbles of the sea-shore played together.

"Surely," said Siegmund, "they take no notice of me; they do not care a jot or a tittle for me. I am a fool to think myself one with them."

He contrasted this with the kindness of the morning as he had stood on the cliffs.

"I was mistaken," he said. "It was an illusion."

He looked wistfully out again. Like neighbours leaning from opposite windows of an overhanging street, the headlands were occupied one with another. White rocks strayed out to sea, followed closely by other white rocks. Everything was busy, interested, occupied with its own pursuit and with its own comrades. Siegmund alone was without pursuit or comrade.

"They will all go on the same; they will be just as gay. Even Helena, after a while, will laugh and take interest in others. What do I matter?"

Siegmund thought of the futility of death:

> "We are not long for music and laughter,
>   Love and desire and hate;
> I think we have no portion in them after
>   We pass the gate."

"Why should I be turned out of the game?" he asked himself, rebelling. He frowned, and answered: "Oh, Lord!—the old argument!"

But the thought of his own expunging from the picture was very bitter.

"Like the puff from the steamer's funnel, I should be gone."

He looked at himself, at his limbs and his body in the pride of his maturity. He was very beautiful to himself.

"Nothing, in the place where I am," he said. "Gone, like a puff of steam that melts on the sunshine."

Again Siegmund looked at the sea. It was glittering with laughter as at a joke.

"And I," he said, lying down in the warm sand, "I am nothing. I do not count; I am inconsiderable."

He set his teeth with pain. There were no tears, there was no relief. A convulsive gasping shook him as he lay on the sands. All the while he was arguing with himself.

"Well," he said, "if I am nothing dead I am nothing alive."

But the vulgar proverb arose—"Better a live dog than a dead lion," to answer him. It seemed an ignominy to be dead. It meant, to be overlooked, even by the smallest creature of God's earth. Surely that was a great ignominy.

Helena, meanwhile, was bathing, for the last time, by the same sea-shore with him. She was no swimmer. Her endless delight was to explore, to discover small treasures. For her the world was still a great wonder-box which hid innumerable sweet toys for surprises in all its crevices. She had bathed in many rock-pools' tepid baths, trying first one, then another. She had lain on the sand where the cold arms of the ocean lifted her and smothered her impetuously, like an awful lover.

"The sea is a great deal like Siegmund," she said, as she rose

panting, trying to dash her nostrils free from water. It was
true; the sea as it flung over her filled her with the same uncontrollable terror as did Siegmund when he sometimes grew
silent and strange in a tide of passion.

She wandered back to her rock-pools; they were bright and
docile; they did not fling her about in a game of terror. She
bent over watching the anemone's fleshy petals shrink from
the touch of her shadow, and she laughed to think they should
be so needlessly fearful. The flowing tide trickled noiselessly
among the rocks, widening and deepening insidiously her little
pools. Helena retreated towards a large cave round the bend.
There the water gurgled under the bladder-wrack of the large
stones; the air was cool and clammy. She pursued her way
into the gloom, bending, though there was no need, shivering
at the coarse feel of the seaweed beneath her naked feet. The
water came rustling up beneath the fucus as she crept along on
the big stones; it returned with a quiet gurgle which made her
shudder, though even that was not disagreeable. It needed, for
all that, more courage than was easy to summon before she
could step off her stone into the black pool that confronted her.
It was festooned thick with weeds that slid under her feet like
snakes. She scrambled hastily upwards towards the outlet.

Turning, the ragged arch was before her, brighter than the
brightest window. It was easy to believe the light-fairies stood
outside in a throng, excited with fine fear, throwing handfuls
of light into the dragon's hole.

"How surprised they will be to see me!" said Helena,
scrambling forward, laughing.

She stood still in the archway, astounded. The sea was
blazing with white fire, and glowing with azure as coals glow
red with heat below the flames. The sea was transfused with
white burning, while over it hung the blue sky in a glory, like
the blue smoke of the fire of God. Helena stood still and
worshipped. It was a moment of astonishment, when she
stood breathless and blinded, involuntarily offering herself for
a thank-offering. She felt herself confronting God at home in
His white incandescence, His fire settling on her like the Holy
Spirit. Her lips were parted in a woman's joy of adoration.

The moment passed, and her thoughts hurried forward in
confusion.

"It is good," said Helena; "it is very good." She looked
again, and saw the waves like a line of children racing hand

in hand, the sunlight pursuing, catching hold of them from behind, as they ran wildly till they fell, caught, with the sunshine dancing upon them like a white dog.

"It is really wonderful here!" said she; but the moment had gone, she could not see again the grand burning of God among the waves. After a while she turned away.

As she stood dabbling her bathing-dress in a pool, Siegmund came over the beach to her.

"You are not gone, then?" he said.

"Siegmund!" she exclaimed, looking up at him with radiant eyes, as if it could not be possible that he had joined her in this rare place. His face was glowing with the sun's inflaming, but Helena did not notice that his eyes were full of misery.

"I, actually," he said, smiling.

"I did not expect you," she said, still looking at him in radiant wonder. "I could easier have expected"—she hesitated, struggled, and continued—"Eros walking by the sea. But you are like him," she said, looking radiantly up into Siegmund's face. "Isn't it beautiful this morning?" she added.

Siegmund endured her wide, glad look for a moment, then he stooped and kissed her. He remained moving his hand in the pool, ashamed, and full of contradiction. He was at the bitter point of farewell; could see, beyond the glamour around him, the ugly building of his real life.

"Isn't the sea wonderful this morning?" asked Helena, as she wrung the water from her costume.

"It is very fine," he answered. He refrained from saying what his heart said: "It is my last morning; it is not yours. It is my last morning, and the sea is enjoying the joke, and you are full of delight."

"Yes," said Siegmund, "the morning is perfect."

"It is," assented Helena warmly. "Have you noticed the waves? They are like a line of children chased by a white dog."

"Ay!" said Siegmund.

"Didn't you have a good time?" she asked, touching with her finger-tips the nape of his neck as he stooped beside her.

"I swam to my little bay again," he replied.

"Did you?" she exclaimed, pleased.

She sat down by the pool, in which she washed her feet free from sand, holding them to Siegmund to dry.

"I am very hungry," she said.

"And I," he agreed.

"I feel quite established here," she said gaily, something in his position having reminded her of their departure.

He laughed.

"It seems another eternity before the three-forty-five train, doesn't it?" she insisted.

"I wish we might never go back," he said.

Helena sighed.

"It would be too much for life to give. We have had something, Siegmund," she said.

He bowed his head, and did not answer.

"It has been something, dear," she repeated.

He rose and took her in his arms.

"Everything," he said, his face muffled in the shoulder of her dress. He could smell her fresh and fine from the sea. "Everything!" he said.

She pressed her two hands on his head.

"I did well, didn't I, Siegmund?" she asked. Helena felt the responsibility of this holiday. She had proposed it; when he had withdrawn, she had insisted, refusing to allow him to take back his word, declaring that she should pay the cost. He permitted her at last.

"Wonderfully well, Helena," he replied.

She kissed his forehead.

"You are everything," he said.

She pressed his head on her bosom.

CHAPTER XVIII

SIEGMUND had shaved and dressed, and come down to breakfast. Mrs. Curtiss brought in the coffee. She was a fragile little woman, of delicate, gentle manner.

"The water would be warm this morning," she said, addressing no one in particular.

Siegmund stood on the hearth-rug with his hands behind him, swaying from one leg to the other. He was embarrassed always by the presence of the amiable little woman; he could not feel at ease before strangers, in his capacity of accepted swain of Helena.

"It was," assented Helena. "It was as warm as new milk."

"Ay, it would be," said the old lady. looking in admiration upon the experience of Siegmund and his beloved. "And did ye see the ships of war?" she asked.

"No, they had gone," replied Helena.

Siegmund swayed from foot to foot, rhythmically.

"You'll be coming in to dinner to-day?" asked the old lady.

Helena arranged the matter.

"I think ye both look better," Mrs. Curtiss said. She glanced at Siegmund.

He smiled constrainedly.

"I thought ye looked so worn when you came," she said sympathetically.

"He had been working hard," said Helena, also glancing at him.

He bent his head, and was whistling without making any sound.

"Ay," sympathised the little woman. "And it's a very short time for you. What a pity ye can't stop for the fireworks at Cowes on Monday. They are grand, so they say."

Helena raised her eyebrows in polite interest. "Have you never seen them?" she asked.

"No," replied Mrs. Curtiss. "I've never been able to get; but I hope to go yet."

"I hope you may," said Siegmund.

The little woman beamed on him. Having won a word from him, she was quite satisfied.

"Well," she said brightly, "the eggs must be done by now.' She tripped out, to return directly.

"I've brought you," she said, "some of the Island cream, and some white currants, if ye'll have them. You must think well of the Island, and come back."

"How could we help?" laughed Helena.

"We will," smiled Siegmund.

When finally the door was closed on her, Siegmund sat down in relief. Helena looked in amusement at him. She was perfectly self-possessed in presence of the delightful little lady.

"This is one of the few places that has ever felt like home to me," she said. She lifted a tangled bunch of fine white currants.

"Ah!" exclaimed Siegmund, smiling at her.

"One of the few places where everything is friendly," she said. "And everybody."

"You have made so many enemies?" he asked, with gentle irony.

"Strangers," she replied. "I seem to make strangers of all the people I meet."

She laughed in amusement at this *mot*. Siegmund looked at her intently. He was thinking of her left alone amongst strangers.

"Need we go—need we leave this place of friends?" he said, as if ironically. He was very much afraid of tempting her.

She looked at the clock on the mantelpiece and counted: "One, two, three, four, five hours, thirty-five minutes. It is an age yet," she laughed.

Siegmund laughed too, as he accepted the particularly fine bunch of currants she had extricated for him.

CHAPTER XIX

THE air was warm and sweet in the little lane, remote from the sea, which led them along their last walk. On either side the white path was a grassy margin thickly woven with pink convolvuli. Some of the reckless little flowers, so gay and evanescent, had climbed the trunk of an old yew tree, and were looking up pertly at their rough host.

Helena walked along, watching the flowers, and making fancies out of them.

"Who called them 'fairies' telephones'?" she said to herself. "They are tiny children in pinafores. How gay they are! They are children dawdling along the pavement of a morning. How fortunate they are! See how they take a wind-thrill! See how wide they are set to the sunshine! And when they are tired, they will curl daintily to sleep, and some fairies in the dark will gather them away. They won't be here in the morning, shrivelled and dowdy. . . . If only we could curl up and be gone, after our day . . ."

She looked at Siegmund. He was walking moodily beside her.

"It is good when life holds no anti-climax," she said.

"Ay!" he answered. Of course, he could not understand her meaning.

She strayed into the thick grass, a sturdy white figure that walked with bent head, abstract, but happy.

"What is she thinking?" he asked himself. "She is sufficient to herself—she doesn't want me. She has her own private way of communing with things, and is friends with them."

"The dew has been very heavy," she said, turning, and looking up at him from under her brows, like a smiling witch.

"I see it has," he answered. Then to himself he said: "She can't translate herself into language. She is incommunicable; she can't render herself to the intelligence. So she is alone and a law unto herself: she only wants me to explore me, like a rock-pool, and to bathe in me. After a while, when I am gone, she will see I was not indispensable. . . ."

The lane led up to the eastern down. As they were emerging, they saw on the left hand an extraordinarily spick and span red bungalow. The low roof of dusky red sloped down towards the coolest green lawn, that was edged and ornamented with scarlet, and yellow, and white flowers brilliant with dew.

A stout man in an alpaca jacket and panama hat was seated on the bare lawn, his back to the sun, reading a newspaper. He tried in vain to avoid the glare of the sun on his reading. At last he closed the paper and looked angrily at the house—not at anything in particular.

He irritably read a few more lines, then jerked up his head in sudden decision, glared at the open door of the house, and called:

"Amy! Amy!"

No answer was forthcoming. He flung down the paper and strode off indoors, his mien one of wrathful resolution. His voice was heard calling curtly from the dining-room. There was a jingle of crockery as he bumped the table leg in sitting down.

"He is in a bad temper," laughed Siegmund.

"Breakfast is late," said Helena with contempt.

"Look!" said Siegmund.

An elderly lady in black and white striped linen, a young lady in holland, both carrying some wild flowers, hastened towards the garden gate. Their faces were turned anxiously to the house. They were hot with hurrying, and had no breath for words. The girl pressed forward, opened the gate for the lady in striped linen, who hastened over the lawn. Then the daughter followed, and vanished also under the shady veranda.

There was a quick sound of women's low, apologetic voices, overridden by the resentful abuse of the man.

The lovers moved out of hearing.

"Imagine that breakfast-table!" said Siegmund.

"I feel," said Helena, with a keen twang of contempt in her voice, "as if a fussy cock and hens had just scuffled across my path."

"There are many such roosts," said Siegmund pertinently.

Helena's cold scorn was very disagreeable to him. She talked to him winsomely and very kindly as they crossed the open down to meet the next incurving of the coast, and Siegmund was happy. But the sense of humiliation, which he had got from her the day before, and which had fixed itself, bled him secretly, like a wound. This hæmorrhage of self-esteem tortured him to the end.

Helena had rejected him. She gave herself to her fancies only. For some time she had confused Siegmund with her god. Yesterday she had cried to her ideal lover, and found only Siegmund. It was the spear in the side of his tortured self-respect.

"At least," he said, in mortification of himself—"at least, someone must recognise a strain of God in me—and who does? I don't believe in it myself."

And, moreover, in the intense joy and suffering of his realised passion, the island, with its sea and sky, had fused till, like a brilliant bead, all their beauty ran together out of the common ore, and Siegmund saw it naked, saw the beauty of everything naked in the shifting magic of this bead. The island would be gone to-morrow: he would look for the beauty and find the dirt. What was he to do?

"You know, Domine," said Helena—it was his old nickname she used—"you look quite stern to-day."

"I feel anything but stern," he laughed. "Weaker than usual, in fact."

"Yes, perhaps so, when you talk. Then you are really surprisingly gentle. But when you are silent, I am even afraid of you—you seem so grave."

He laughed.

"And shall I not be brave?" he said. "Can't you smell *Fumum et opes strepitumque Romæ?*" He turned quickly to Helena. "I wonder if that's right," he said. "It's years since I did a line of Latin, and I thought it had all gone."

"In the first place, what does it mean?" said Helena calmly, "for I can only half translate. I have thrown overboard all my scrap-books of such stuff."

"Why," said Siegmund, rather abashed, "only 'the row and the smoke of Rome'. But it is remarkable, Helena"—here the peculiar look of interest came on his face again—"it is really remarkable that I should have said that."

"Yes, you look surprised," smiled she.

"But it must be twenty"—he counted—"twenty-two or three years since I learned that, and I forgot it—goodness knows how long ago. Like a drowning man, I have these memories before . . ." He broke off, smiling mockingly, to tease her.

"Before you go back to London," said she, in a matter-of-fact, almost ironical tone. She was inscrutable. This morning she could not bear to let any deep emotion come uppermost. She wanted rest. "No," she said, with calm distinctness, a few moments after, when they were climbing the rise to the cliff's edge. "I can't say that I smell the smoke of London. The mist-curtain is thick yet. There it is"—she pointed to the heavy, purple-grey haze that hung like arras on a wall, between the sloping sky and the sea. She thought of yesterday morning's mist-curtain, thick and blazing gold, so heavy that no wind could sway its fringe.

They lay down in the dry grass, upon the gold bits of bird's-foot trefoil of the cliff's edge, and looked out to sea. A warm, drowsy calm drooped over everything.

"Six hours," thought Helena, "and we shall have passed the mist-curtain. Already it is thinning. I could break it open with waving my hand. I will not wave my hand."

She was exhausted by the suffering of the last night, so she refused to allow any emotion to move her this morning, till she was strong. Siegmund was also exhausted; but his thoughts laboured like ants, in spite of himself, striving towards a conclusion.

Helena had rejected him. In his heart he felt that in this love affair also he had been a failure. No matter how he contradicted himself, and said it was absurd to imagine he was a failure as Helena's lover, yet he felt a physical sensation of defeat, a kind of knot in his breast which reason, nor dialectics, nor circumstance, not even Helena, could untie. He had failed as lover to Helena.

It was not surprising his marriage with Beatrice should prove disastrous. Rushing into wedlock as he had done, at the ripe age of seventeen, he had known nothing of his woman, nor she of him. When his mind and soul set to develop, as Beatrice could not sympathise with his interests, he naturally inclined away from her, so that now, after twenty years, he was almost a stranger to her. That was not very surprising.

But why should he have failed with Helena?

The bees droned fitfully over the scented grass, aimlessly swinging in the heat. Siegmund watched one gold and amber fellow lazily let go a white clover-head, and boom in a careless curve out to sea, humming softer and softer as he reeled along in the giddy space.

"The little fool!" said Siegmund, watching the black dot swallowed into the light.

No ship sailed the curving sea. The light danced in a whirl upon the ripples. Everything else watched with heavy eyes of heat entrancement the wild spinning of the lights.

"Even if I were free," he continued to think, "we should only grow apart, Helena and I. She would leave me. This time I should be the laggard. She is young and vigorous; I am beginning to set.

"Is that why I have failed? I ought to have had her in love sufficiently to keep her these few days. I am not quick. I do not follow her or understand her swiftly enough. And I am always timid of compulsion. I cannot compel anybody to follow me.

"So we are here. I am out of my depth. Like the bee, I was mad with the sight of so much joy, such a blue space, and now I shall find no footing to alight on. I have flown out into life beyond my strength to get back. When can I set my feet on when this is gone?"

The sun grew stronger. Slower and more slowly went the hawks of Siegmund's mind, after the quarry of conclusion. He lay bare-headed, looking out to sea. The sun was burning deeper into his face and head.

"I feel as if it were burning into me," thought Siegmund abstractedly. "It is certainly consuming some part of me.

Perhaps it is making me ill." Meanwhile, perversely, he gave his face and his hot black hair to the sun.

Helena lay in what shadow he afforded. The heat put out all her thought-activity. Presently she said:

"This heat is terrible, Siegmund. Shall we go down to the water?"

They climbed giddily down the cliff path. Already they were somewhat sun-intoxicated. Siegmund chose the hot sand, where no shade was, on which to lie.

"Shall we not go under the rocks?" said Helena.

"Look!" he said, "the sun is beating on the cliffs. It is hotter, more suffocating, there."

So they lay down in the glare, Helena watching the foam retreat slowly with a cool splash; Siegmund thinking. The naked body of heat was dreadful.

"My arms, Siegmund," said she. "They feel as if they were dipped in fire."

Siegmund took them, without a word, and hid them under his coat.

"Are you sure it is not bad for you—your head, Siegmund? Are you sure?"

He laughed stupidly.

"That is all right," he said. He knew that the sun was burning through him, and doing him harm, but he wanted the intoxication.

As he looked wistfully far away over the sea at Helena's mist-curtain, he said:

"I *think* we should be able to keep together if"—he faltered —"if only I could have you a little longer. I have never had you . . ."

Some sound of failure, some tone telling her it was too late, some ring of despair in his quietness, made Helena cling to him wildly, with a savage little cry as if she were wounded. She clung to him, almost beside herself. She could not lose him, she could not spare him. She would not let him go. Helena was, for the moment, frantic.

He held her safely, saying nothing until she was calmer, when, with his lips on her cheek, he murmured:

"I should be able, shouldn't I, Helena?"

"You are always able!" she cried. "It is I who play with you at hiding."

"I have really had you so little," he said.

"Can't you forget it, Siegmund?" she cried. "Can't you forget it? It was only a shadow, Siegmund. It was a lie, it was nothing real. Can't you forget it, dear?"

"You can't do without me?" he asked.

"If I lose you I am lost," answered she with swift decision. She had no knowledge of weeping, yet her tears were wet on his face. He held her safely; her arms were hidden under his coat.

"I will have no mercy on those shadows the next time they come between us," said Helena to herself. "They may go back to hell."

She still clung to him, craving so to have him that he could not be reft away.

Siegmund felt very peaceful. He lay with his arms about her, listening to the backward-creeping tide. All his thoughts, like bees, were flown out to sea and lost.

"If I had her more, I should understand her through and through. If we were side by side we should grow together. If we could stay here, I should get stronger and more upright."

This was the poor heron of quarry the hawks of his mind had struck.

Another hour fell like a foxglove bell from the stalk. There were only two red blossoms left. Then the stem would have set to seed. Helena leaned her head upon the breast of Siegmund, her arms clasping, under his coat, his body, which swelled and sank gently, with the quiet of great power.

"If," thought she, "the whole clock of the world could stand still now, and leave us thus, me with the lift and fall of the strong body of Siegmund in my arms. . . ."

But the clock ticked on in the heat, the seconds marked off by the falling of the waves, repeated so lightly, and in such fragile rhythm, that it made silence sweet.

"If now," prayed Siegmund, "death would wipe the sweat from me, and it were dark . . ."

But the waves softly marked the minutes, retreating farther, leaving the bare rocks to bleach and the weed to shrivel.

Gradually, like the shadow on a dial, the knowledge that it was time to rise and go crept upon them. Although they remained silent, each knew that the other felt the same weight of responsibility, the shadow-finger of the sundial travelling over them. The alternative was, not to return, to let the finger travel and be gone. But then . . . Helena knew she must not let the time cross her; she must rise before it was too late, and travel before the coming finger. Siegmund hoped she would not get up. He lay in suspense, waiting.

At last she sat up abruptly.

"It is time, Siegmund," she said.

He did not answer, he did not look at her, but lay as she had left him. She wiped her face with her handkerchief, waiting. Then she bent over him. He did not look at her. She saw his forehead was swollen and inflamed with the sun. Very gently she wiped from it the glistening sweat. He closed his eyes, and she wiped his cheeks and his mouth. Still he did not look at her. She bent very close to him, feeling her heart crushed with grief for him.

"We must go, Siegmund," she whispered.

"All right," he said, but still he did not move.

She stood up beside him, shook herself, and tried to get a breath of air. She was dazzled blind by the sunshine.

Siegmund lay in the bright light, with his eyes closed, never moving. His face was inflamed, but fixed like a mask.

Helena waited, until the terror of the passing of the hour was too strong for her. She lifted his hand, which lay swollen with heat on the sand, and she tried gently to draw him.

"We shall be too late," she said in distress.

He sighed and sat up, looking out over the water.

Helena could not bear to see him look so vacant and expressionless. She put her arm round his neck, and pressed his head against her skirt.

Siegmund knew he was making it unbearable for her. Pulling himself together, he bent his head from the sea, and said:

"Why, what time is it?"

He took out his watch, holding it in his hand. Helena still held his left hand, and had one arm round his neck.

"I can't see the figures," he said. "Everything is dimmed, as if it were coming dark."

"Yes," replied Helena, in that reedy, painful tone of hers. "My eyes were the same. It is the strong sunlight."

"I can't," he repeated, and he was rather surprised—"I can't see the time. Can you?"

She stooped down and looked.

"It is half-past one," she said.

Siegmund hated her voice as she spoke. There was still sufficient time to catch the train. He stood up, moved inside his clothing, saying: "I feel almost stunned by the heat. I can hardly see, and all my feeling in my body is dulled."

"Yes," answered Helena, "I am afraid it will do you harm."

"At any rate," he smiled as if sleepily, "I have had enough. If it's too much—what *is* too much?"

They went unevenly over the sand, their eyes sun-dimmed.

"We are going back—we are going back!" the heart of Helena seemed to run hot, beating these words.

They climbed the cliff path toilsomely. Standing at the top, on the edge of the grass, they looked down the cliffs at the beach and over the sea. The strand was wide, forsaken by the sea, forlorn with rocks bleaching in the sun, and sand and sea-weed breathing off their painful scent upon the heat. The sea crept smaller, farther away; the sky stood still. Siegmund and Helena looked hopelessly out on their beautiful, incandescent world. They looked hopelessly at each other. Siegmund's mood was gentle and forbearing. He smiled faintly at Helena, then turned, and, lifting his hand to his mouth in a kiss for the beauty he had enjoyed, "*Addio!*" he said.

He turned away, and, looking from Helena landwards, he said, smiling peculiarly:

"It reminds me of Traviata—an '*Addio*' at every verse-end."

She smiled with her mouth in acknowledgment of his facetious irony; it jarred on her. He was pricked again by her supercilious reserve.

"*Addi-i-i-i-o, Addi-i-i-o!*" he whistled between his teeth, hissing out the Italian's passion-notes in a way that made Helena clench her fists.

"I suppose," she said, swallowing, and recovering her voice to check this discord—"I suppose we shall have a fairly easy journey—Thursday."

"I don't know," said Siegmund.

"There will not be very many people," she insisted.

"I think," he said, in a very quiet voice, "you'd better let me go by the South-Western from Portsmouth while you go on by the Brighton."

"But why?" she exclaimed in astonishment.

"I don't want to sit looking at you all the way," he said.

"But why should you?" she exclaimed.

He laughed.

"Indeed, no!" she said. "We shall go together."

"Very well," he answered.

They walked on in silence towards the village. As they drew near the little post office, he said:

"I suppose I may as well wire them that I shall be home to-night."

"You haven't sent them any word?" she asked.

He laughed. They came to the open door of the little shop. He stood still, not entering. Helena wondered what he was thinking.

"Shall I?" he asked, meaning, should he wire to Beatrice. His manner was rather peculiar.

"Well, I should think so," faltered Helena, turning away to look at the postcards in the window. Siegmund entered the shop. It was dark and cumbered with views, cheap china ornaments, and toys. He asked for a telegraph form.

"My God!" he said to himself bitterly as he took the pencil. He could not sign the abbreviated name his wife used towards him. He scribbled his surname, as he would have done to a stranger. As he watched the amiable, stout woman counting up his words carefully, pointing with her finger, he felt sick with irony.

"That's right," she said, picking up the sixpence and taking the form to the instrument. "What beautiful weather!" she continued. "It will be making you sorry to leave us."

"There goes my warrant," thought Siegmund, watching the flimsy bit of paper under the post-mistress's heavy hand.

"Yes—it is too bad, isn't it," he replied, bowing and laughing to the woman.

"It is, sir," she answered pleasantly. "Good-morning."

He came out of the shop still smiling, and when Helena turned from the postcards to look at him, the lines of laughter remained over his face like a mask. She glanced at his eyes for a sign; his facial expression told her nothing; his eyes were just as inscrutable, which made her falter with dismay.

"What is he thinking of?" she asked herself. Her thoughts flashed back. "And why did he ask me so peculiarly whether he should wire them at home?"

"Well," said Siegmund, "are there any postcards?"

"None that I care to take," she replied. "Perhaps you would like one of these?"

She pointed to some faded-looking cards which proved to be imaginary views of Alum Bay done in variegated sand. Siegmund smiled.

"I wonder if they dribbled the sand on with a fine glass tube," he said.

"Or a brush," said Helena.

"She does not understand," said Siegmund to himself. "And whatever I do I must not tell her. I should have thought she would understand."

As he walked home beside her there mingled with his other feelings resentment against her. Almost he hated her.

CHAPTER XX

AT first they had a carriage to themselves. They sat opposite each other with averted faces, looking out of the windows and watching the houses, the downs dead asleep in the sun, the embankments of the railway with exhausted hot flowers go slowly past out of their reach. They felt as if they were being dragged away like criminals. Unable to speak or think, they stared out of the windows, Helena struggling in vain to keep back her tears, Siegmund labouring to breathe normally.

At Yarmouth the door was snatched open, and there was a confusion of shouting and running; a swarm of humanity, clamouring, attached itself at the carriage doorway, which was immediately blocked by a stout man who heaved a leather bag in front of him as he cried in German that here was room for all. Faces innumerable—hot, blue-eyed faces—strained to look over his shoulders at the shocked girl and the amazed Siegmund.

There entered eight Germans into the second-class compartment, five men and three ladies. When at last the luggage was stowed away they sank into the seats. The last man on either side to be seated lowered himself carefully, like a wedge, between his two neighbours. Siegmund watched the stout man, the one who had led the charge, settling himself between his large lady and the small Helena. The latter crushed herself against the side of the carriage. The German's hips came down tight against her. She strove to lessen herself against the window, to escape the pressure of his flesh, whose heat was transmitted to her. The man squeezed in the opposite direction.

"I am afraid I press you," he said, smiling in his gentle, chivalric German fashion. Helena glanced swiftly at him. She liked his grey eyes, she liked the agreeable intonation, and the pleasant sound of his words.

"Oh no," she answered. "You do not crush me."

Almost before she had finished the words she turned away to the window. The man seemed to hesitate a moment, as if recovering himself from a slight rebuff, before he could address his lady with the good-humoured remark in German: "Well, and have we not managed it very nicely, eh?"

The whole party began to talk in German with great animation. They told each other of the quaint ways of this or the other; they joked loudly over "Billy"—this being a nickname discovered for the German Emperor—and what he would be saying of the Czar's trip; they questioned each other, and answered each other concerning the places they were going to see, with great interest, displaying admirable knowledge. They were pleased with everything; they extolled things English.

Helena's stout neighbour, who, it seemed, was from Dresden, began to tell anecdotes. He was a *raconteur* of the naïve type: he talked with face, hands, with his whole body. Now and again he would give little spurts in his seat. After one of these he must have become aware of Helena—who felt as if she were enveloped by a soft stove—struggling to escape his compression. He stopped short, lifted his hat, and smiling beseechingly, said in his persuasive way:

"I am sorry. I am sorry. I compress you!" He glanced round in perplexity, seeking some escape or remedy. Finding none, he turned to her again, after having squeezed hard against his lady to free Helena, and said:

"Forgive me, I am sorry."

"You are forgiven," replied Helena, suddenly smiling into his face with her rare winsomeness. The whole party, attentive, relaxed into a smile at this. The good humour was complete.

"Thank you," said the German gratefully.

Helena turned away. The talk began again like the popping of corn; the *raconteur* resumed his anecdote. Everybody was waiting to laugh. Helena rapidly wearied of trying to follow the tale. Siegmund had made no attempt. He had watched, with the others, the German's apologies, and the sight of his lover's face had moved him more than he could tell.

She had a peculiar, childish wistfulness at times, and with this an intangible aloofness that pierced his heart. It seemed to him he should never know her. There was a remoteness about her, an estrangement between her and all natural daily things, as if she were of an unknown race that never can tell its own story. This feeling always moved Siegmund's pity to its deepest, leaving him poignantly helpless. This same foreignness, revealed in other ways, sometimes made him hate her. It was as if she would sacrifice him rather than renounce her foreign birth. There was something in her he could never understand, so that never, never could he say he was master of her as she was of him the mistress.

As she smiled and turned away from the German, mute, un-complaining, like a child wise in sorrow beyond its years, Siegmund's resentment against her suddenly took fire, and blazed him with sheer pain of pity. She was very small. Her quiet ways, and sometimes her impetuous clinging made her seem small; for she was very strong. But Siegmund saw her now, small, quiet, uncomplaining, living for him who sat and looked at her. But what would become of her when he had left her, when she was alone, little foreigner as she was, in this world, which apologises when it has done the hurt, too blind to see beforehand? Helena would be left behind; death was no way for her. She could not escape thus with him from this house of strangers which she called "life". She had to go on alone, like a foreigner who cannot learn the strange language.

"What will she do?" Siegmund asked himself, "when her loneliness comes upon her like a horror, and she has no one to go to. She will come to the memory of me for a while, and that will take her over till her strength is established. But what then?"

Siegmund could find no answer. He tried to imagine her life. It would go on, after his death, just in the same way, for a while, and then? He had not the faintest knowledge of how she would develop. What would she do when she was thirty-eight, and as old as himself? He could not conceive. Yet she would not die, of that he was certain.

Siegmund suddenly realised that he knew nothing of her life, her real inner life. She was a book written in characters un-intelligible to him and to everybody. He was tortured with the problem of her till it became acute, and he felt as if his heart would burst inside him. As a boy he had experienced the same sort of feeling after wrestling for an hour with a problem in Euclid, for he was capable of great concentration.

He felt Helena looking at him. Turning, he found her steady, unswerving eyes fixed on him, so that he shrank confused from them. She smiled: by an instinctive movement she made him know that she wanted him to hold her hand. He leaned forward and put his hand over hers. She had peculiar hands, small, with a strange, delightful silkiness. Often they were cool or cold; generally they lay unmoved within his clasp, but then they were instinct with life, not inert. Sometimes he would feel a peculiar jerking in his pulse, very much like electricity, when he held her hand. Occasionally it was almost painful, and felt as if a little virtue were passing out of his blood. But that he dismissed as nonsense.

The Germans were still rattling away, perspiring freely, wiping their faces with their handkerchiefs as they laughed, moving inside their clothing, which was sticking to their sides. Siegmund had not noticed them for some time, he was so much absorbed. But Helena, though she sympathised with her fellow-passengers, was tormented almost beyond endurance by the noise, the heat of her neighbour's body, the atmosphere of the crowded carriage, and her own emotion. The only thing that could relieve her was the hand of Siegmund soothing her in its hold.

She looked at him with the same steadiness which made her eyes feel heavy upon him, and made him shrink. She wanted his strength of nerve to support her, and he submitted at once, his one aim being to give her out of himself whatever she wanted.

CHAPTER XXI

THE tall white yachts in a throng were lounging off the roads of Ryde. It was near the regatta time, so these proud creatures had flown loftily together, and now flitted hither and thither among themselves, like a concourse of tall women, footing the waves with superb touch. To Siegmund they were very beautiful, but removed from him, as dancers crossing the window-lights are removed from the man who looks up from the street. He saw the Solent and the world of glamour flying gay as snow outside, where inside was only Siegmund, tired, dispirited, without any joy.

He and Helena had climbed among coils of rope on to the prow of their steamer, so they could catch a little spray of speed on their faces to stimulate them. The sea was very bright and crowded. White sails leaned slightly and filed along the roads; two yachts with sails of amber floated, it seemed without motion, amid the eclipsed blue of the day; small boats with red and yellow flags fluttered quickly, trailing the sea with colour; a pleasure steamer coming from Cowes swung her soft stout way among the fleeting ships; high in the background were men-of-war, a long line, each one threading tiny triangles of flags through a sky dim with distance.

"It is all very glad," said Siegmund to himself, "but it seems to be fanciful."

He was out of it. Already he felt detached from life. He belonged to his destination. It is always so: we have no share in the beauty that lies between us and our goal.

Helena watched with poignant sorrow all the agitation of colour on the blue afternoon.

"We must leave it; we must pass out of it," she lamented, over and over again. Each new charm she caught eagerly.

"I like the steady purpose of that brown-sailed tramp," she said to herself, watching a laden coaster making for Portsmouth.

They were still among the small shipping of Ryde. Siegmund and Helena, as they looked out, became aware of a small motor-launch heading across their course towards a yacht whose tall masts were drawn clean on the sky. The eager launch, its nose up as if to breathe, was racing over the swell like a coursing dog. A lady, in white, and a lad with dark head and white jersey were leaning in the bows; a gentleman was bending over some machinery in the middle of the boat, while the sailor in the low stern was also stooping forward attending to some-thing. The steamer was sweeping onwards, huge above the water; the dog of a boat was coursing straight across her track. The lady saw the danger first. Stretching forward, she seized the arm of the lad and held him firm, making no sound, but watching the forward menace of the looming steamer.

"Look!" cried Helena, catching hold of Siegmund. He was
already watching. Suddenly the steamer bell clanged. The
gentleman looked up, with startled, sunburned face; then he
leaped to the stern. The launch veered. It and the steamer
closed together like a pair of scissors. The lady, still holding
the boy, looked up with an expressionless face at the high
sweeping chisel of the steamer's bows; the husband stood rigid,
staring ahead. No sound was to be heard save the rustling of
water under the bows. The scissors closed, the launch skelped
forward like a dog from in front of the traffic. It escaped by
a yard or two. Then, like a dog, it seemed to look round. The
gentleman in the stern glanced back quickly. He was a handsome, dark-haired man with dark eyes. His face was as if
carven out of oak, set and grey-brown. Then he looked to the
steering of his boat. No one had uttered a sound. From the
tiny boat coursing low on the water, not a sound, only tense
waiting. The launch raced out of danger towards the yacht.
The gentleman, with a brief gesture, put his man in charge
again, whilst he himself went forward to the lady. He was a
handsome man, very proud in his movements; and she, in her
bearing, was prouder still. She received him almost with
indifference.

Helena turned to Siegmund. He took both her hands and
pressed them, whilst she looked at him with eyes blind with
emotion. She was white to the lips, and heaving like the buoy
in the wake of the steamer. The noise of life had suddenly
been hushed, and each heart had heard for a moment the noise-
lessness of death. How everyone was white and gasping! They
strove, on every hand, to fill the day with noise and the colour
of life again.

"By Jove, that was a near thing!"

"Ah, that has made me feel bad!" said a woman.

"A French yacht," said somebody.

Helena was waiting for the voice of Siegmund. But he did
not know what to say. Confused, he repeated:

"That was a close shave."

Helena clung to him, searching his face. She felt his
difference from herself. There was something in his experience that made him different, quiet, with a peculiar expression
as if he were pained.

"Ah, dear Lord!" he was saying to himself. "How bright
and whole the day is for them! If God had suddenly put His

hand over the sun, and swallowéd us up in a shadow, they could not have been more startled. That man, with his fine, white-flannelled limbs and his dark head, has no suspicion of the shadow that supports it all. Between the blueness of the sea and the sky he passes easy as a gull, close to the fine white seamew of his mate, amid red flowers of flags, and soft birds of ships, and slow-moving monsters of steamboats.

"For me the day is transparent and shrivelling. I can see the darkness through its petals. But for him it is a fresh bell-flower, in which he fumbles with delights like a bee.

"For me, quivering in the interspaces of the atmosphere, is the darkness the same that fills in my soul. I can see death urging itself into life, the shadow supporting the substance. For my life is burning an invisible flame. The glare of the light of myself, as I burn on the fuel of death, is not enough to hide from me the source and the issue. For what is a life but a flame that bursts off the surface of darkness, and tapers into the darkness again? But the death that issues differs from the death that was the source. At least, I shall enrich death with a potent shadow, if I do not enrich life."

"Wasn't that woman fine!" said Helena.

"So perfectly still," he answered.

"The child realised nothing," she said.

Siegmund laughed, then leaned forward impulsively to her.

"I am always so sorry," he said, "that the human race is urged inevitably into a deeper and deeper realisation of life."

She looked at him, wondering what provoked such a remark.

"I guess," she said slowly, after a while, "that the man, the sailor, will have a bad time. He was abominably careless."

"He was careful of something else just then," said Siegmund, who hated to hear her speak in cold condemnation. "He was attending to the machinery or something."

"That was scarcely his first business," said she, rather sarcastic.

Siegmund looked at her. She seemed very hard in judgment —very blind. Sometimes his soul surged against her in hatred.

"Do you think the man *wanted* to drown the boat?" he asked.

"He nearly succeeded," she replied.

There was antagonism between them. Siegmund recognised in Helena the world sitting in judgment, and he hated it. But, after all," he thought, "I suppose it is the only way to get along, to judge the event and not the person. I have a disease of sympathy, a vice of exoneration."

Nevertheless, he did not love Helena as a judge. He thought rather of the woman in the boat. She was evidently one who watched the sources of life, saw it great and impersonal.

"Would the woman cry, or hug and kiss the boy when she got on board?" he asked.

"I rather think not. Why?" she replied.

"I hope she didn't," he said.

Helena sat watching the water spurt back from the bows. She was very much in love with Siegmund. He was suggestive; he stimulated her. But to her mind he had not his own dark eyes of hesitation; he was swift and proud as the wind. She never realised his helplessness.

Siegmund was gathering strength from the thought of that other woman's courage. If she had so much restraint as not to cry out, or alarm the boy, if she had so much grace not to complain to her husband, surely he himself might refrain from revealing his own fear to Helena, and from lamenting his hard fate.

They sailed on past the chequered round towers. The sea opened, and they looked out to eastward into the sea-space. Siegmund wanted to flee. He yearned to escape down the open ways before him. Yet he knew he would be carried on to London. He watched the sea-ways closing up. The shore came round. The high old houses stood flat on the right hand. The shore swept round in a sickle, reaping them into the harbour. There the old *Victory*, gay with myriad pointed pennons, was harvested, saved for a trophy.

"It is a dreadful thing," thought Siegmund, "to remain as a trophy when there is nothing more to do." He watched the landing-stage swooping nearer. There were the trains drawn up in readiness. At the other end of the train was London.

He could scarcely bear to have Helena before him for another two hours. The suspense of that protracted farewell, while he sat opposite her in the beating train, would cost too much. He longed to be released from her.

They had got their luggage, and were standing at the foot of the ladder, in the heat of the engines and the smell of hot oil, waiting for the crowd to pass on, so that they might ascend and step off the ship on to the mainland.

"Won't you let me go by the South-Western, and you by

the Brighton?" asked Siegmund, hesitating, repeating the morning's question.

Helena looked at him, knitting her brows with misgiving and perplexity.

"No," she replied. "Let us go together."

Siegmund followed her up the iron ladder to the quay.

There was no great crowd on the train. They easily found a second-class compartment without occupants. He swung the luggage on the rack and sat down, facing Helena.

"Now," said he to himself, "I wish I were alone."

He wanted to think and prepare himself.

Helena, who was thinking actively, leaned forward to him to say:

"Shall I not go down to Cornwall?"

By her soothing willingness to do anything for him, Siegmund knew that she was dogging him closely. He could not bear to have his anxiety protracted.

"But you have promised Louisa, have you not?" he replied.

"Oh, well!" she said, in the peculiar slighting tone she had when she wished to convey the unimportance of affairs not touching him.

"Then you must go," he said.

"But," she began, with harsh petulance, "I do not want to go down to Cornwall with *Louisa* and *Olive*"—she accentuated the two names—"after *this*," she added.

"Then Louisa will have no holiday—and you have promised," he said gravely.

Helena looked at him. She saw he had decided that she should go.

"Is my promise so *very* important?" she asked. She glanced angrily at the three ladies who were hesitating in the doorway. Nevertheless, the ladies entered, and seated themselves at the opposite end of the carriage. Siegmund did not know whether he were displeased or relieved by their intrusion. If they had stayed out, he might have held Helena in his arms for still another hour. As it was, she could not harass him with words. He tried not to look at her, but to think.

The train at last moved out of the station. As it passed through Portsmouth, Siegmund remembered his coming down, on the Sunday. It seemed an indefinite age ago. He was thankful that he sat on the side of the carriage opposite from the one he had occupied five days before. The afternoon of the flawless sky was ripening into evening. The chimneys and the sides of the houses of Portsmouth took on that radiant appearance which transfigures the end of day in town. A rich bloom of light appears on the surfaces of brick and stone.

"It will go on," thought Siegmund, "being gay of an evening, for ever. And I shall miss it all!"

But as soon as the train moved into the gloom of the Town station, he began again:

"Beatrice will be proud, and silent as steel when I get home. She will say nothing, thank God—nor shall I. That will expedite matters: there will be no interruptions . . .

"But we cannot continue together after this. Why should I discuss reasons for and against? We cannot. She goes to a cottage in the country. Already I have spoken of it to her. I allow her all I can of my money, and on the rest I manage for myself in lodgings in London. Very good.

"But when I am comparatively free I cannot live alone. I shall want Helena; I shall remember the children. If I have the one, I shall be damned by the thought of the other. This bruise on my mind will never get better. Helena says she would never come to me; but she would, out of pity for me. I know she would.

"But then, what then? Beatrice and the children in the country, and me not looking after the children. Beatrice is thriftless. She would be in endless difficulty. It would be a degradation to me. She would keep a red sore inflamed against me; I should be a shameful thing in her mouth. Besides, there would go all her strength. She would not make any efforts. 'He has brought it on us,' she would say; 'let him see what the result is.' And things would go from bad to worse with them. It would be a gangrene of shame.

"And Helena—I should have nothing but mortification. When she was asleep I could not look at her. She is such a strange, incongruous creature. But I should be responsible for her. She believes in me as if I had the power of God. What should I think of myself?"

Siegmund leaned with his head against the window, watching the country whirl past, but seeing nothing. He thought imaginatively, and his imagination destroyed him. He pictured Beatrice in the country. He sketched the morning—breakfast haphazard at a late hour; the elder children rushing off without food, miserable and untidy, the youngest bewildered under her swift, indifferent preparations for school. He thought of Beatrice in the evening, worried and irritable, her bills unpaid, the work undone, declaiming lamentably against the cruelty of her husband, who had abandoned her to such a burden of care while he took his pleasure elsewhere.

This line exhausted or intolerable, Siegmund switched off to the consideration of his own life in town. He would go to America; the agreement was signed with the theatre manager. But America would be only a brief shutting of the eyes and closing of the mouth. He would wait for the home-coming to Helena, and she would wait for him. It was inevitable; then would begin—what? He would never have enough money to keep Helena, even if he managed to keep himself. Their meetings would then be occasional and clandestine. Ah, it was intolerable!

"If I were rich," said Siegmund, "all would be plain. I would give each of my children enough, and Beatrice, and we would go away; but I am nearly forty; I have no genius; I shall never be rich." Round and round went his thoughts like oxen over a threshing floor, treading out the grain. Gradually the chaff flew away; gradually the corn of conviction gathered small and hard upon the floor.

As he sat thinking, Helena leaned across to him and laid her hand on his knee.

"If I have made things more difficult," she said, her voice harsh with pain, "you will forgive me."

He started. This was one of the cruel cuts of pain that love gives, filling the eyes with blood. Siegmund stiffened himself; slowly he smiled, as he looked at her childish, plaintive lips, and her large eyes haunted with pain.

"Forgive you?" he repeated. "Forgive you for five days of perfect happiness; the only real happiness I have ever known!"

Helena tightened her fingers on his knee. She felt herself stinging with painful joy; but one of the ladies was looking at her curiously. She leaned back in her place, and turned to watch the shocks of corn strike swiftly, in long rows, across her vision.

Siegmund, also quivering, turned his face to the window, where the rotation of the wide sea-flat helped the movement of his thought. Helena had interrupted him. She had be-wildered his thoughts from their hawking, so that they struck here and there, wildly, among small, pitiful prey that was useless, conclusions which only hindered the bringing home of the final convictions.

"What will she do?" cried Siegmund. "What will she do when I am gone? What will become of her? Already she has no aim in life; then she will have no object. Is it any good my going if I leave her behind? What an inextricable knot this is! But what will she do?"

It was a question she had aroused before, a question which he could never answer; indeed, it was not for him to answer.

They wound through the pass of the South Downs. As Siegmund, looking backward, saw the northern slope of the downs swooping smoothly, in a great, broad bosom of sward, down to the body of the land, he warmed with sudden love for the earth; there the great downs were, naked like a breast, leaning kindly to him. The earth is always kind; it loves us, and would foster us like a nurse. The downs were big and tender and simple. Siegmund looked at the farm, folded in a hollow, and he wondered what fortunate folk were there, nourished and quiet, hearing the vague roar of the train that was carrying him home.

Up towards Arundel the cornfields of red wheat were heavy with gold. It was evening, when the green of the trees went out, leaving dark shapes proud upon the sky; but the red wheat was forged in the sunset, hot and magnificent. Siegmund almost gloated as he smelled the ripe corn, and opened his eyes to its powerful radiation. For a moment he forgot everything, amid the forging of red fields of gold in the smithy of the sunset. Like sparks, poppies blew along the railway-banks, a crimson train. Siegmund waited, through the meadows, for the next wheat-field. It came like the lifting of yellow-hot metal out of the gloom of darkened grass-lands.

Helena was reassured by the glamour of evening over ripe Sussex. She breathed the land now and then, while she watched the sky. The sunset was stately. The blue-eyed day, with great limbs, having fought its victory and won, now mounted triumphant on its pyre, and with white arms uplifted took the flames, which leaped like blood about its feet. The day died nobly, so she thought.

One gold cloud, as an encouragement tossed to her, followed the train.

"Surely that cloud is for us," said she, as she watched it anxiously. Dark trees brushed between it and her, while she waited in suspense. It came, unswerving, from behind the trees.

"I am sure it is for us," she repeated. A gladness came into her eyes. Still the cloud followed the train. She leaned forward to Siegmund and pointed out the cloud to him. She was very eager to give him a little of her faith.

"It has come with us quite a long way. Doesn't it seem to you to be travelling with us? It is the golden hand; it is the good omen."

She then proceeded to tell him the legend from "Aylwin".

Siegmund listened, and smiled. The sunset was handsome on his face.

Helena was almost happy.

"I am right," said he to himself. "I am right in my conclusions, and Helena will manage by herself afterwards. I am right; there is the hand to confirm it."

The heavy train settled down to an easy, unbroken stroke, swinging like a greyhound over the level northwards. All the time Siegmund was mechanically thinking the well-known movement from the Valkyrie Ride, his whole self beating to the rhythm. It seemed to him there was a certain grandeur in this flight, but it hurt him with its heavy insistence of catastrophe. He was afraid; he had to summon his courage to sit quiet. For a time he was reassured; he believed he was going on towards the right end. He hunted through the country and the sky, asking of everything, "Am I right? Am I right?" He did not mind what happened to him, so long as he felt it was right. What he meant by "right" he did not trouble to think, but the question remained. For a time he had been re-assured; then a dullness came over him, when his thoughts were stupid, and he merely submitted to the rhythm of the train, which stamped him deeper and deeper with a brand of catastrophe.

The sun had gone down. Over the west was a gush of brightness as the fountain of light bubbled lower. The stars, like specks of froth from the foaming of the day, clung to the blue ceiling. Like spiders they hung overhead, while the hosts of the gold atmosphere poured out of the hive by the western low door. Soon the hive was empty, a hollow dome of purple, with here and there on the floor a bright brushing of wings—a village; then, overhead, the luminous star-spiders began to run.

"Ah, well!" thought Siegmund—he was tired—"if one bee dies in a swarm, what is it, so long as the hive is all right? Apart from the gold light, and the hum and the colour of day, what was I? Nothing! Apart from these rushings out of the hive, along with swarm, into the dark meadows of night, gathering God knows what, I was a pebble. Well, the day will swarm in golden again, with colour on the wings of every bee, and humming in each activity. The gold and the colour and sweet smell and the sound of life, they exist, even if there is no bee; it only happens we see the iridescence on the wings of a bee. It exists whether or not, bee or no bee. Since the iridescence and the humming of life *are* always, and since it was they who made me, then I am not lost. At least, I do not care. If the spark goes out, the essence of the fire is there in the darkness. What does it matter? Besides, I *have* burned bright; I have laid up a fine cell of honey somewhere—I wonder where? We can never point to it; but it *is* so—what does it matter, then!"

They had entered the north downs, and were running through Dorking towards Leatherhead. Box Hill stood dark in the dusky sweetness of the night. Helena remembered that here she and Siegmund had come for their first walk together. She would like to come again Presently she saw the quick stilettos of stars on the small, baffled river; they ran between high embankments. Siegmund recollected that these were covered with roses of Sharon—the large golden St. John's wort of finest silk. He looked, and could just distinguish the full-blown, delicate flowers, ignored by the stars. At last he had something to say to Helena:

"Do you remember," he asked, "the roses of Sharon all along here?"

"I do," replied Helena, glad he spoke so brightly. "Weren't they pretty?"

After a few moments of watching the bank, she said:

"Do you know, I have never gathered one? I think I should like to; I should like to feel them, and they should have an orangy smell."

He smiled, without answering.

She glanced up at him, smiling brightly.

"But shall we come down here in the morning, and find some?" she asked. She put the question timidly. "Would you care to?" she added.

Siegmund darkened and frowned. Here was the pain revived again.

"No," he said gently; "I think we had better not." Almost for the first time he did not make apologetic explanation.

Helena turned to the window, and remained, looking out at the spinning of the lights of the towns without speaking, until they were near Sutton. Then she rose and pinned on her hat, gathering her gloves and her basket. She was, in spite of herself, slightly angry. Being quite ready to leave the train, she sat down to wait for the station. Siegmund was aware that she was displeased, and again, for the first time, he said to himself, "Ah, well, it must be so."

She looked at him. He was sad, therefore she softened instantly.

"At least," she said doubtfully, "I shall see you at the station."

"At Waterloo?" he asked.

"No, at Wimbledon," she replied, in her metallic tone.

"But——" he began.

"It will be the best way for us," she interrupted, in the calm tone of conviction. "Much better than crossing London from Victoria to Waterloo."

"Very well," he replied.

He looked up a train for her in his little time-table.

"You will get in Wimbledon 10.5—leave 10.40—leave Waterloo 11.30," he said.

"Very good," she answered.

The brakes were grinding. They waited in a burning suspense for the train to stop.

"If only she will soon go!" thought Siegmund. It was an intolerable minute. She rose; everything was a red blur. She stood before him, pressing his hand; then he rose to give her the bag. As he leaned upon the window-frame and she stood below on the platform, looking up at him, he could scarcely breathe. "How long will it be?" he said to himself, looking at the open carriage doors. He hated intensely the lady who could not get a porter to remove her luggage; he could have killed her; he could have killed the dilatory guard. At last the doors slammed and the whistle went. The train started imperceptibly into motion.

"Now I lose her," said Siegmund.

She looked up at him; her face was white and dismal.

"Good-bye, then!" she said, and she turned away.

Siegmund went back to his seat. He was relieved, but he trembled with sickness. We are all glad when intense moments are done with; but why did she fling round in that manner, stopping the keen note short; what would she do?

CHAPTER XXII

SIEGMUND went up to Victoria. He was in no hurry to get down to Wimbledon. London was warm and exhausted after the hot day, but this peculiar lukewarmness was not unpleasant to him. He chose to walk from Victoria to Waterloo.

The streets were like polished gun-metal glistened over with gold. The taxi-cabs, the wild cats of the town, swept over the gleaming floor swiftly, soon lessening in the distance, as if scornful of the other clumsy-footed traffic. He heard the merry click-clock of the swinging hansoms, then the excited whirring of the motor-buses as they charged full-tilt heavily down the road, their hearts, as it seemed, beating with trepidation; they drew up with a sigh of relief by the kerb, and stood there panting—great, nervous, clumsy things. Siegmund was always amused by the headlong, floundering career of the buses. He was pleased with this scampering of the traffic; anything for distraction. He was glad Helena was not with him, for the streets would have irritated her with their coarse noise. She would stand for a long time to watch the rabbits pop and hobble along on the common at night; but the tearing along of the taxis and the charge of a great motor-bus was painful to her. "Discords," she said, "after the trees and sea." She liked the glistening of the streets; it seemed a fine alloy of gold laid down for pavement, such pavement as drew near to the pure gold streets of Heaven; but this noise could not be endured near any wonderland.

Siegmund did not mind it; it drummed out his own thoughts. He watched the gleaming magic of the road, raced over with shadows, project itself far before him into the night. He watched the people. Soldiers, belted with scarlet, went jauntily on in front. There was a peculiar charm in their movement.

There was a soft vividness of life in their carriage; it reminded Siegmund of the soft swaying and lapping of a poised candle-flame. The women went blithely alongside. Occasionally, in passing, one glanced at him; then, in spite of himself, he smiled; he knew not why. The women glanced at him with approval, for he was ruddy; besides, he had that carelessness and abstraction of despair. The eyes of the women said, "You are comely, you are lovable," and Siegmund smiled.

When the street opened, at Westminster, he noticed the city sky, a lovely deep purple, and the lamps in the square steaming out a vapour of grey-gold light.

"It is a wonderful night," he said to himself. "There are not two such in a year."

He went forward to the Embankment, with a feeling of elation in his heart. This purple and gold-grey world, with the fluttering flame-warmth of soldiers and the quick brightness of women, like lights that clip sharply in a draught, was a revelation to him.

As he leaned upon the Embankment parapet the wonder did not fade, but rather increased. The trams, one after another, floated loftily over the bridge. They went like great burning bees in an endless file into a hive, past those which were drifting dreamily out, while below, on the black, distorted water, golden serpents flashed and twisted to and fro.

"Ah!" said Siegmund to himself; "it is far too wonderful for me. Here, as well as by the sea, the night is gorgeous and un-couth. Whatever happens, the world is wonderful."

So he went on amid all the vast miracle of movement in the city night, the swirling of water to the sea, the gradual sweep of the stars, the floating of many lofty, luminous cars through the bridged darkness, like an army of angels filing past on one of God's campaigns, the purring haste of the taxis, the slightly dancing shadows of people. Siegmund went on slowly, like a slow bullet winging into the heart of life. He did not lose this sense of wonder, not in the train, nor as he walked home in the moonless dark.

When he closed the door behind him and hung up his hat he frowned. He did not think definitely of anything, but his frown meant to him: "Now for the beginning of Hell!"

He went towards the dining-room, where the light was, and the uneasy murmur. The clock, with its deprecating, suave chime, was striking ten. Siegmund opened the door of the room. Beatrice was sewing, and did not raise her head. Frank, a tall, thin lad of eighteen, was bent over a book. He did not look up. Vera had her fingers thrust in among her hair, and continued to read the magazine that lay on the table before her. Siegmund looked at them all. They gave no sign to show they were aware of his entry; there was only that unnatural tenseness of people who cover their agitation. He glanced round to see where he should go. His wicker arm-chair remained by the fireplace; his slippers were standing under the sideboard, as he had left them. Siegmund sat down in the creaking chair; he began to feel sick and tired.

"I suppose the children are in bed," he said.

His wife sewed on as if she had not heard him; his daughter noisily turned over a leaf and continued to read, as if she were pleasantly interested and had known no interruption. Siegmund waited, with his slipper dangling from his hand, looking from one to another.

"They've been gone two hours," said Frank at last, still without raising his eyes from his book. His tone was contemptuous, his voice was jarring, not yet having developed a man's fullness.

Siegmund put on his slipper, and began to unlace the other boot. The slurring of the lace through the holes and the snacking of the tag seemed unnecessarily loud. It annoyed his wife. She took a breath to speak, then refrained, feeling suddenly her daughter's scornful restraint upon her. Siegmund rested his arms upon his knees, and sat leaning forward, looking into the barren fireplace, which was littered with paper, and orange-peel, and a banana-skin.

"Do you want any supper?" asked Beatrice, and the sudden harshness of her voice startled him into looking at her.

She had her face averted, refusing to see him. Siegmund's heart went down with weariness and despair at the sight of her.

"Aren't *you* having any?" he asked.

The table was not laid. Beatrice's work-basket, a little wicker fruit-skep, overflowed scissors, and pins, and scraps of holland, and reels of cotton on the green serge cloth. Vera leaned both her elbows on the table.

Instead of replying to him, Beatrice went to the sideboard. She took out a table-cloth, pushed her sewing litter aside, and spread the cloth over one end of the table. Vera gave her magazine a little knock with her hand.

"Have you read this tale of a French convent school in here, Mother?" she asked.

"In where?" said Beatrice.

"In this month's *Nash's*."

"No," replied Beatrice. "What time have I for reading, much less for anything else?"

"You should think more of yourself, and a little less of other people, then," said Vera, with a sneer at the "other people". She rose. "Let me do this. You sit down; you are tired, Mother," she said.

Her mother, without replying, went out to the kitchen. Vera followed her. Frank, left alone with his father, moved uneasily, and bent his thin shoulders lower over his book. Siegmund remained with his arms on his knees, looking into the grate. From the kitchen came the chinking of crockery, and soon the smell of coffee. All the time Vera was heard chatting with affected brightness to her mother, addressing her in fond tones, using all her wits to recall bright little incidents to retail to her. Beatrice answered rarely, and then with utmost brevity.

Presently Vera came in with the tray. She put down a cup of coffee, a plate with boiled ham, pink and thin, such as is bought from a grocer, and some bread-and-butter. Then she sat down, noisily turning over the leaves of her magazine. Frank glanced at the table; it was laid solely for his father. He looked at the bread and the meat, but restrained himself, and went on reading, or pretended to do so. Beatrice came in with the small cruet; it was conspicuously bright.

Everything was correct: knife and fork, spoon, cruet, all perfectly clean, the crockery fine, the bread and butter thin— in fact, it was just as it would have been for a perfect stranger. This scrupulous neatness, in a household so slovenly and easy-going, where it was an established tradition that something should be forgotten or wrong, impressed Siegmund. Beatrice put the serving knife and fork by the little dish of ham, saw that all was proper, then went and sat down. Her face showed no emotion; it was calm and proud. She began to sew.

"What do you say, Mother?" said Vera, as if resuming a conversation. "Shall it be Hampton Court or Richmond on Sunday?"

"I say, as I said before," replied Beatrice: "I cannot afford to go out."

"But you must begin, my dear, and Sunday shall see the beginning. *Dîtes donc!*"

"There are other things to think of," said Beatrice.

"Now, maman, *nous avons changé tout cela*! We are going out—a jolly little razzle!" Vera, who was rather handsome, lifted up her face and smiled at her mother gaily.

"I am afraid there will be no *razzle*"—Beatrice accented the word, smiling slightly—"for me. You are slangy, Vera."

"*Un doux argot, ma mère.* You look tired."

Beatrice glanced at the clock.

"I will go to bed when I have cleared the table," she said.

Siegmund winced. He was still sitting with his head bent down, looking in the grate. Vera went on to say something more. Presently Frank looked up at the table, and remarked in his grating voice:

"There's your supper, Father."

The women stopped and looked round at this. Siegmund bent his head lower. Vera resumed her talk. It died out, and there was silence.

Siegmund was hungry.

"Oh, good Lord, good Lord! bread of humiliation to-night!" he said to himself before he could muster courage to rise and go to the table. He seemed to be shrinking inwards. The women glanced swiftly at him and away from him as his chair creaked and he got up. Frank was watching from under his eyebrows.

Siegmund went through the ordeal of eating and drinking in presence of his family. If he had not been hungry, he could not have done it, despite the fact that he was content to receive humiliation this night. He swallowed the coffee with effort. When he had finished he sat irresolute for some time; then he arose and went to the door.

"Good-night!" he said.

Nobody made any reply. Frank merely stirred in his chair. Siegmund shut the door and went.

There was absolute silence in the room till they heard him turn on the tap in the bathroom; then Beatrice began to breathe spasmodically, catching her breath as if she would sob. But she restrained herself. The faces of the two children set hard with hate.

"He is not worth the flicking of your little finger, Mother," said Vera.

Beatrice moved about with pitiful, groping hands, collecting her sewing and her cottons.

"At any rate, he's come back red enough," said Frank, in his grating tone of contempt. "He's like boiled salmon."

Beatrice did not answer anything. Frank rose, and stood with his back to the grate, in his father's characteristic attitude.

"I *would* come slinking back in a funk!" he said, with a young man's sneer.

Stretching forward, he put a piece of ham between two pieces of bread, and began to eat the sandwich in large bites. Vera came to the table at this, and began to make herself a more dainty sandwich. Frank watched her with jealous eyes.

"There is a little more ham, if you'd like it," said Beatrice to him. "I kept you some."

"All right, Ma," he replied. "Fetch it in."

Beatrice went out to the kitchen.

"And bring the bread and butter, too, will you?" called Vera after her.

"The damned coward! Ain't he a rotten funker?" said Frank, *sotto voce*, while his mother was out of the room.

Vera did nct reply, but she seemed tacitly to agree.

They petted their mother, while she waited on them. At length Frank yawned. He fidgeted a moment or two, then he went over to his mother, and, putting his hand on her arm— the feel of his mother's round arm under the black silk sleeve made his tears rise—he said, more gratingly than ever:

"Ne'er mind, Ma; we'll be all right to you." Then he bent and kissed her. "Good-night, Mother," he said awkwardly, and he went out of the room.

Beatrice was crying.

CHAPTER XXIII

"I SHALL never re-establish myself," said Siegmund as he closed behind him the dining-room door and went upstairs in the dark. "I am a family criminal. Beatrice might come round, but the

children's insolent judgment is too much. And I am like a dog
that creeps round the house from which it escaped with joy.
I have nowhere else to go. Why did I come back? But I am
sleepy. I will not bother to-night."

He went into the bathroom and washed himself. Everything
he did gave him a grateful sense of pleasure, notwithstanding
the misery of his position. He dipped his arms deeper into the
cold water, that he might feel the delight of it a little farther.
His neck he swilled time after time, and it seemed to him he
laughed with pleasure as the water caught him and fell away.
The towel reminded him how sore were his forehead and his
neck, blistered both to a state of rawness by the sun. He
touched them very cautiously to dry them, wincing, and
smiling at his own childish touch-and-shrink.

Though his bedroom was very dark, he did not light the gas.
Instead, he stepped out into the small balcony. His shirt was
open at the neck and wrists. He pulled it farther apart, baring
his chest to the deliciously soft night. He stood looking out at
the darkness for some time. The night was as yet moonless,
but luminous with a certain atmosphere of light. The stars
were small. Near at hand, large shapes of trees rose up.
Farther, lamps like little mushroom groups shone amid an
undergrowth of darkness. There was a vague hoarse noise filling the sky, like the whispering in a shell, and this breathing
of the summer night occasionally swelled into a restless sigh
as a train roared across the distance.

"What a big night!" thought Siegmund. "The night gathers
everything into a oneness. I wonder what is in it."

He leaned forward over the balcony, trying to catch something out of the night. He felt his soul like tendrils stretched
out anxiously to grasp a hold. What could he hold to in this
great, hoarse-breathing night? A star fell. It seemed to burst
into sight just across his eyes with a yellow flash. He looked
up, unable to make up his mind whether he had seen it or not.
There was no gap in the sky.

"It is a good sign—a shooting star," he said to himself.
"It is a good sign for me. I know I am right. That was my
sign."

Having assured himself, he stepped indoors, unpacked his
bag, and was soon in bed.

"This is a good bed," he said. "And the sheets are very
fresh."

He lay for a little while with his head bending forwards, look-ing from his pillow out at the stars, then he went to sleep.

At half-past six in the morinng he suddenly opened his eyes.

"What is it?" he asked, and almost without interruption answered: "Well, I've got to go through it."

His sleep had shaped him perfect premonition, which, like a dream, he forgot when he awoke. Only this naïve question and answer betrayed what had taken place in his sleep. Immediately he awoke this subordinate knowledge vanished.

Another fine day was striding in triumphant. The first thing Siegmund did was to salute the morning, because of its bright-ness. The second thing was to call to mind the aspect of that bay in the Isle of Wight. "What would it just be like now?" said he to himself. He had to give his heart some justification for the peculiar pain left in it from his sleep activity, so he began poignantly to long for the place which had been his during the last mornings. He pictured the garden with roses and nasturtiums; he remembered the sunny way down the shore, and all the expanse of sea hung softly between the tall white cliffs.

"It is impossible it is gone!" he cried to himself. "It can't be gone. I looked forward to it as if it never would come. It can't be gone now. Helena is not lost to me, surely." Then he began a long pining for the departed beauty of his life. He turned the jewel of memory, and facet by facet it wounded him with its brilliant loveliness. This pain, though it was keen, was half pleasure.

Presently he heard his wife stirring. She opened the door of the room next to his, and he heard her:

"Frank, it's a quarter to eight. You *will* be late."

"All right, Mother. Why didn't you call me sooner?" grumbled the lad.

"I didn't wake myself. I didn't go to sleep till morning, and then I slept."

She went downstairs. Siegmund listened for his son to get out of bed. The minutes passed.

"The young donkey, why doesn't he get out?" said Siegmund angrily to himself. He turned over, pressing himself upon the bed in anger and humiliation, because now he had no authority to call to his son and keep him to his duty. Siegmund waited, writhing with anger, shame, and anxiety. When the suave, velvety "Pan-n-n! pan-n-n-n!" of the clock was heard striking, Frank stepped with a thud on to the floor. He could be heard dressing in clumsy haste. Beatrice called from the bottom of the stairs:

"Do you want any hot water?"

"You know there isn't time for me to shave now," answered her son, lifting his voice to a kind of broken falsetto.

The scent of the cooking of bacon filled the house. Siegmund heard his second daughter, Marjory, aged nine, talking to Vera, who occupied the same room with her. The child was evidently questioning, and the elder girl answered briefly. There was a lull in the household noises, broken suddenly by Marjory, shouting from the top of the stairs:

"Mam!" She waited. "Mam!" Still Beatrice did not hear her. "Mam! Mamma!" Beatrice was in the scullery. "Mamma-a!" The child was getting impatient. She lifted her voice and shouted: "Mam? Mamma!" Still no answer. "Mam-mee-e!" she squealed.

Siegmund could hardly contain himself.

"Why don't you go down and ask?" Vera called crossly from the bedroom.

And at the same moment Beatrice answered, also crossly: "What do you want?"

"Where's my stockings?" cried the child at the top of her voice.

"Why do you ask me? Are they down here?" replied her mother. "What are you shouting for?"

The child plodded downstairs. Directly she returned, and as she passed into Vera's room, she grumbled: "And now they're not mended."

Siegmund heard a sound that made his heart beat. It was the crackling of the sides of the crib, as Gwen, his little girl of five, climbed out. She was silent for a space. He imagined her sitting on the white rug and pulling on her stockings. Then there came the quick little thud of her feet as she went downstairs.

"Mam," Siegmund heard her say as she went down the hall, "has dad come?"

The answer and the child's further talk were lost in the distance of the kitchen. The small, anxious question, and the quick thudding of Gwen's feet, made Siegmund lie still with torture. He wanted to hear no more. He lay shrinking within himself. It seemed that his soul was sensitive to madness. He felt that he could not, come what might, get up and meet them all.

The front door banged, and he heard Frank's hasty call: "Good-bye!" Evidently the lad was in an ill-humour. Siegmund listened for the sound of the train; it seemed an age; the boy would catch it. Then the water from the wash-hand bowl in the bathroom ran loudly out. That, he suggested, was Vera, who was evidently not going up to town. At the thought of this, Siegmund almost hated her. He listened for her to go downstairs. It was nine o'clock.

The footsteps of Beatrice came upstairs. She put something down in the bathroom—his hot water. Siegmund listened intently for her to come to his door. Would she speak? She approached hurriedly, knocked, and waited. Siegmund, startled, for the moment, could not answer. She knocked loudly.

"All right," said he.

Then she went downstairs.

He lay probing and torturing himself for another half-hour, till Vera's voice said coldly, beneath his window outside:

"You should clear away, then. We don't want the breakfast things on the table for a week."

Siegmund's heart set hard. He rose, with a shut mouth, and went across to the bathroom. There he started. The quaint figure of Gwen stood at the bowl, her back was towards him; she was sponging her face gingerly. Her hair, all blowsed from the pillow, was tied in a stiff little pigtail, standing out from her slender, childish neck. Her arms were bare to the shoulder. She wore a bodiced petticoat of pink flannelette, which hardly reached her knees. Siegmund felt slightly amused to see her stout little calves planted so firmly close together. She carefully sponged her cheeks, her pursed-up mouth, and her neck, soaping her hair, but not her ears. Then, very deliberately, she squeezed out the sponge and proceeded to wipe away the soap.

For some reason or other she glanced round. Her startled eyes met his. She, too, had beautiful dark blue eyes. She stood, with the sponge at her neck, looking full at him. Siegmund felt himself shrinking. The child's look was steady, calm, inscrutable.

"Hello!" said her father. "Are you here!"

The child, without altering her expression in the slightest, turned her back on him, and continued wiping her neck. She dropped the sponge in the water and took the towel from off the side of the bath. Then she turned to look again at Siegmund, who stood in his pyjamas before her, his mouth shut hard, but his eyes shrinking and tender. She seemed to be trying to discover something in him.

"Have you washed your ears?" he said gaily.

She paid no heed to this, except that he noticed her face now wore a slight constrained smile as she looked at him. She was shy. Still she continued to regard him curiously.

"There is some chocolate on my dressing-table," he said.

"Where have you been to?" she asked suddenly.

"To the seaside," he answered, smiling.

"To Brighton?" she asked. Her tone was still condemning.

"Much farther than that," he replied.

"To Worthing?" she asked.

"Farther—in a steamer," he replied.

"But who did you go with?" asked the child.

"Why, I went all by myself," he answered.

"Twuly?" she asked.

"Weally and twuly," he answered, laughing.

"Couldn't you take me?" she asked.

"I will next time," he replied.

The child still looked at him, unsatisfied.

"But what did you go for?" she asked, goading him suspiciously.

"To see the sea and the ships and the fighting ships with cannons——"

"You *might* have taken me," said the child reproachfully.

"Yes, I ought to have done, oughtn't I?" he said, as if regretful.

Gwen still looked full at him.

"You *are* red," she said.

He glanced quickly in the glass, and replied:

"That is the sun. Hasn't it been hot?"

"Mm! It made my nose all peel. Vera said she would scrape me like a new potato." The child laughed and turned shyly away.

"Come here," said Siegmund. "I believe you've got a tooth out, haven't you?"

He was very cautious and gentle. The child drew back. He hesitated, and she drew away from him, unwilling.

"Come and let me look," he repeated.

She drew farther away, and the same constrained smile appeared on her face, shy, suspicious, condemning.

"Aren't you going to get your chocolate?" he asked, as the child hesitated in the doorway.

She glanced into his room, and answered:

"I've got to go to mam and have my hair done."

Her awkwardness and her lack of compliance insulted him. She went downstairs without going into his room.

Siegmund, rebuffed by the only one in the house from whom he might have expected friendship, proceeded slowly to shave, feeling sick at heart. He was a long time over his toilet. When he stripped himself for the bath, it seemed to him he could smell the sea. He bent his head and licked his shoulder. It tasted decidedly salt.

"A pity to wash it off," he said.

As he got up dripping from the cold bath, he felt for the moment exhilarated. He rubbed himself smooth. Glancing down at himself, he thought: "I look young. I look as young as twenty-six."

He turned to the mirror. There he saw himself a mature, complete man of forty, with grave years of experience on his countenance.

"I used to think that, when I was forty," he said to himself, "I should find everything straight as the nose on my face, walking through my affairs as easily as you like. Now I am no more sure of myself, have no more confidence than a boy of twenty. What can I do? It seems to me a man needs a mother all his life. I don't feel much like a lord of creation."

Having arrived at this cynicism, Siegmund prepared to go downstairs. His sensitiveness had passed off; his nerves had become callous. When he was dressed he went down to the kitchen without hesitation. He was indifferent to his wife and children. No one spoke to him as he sat to the table. That was as he liked it; he wished for nothing to touch him. He ate his breakfast alone, while his wife bustled about upstairs and Vera bustled about in the dining-room. Then he retired to the solitude of the drawing-room. As a reaction against his poetic activity, he felt as if he were gradually becoming more stupid and blind. He remarked nothing, not even the extravagant bowl of grasses placed where he would not have allowed it— on his piano; nor his fiddle, laid cruelly on the cold, polished floor near the window. He merely sat down in an arm-chair, and felt sick.

All his unnatural excitement, all the poetic stimulation of the past few days, had vanished. He sat flaccid, while his life struggled slowly through him. After an intoxication of passion and love, and beauty, and of sunshine, he was prostrate. Like a plant that blossoms gorgeously and madly, he had wasted the tissue of his strength, so that now his life struggled in a clogged and broken channel.

Siegmund sat with his head between his hands, leaning upon the table. He would have been stupidly quiescent in his feeling of loathing and sickness had not an intense irritability in all his nerves tormented him into consciousness.

"I suppose this is the result of the sun—a sort of sunstroke," he said, realising an intolerable stiffness of his brain, a stunned condition in his head.

"This is hideous!" he said. His arms were quivering with intense irritation. He exerted all his will to stop them, and then the hot irritability commenced in his belly. Siegmund fidgeted in his chair without changing his position. He had not the energy to get up and move about. He fidgeted like an insect pinned down.

The door opened. He felt violently startled; yet there was no movement perceptible. Vera entered, ostensibly for an autograph-album into which she was going to copy a drawing from the *London Opinion*, really to see what her father was doing. He did not move a muscle. He only longed intensely for his daughter to go out of the room, so that he could let go. Vera went out of the drawing-room humming to herself. Apparently she had not even glanced at her father. In reality, she had observed him closely.

"He is sitting with his head in his hands," she said to her mother.

Beatrice replied: "I'm glad he's nothing else to do."

"I should think he's pitying himself," said Vera.

"He's a good one at it," answered Beatrice.

Gwen came forward and took hold of her mother's skirt, looking up anxiously.

"What is he doing, Mam?" she asked.

"Nothing," replied her mother—"nothing; only sitting in the drawing-room."

"But what has he *been* doing?" persisted the anxious child.

"Nothing—nothing that I can tell *you*. He's only spoilt all our lives."

The little girl stood regarding her mother in the greatest distress and perplexity.

"But what will he do, Mam?" she asked.

"Nothing. Don't bother. Run and play with Marjory now. Do you want a nice plum?"

She took a yellow plum from the table. Gwen accepted it without a word. She was too much perplexed.

"What do you say?" asked her mother.

"Thank you," replied the child, turning away.

Siegmund sighed with relief when he was again left alone. He twisted in his chair, and sighed again, trying to drive out the intolerable clawing irritability from his belly.

"Ah, this is horrible!" he said.

He stiffened his muscles to quieten them.

"I've never been like this before. What is the matter?" he asked himself.

But the question died out immediately. It seemed useless and sickening to try and answer it. He began to cast about for an alleviation. If he could only do something, or have something he wanted, it would be better.

"What do I want?" he asked himself, and he anxiously strove to find this out.

Everything he suggested to himself made him sicken with weariness or distaste: the seaside, a foreign land, a fresh life that he had often dreamed of, farming in Canada.

"I should be just the same there," he answered himself. "Just the same sickening feeling there that I want nothing."

"Helena!" he suggested to himself, trembling.

But he only felt a deeper horror. The thought of her made him shrink convulsively.

"I can't endure this," he said. "If this is the case, I had better be dead. To have no want, no desire—that is death, to begin with."

He rested awhile after this. The idea of death alone seemed entertaining. Then, "Is there really nothing I could turn to?" he asked himself.

To him, in that state of soul, it seemed there was not.

"Helena!" he suggested again, appealingly testing himself. "Ah, no!" he cried, drawing sharply back, as from an approaching touch upon a raw place.

He groaned slightly as he breathed, with a horrid weight of
nausea. There was a fumbling upon the door-knob. Siegmund
did not start. He merely pulled himself together. Gwen pushed
open the door, and stood holding on to the door-knob looking
at him.

"Dad, Mam says dinner's ready," she announced.

Siegmund did not reply. The child waited, at a loss for some
moments, before she repeated, in a hesitating tone:

"Dinner's ready."

"All right," said Siegmund. "Go away."

The little girl returned to the kitchen with tears in her eyes,
very crestfallen.

"What did he say?" asked Beatrice.

"He shouted at me," replied the little one, breaking into
tears.

Beatrice flushed. Tears came into her own eyes. She took
the child in her arms and pressed her to her, kissing her
forehead.

"Did he?" she said very tenderly. "Never mind, then, dearie
—never mind."

The tears in her mother's voice made the child sob bitterly.
Vera and Marjory sat silent at table. The steak and mashed
potatoes steamed and grew cold.

CHAPTER XXIV

WHEN Helena arrived home on the Thursday evening she found
everything repulsive. All the odours of the sordid street
through which she must pass hung about the pavement, having
crept out in the heat. The house was bare and narrow. She
remembered children sometimes to have brought her moths
shut up in matchboxes. As she knocked at the door she felt
like a numbed moth which a boy is pushing off its leaf-rest into
his box.

The door was opened by her mother. She was a woman
whose sunken mouth, ruddy cheeks, and quick brown eyes
gave her the appearance of a bird which walks about pecking
suddenly here and there. As Helena reluctantly entered the

mother drew herself up, and immediately relaxed, seeming to peck forwards as she said:

"Well?"

"Well, here we are!" replied the daughter in a matter-of-fact tone.

Her mother was inclined to be affectionate, therefore she became proportionately cold.

"So I see," exclaimed Mrs. Verden, tossing her head in a peculiar jocular manner. "And what sort of a time have you had?"

"Oh, very good," replied Helena, still more coolly.

"H'm!"

Mrs. Verden looked keenly at her daughter. She recognised the peculiar sulky, childish look she knew so well, therefore, making an effort, she forbore to question.

"You look well," she said.

Helena smiled ironically.

"And are you ready for your supper?" she asked, in the playful, affectionate manner she had assumed.

"If the supper is ready I will have it," replied her daughter.

"Well, it's not ready." The mother shut tight her sunken mouth, and regarded her daughter with playful challenge. "Because," she continued, "I didn't know when you were coming." She gave a jerk with her arm, like an orator who utters the incontrovertible. "But," she added, after a tedious dramatic pause, "I can soon have it ready. What will you have?"

"The full list of your capacious larder," replied Helena.

Mrs. Verden looked at her again, and hesitated.

"Will you have cocoa or lemonade?" she asked, coming to the point curtly.

"Lemonade," said Helena.

Presently Mr. Verden entered—a small, white-bearded man with a gentle voice.

"Oh, so you are back, Nellie!" he said, in his quiet, reserved manner.

"As you see, Pater," she answered.

"H'm!" he murmured, and he moved about at his accounts.

Neither of her parents dared to question Helena. They moved about her on tiptoe, stealthily. Yet neither subserved her. Her father's quiet "H'm!" her mother's curt question, made her draw inwards like a snail which can never retreat far enough from condemning eyes. She made a careless pretence of eating. She was like a child which has done wrong, and will not be punished, but will be left with the humiliating smear of offence upon it.

There was a quick, light palpitating of the knocker. Mrs. Verden went to the door.

"Has she come?"

And there were hasty steps along the passage. Louisa entered. She flung herself upon Helena and kissed her.

"How long have you been in?" she asked, in a voice trembling with affection.

"Ten minutes," replied Helena.

"Why didn't you send me the time of the train, so that I could come and meet you?" Louisa reproached her.

"Why?" drawled Helena.

Louisa looked at her friend without speaking. She was deeply hurt by this sarcasm.

As soon as possible Helena went upstairs. Louisa stayed with her that night. On the next day they were going to Cornwall together for their usual midsummer holiday. They were to be accompanied by a third girl—a minor friend of Louisa, a slight acquaintance of Helena.

During the night neither of the two friends slept much. Helena made confidences to Louisa, who brooded on these, on the romance and tragedy which enveloped the girl she loved so dearly. Meanwhile, Helena's thoughts went round and round, tethered amid the five days by the sea, pulling forwards as far as the morrow's meeting with Siegmund, but reaching no further.

Friday was an intolerable day of silence, broken by little tender advances and playful, affectionate sallies on the part of the mother, all of which were rapidly repulsed. The father said nothing, and avoided his daughter with his eyes. In his humble reserve there was a dignity which made his disapproval far more difficult to bear than the repeated flagrant questionings of the mother's eyes. But the day wore on. Helena pretended to read, and sat thinking. She played her violin a little, mechanically. She went out into the town, and wandered about.

At last the night fell.

"Well," said Helena to her mother, "I suppose I'd better pack."

"Haven't you done it?" cried Mrs. Verden, exaggerating her surprise. "You'll never have it done. I'd better help you. What time does the train go?"

Helena smiled.

"Ten minutes to ten."

Her mother glanced at the clock. It was only half-past eight. There was ample time for everything.

"Nevertheless, you'd better look sharp," Mrs. Verden said.

Helena turned away, weary of this exaggeration.

"I'll come with you to the station," suggested Mrs Verden. "I'll see the last of you. We shan't see much of you just now."

Helena turned round in surprise.

"Oh, I wouldn't bother," she said, fearing to make her dis-approval too evident.

"Yes—I will—I'll see you off."

Mrs. Verden's animation and indulgence were remarkable. Usually she was curt and undemonstrative. On occasions like these, however, when she was reminded of the ideal relations between mother and daughter, she played the part of the affectionate parent, much to the general distress.

Helena lit a candle and went to her bedroom. She quickly packed her dress-basket. As she stood before the mirror to put on her hat, her eyes, gazing heavily, met her heavy eyes in the mirror. She glanced away swiftly as if she had been burned.

"How stupid I look!" she said to herself. "And Siegmund, how is he, I wonder?"

She wondered how Siegmund had passed the day, what had happened to him, how he felt, how he looked. She thought of him protectively.

Having strapped her basket, she carried it downstairs. Her mother was ready, with a white lace scarf round her neck. After a short time Louisa came in. She dropped her basket in the passage, and then sank into a chair.

"I don't want to go, Nell," she said, after a few moments of silence.

"Why, how is that?" asked Helena, not surprised, but con-descending, as to a child.

"Oh, I don't know; I'm tired," said the other petulantly.

"Of course you are. What do you expect, after a day like this?" said Helena.

"And rushing about packing," exclaimed Mrs. Verden, still in an exaggerated manner, this time scolding playfully.

"Oh, I don't know. I don't think I want to go, dear," repeated Louisa dejectedly.

"Well, it is time we set out," replied Helena, rising. "Will you carry the basket or the violin, Mater?"

Louisa rose, and with a forlorn expression took up her light luggage.

The west opposite the door was smouldering with sunset. Darkness is only smoke that hangs suffocatingly over the low red heat of the sunken day. Such was Helena's longed-for night. The tramcar was crowded. In one corner Olive, the third friend, rose excitedly to greet them. Helena sat mute, while the car swung through the yellow, stale lights of a third-rate street of shops. She heard Olive remarking on her sunburned face and arms; she became aware of the renewed inflammation in her blistered arms; she heard her own curious voice answering. Everything was in a maze. To the beat of the car, while the yellow blur of the shops passed over her eyes, she repeated: "Two hundred and forty miles—two hundred and forty miles."

CHAPTER XXV

SIEGMUND passed the afternoon in a sort of stupor. At tea-time Beatrice, who had until then kept herself in restraint, gave way to an outburst of angry hysteria.

"When does your engagement at the Comedy Theatre commence?" she had asked him coldly.

He knew she was wondering about money.

"To-morrow—if ever," he had answered.

She was aware that he hated the work. For some reason or other her anger flashed out like sudden lightning at his "if ever".

"What do you think you *can* do?" she cried. "For I think you have done enough. We can't do as we like altogether—indeed, indeed we cannot. You have had your fling, haven't you? You have had your fling, and you want to keep on. But there's more than one person in the world. Remember that. But there are your children, let me remind you. Whose are they? You talk about shirking the engagement, but who is going to be responsible for your children, do you think?"

"I said nothing about shirking the engagement," replied Siegmund, very coldly.

"No, there was no need to say. I know what it means. You sit there sulking all day. What do you think *I* do? I have to see to the children, I have to work and slave, I go on from day to day. I tell you *I'll* stop, I tell you *I'll* do as I like. *I'll* go as well. No, I wouldn't be such a coward, you know that. You know *I* wouldn't leave little children—to the workhouse or anything. They're my children; they mightn't be yours."

"There is no need for this," said Siegmund contemptuously. The pressure in his temples was excruciating, and he felt loathsomely sick.

Beatrice's dark eyes flashed with rage.

"Isn't there!" she cried. "Oh, isn't there? No, there is need for a great deal more. I don't know what you think I am. How much farther do you think you can go? No, you don't like reminding of us. You sit moping, sulking, because you have to come back to your own children. I wonder how much you think I shall stand? What do you think I am, to put up with it? What do you think I am? Am I a servant to eat out of your hand?"

"Be quiet!" shouted Siegmund. "Don't I know what you are? Listen to yourself!"

Beatrice was suddenly silenced. It was the stillness of white-hot wrath. Even Siegmund was glad to hear her voice again. She spoke low and trembling.

"You coward—you miserable coward! It is I, is it, who am wrong? It is I who am to blame, is it? You miserable thing! I have no doubt you know what I am."

Siegmund looked up at her as her words died off. She looked back at him with dark eyes loathing his cowed, wretched animosity. His eyes were bloodshot and furtive, his mouth was drawn back in a half-grin of hate and misery. She was goading him, in his darkness whither he had withdrawn himself like a sick dog, to die or recover as his strength should prove. She tortured him till his sickness was swallowed by anger, which glared redly at her as he pushed back his chair to rise. He trembled too much, however. His chin dropped again on his chest. Beatrice sat down in her place, hearing footsteps. She was shuddering slightly, and her eyes were fixed.

Vera entered with the two children. All three immediately, as if they found themselves confronted by something threatening, stood arrested. Vera tackled the situation.

"Is the table ready to be cleared yet?" she asked in an unpleasant tone.

Her father's cup was half emptied. He had come to tea late, after the others had left the table. Evidently he had not finished, but he made no reply, neither did Beatrice. Vera glanced disgustedly at her father. Gwen sidled up to her mother, and tried to break the tension.

"Mam, there was a lady had a dog, and it ran into a shop, and it licked a sheep, Mam, what was hanging up."

Beatrice sat fixed, and paid not the slightest attention. The child looked up at her, waited, then continued softly.

"Mam, there was a lady had a dog——"

"Don't bother!" snapped Vera sharply.

The child looked, wondering and resentful, at her sister. Vera was taking the things from the table, snatching them, and thrusting them on the tray. Gwen's eyes rested a moment or two on the bent head of her father; then deliberately she turned again to her mother, and repeated in her softest and most persuasive tones:

"Mam, I saw a dog, and it ran in a butcher's shop and licked a piece of meat. Mam, Mam!"

There was no answer. Gwen went forward and put her hand on her mother's knee.

"Mam!" she pleaded timidly.

No response.

"Mam!" she whispered.

She was desperate. She stood on tiptoe, and pulled with little hands at her mother's breast.

"Mam!" she whispered shrilly.

Her mother, with an effort of self-denial, put off her investment of tragedy, and, laying her arm round the child's shoulders, drew her close. Gwen was somewhat reassured, but not satisfied. With an earnest face upturned to the impassive countence of her mother, she began to whisper, sibilant, coaxing, pleading:

"Mam, there was a lady, she had a dog——"

Vera turned sharply to stop this whispering, which was too much for her nerves, but the mother forestalled her. Taking the child in her arms, she averted her face, put her cheek against the baby cheek, and let the tears run freely. Gwen was too much distressed to cry. The tears gathered very slowly in her eyes, and fell without her having moved a muscle in her face. Vera remained in the scullery, weeping tears of rage, and pity, and shame into the towel. The only sound in the room was the occasional sharp breathing of Beatrice. Siegmund sat without the trace of a movement, almost without breathing. His head was ducked low; he dared never lift it, he dared give no sign of his presence.

Presently Beatrice put down the child, and went to join Vera in the scullery. There came the low sound of women's talking —an angry, ominous sound. Gwen followed her mother. Her little voice could be heard cautiously asking:

"Mam, is dad cross—is he? What did he do?"

"Don't bother!" snapped Vera. "You *are* a little nuisance! Here, take this into the dining-room, and don't drop it."

The child did not obey. She stood looking from her mother to her sister. The latter pushed a dish into her hand.

"Go along," she said, gently thrusting the child forth.

Gwen departed. She hesitated in the kitchen. Her father still remained unmoved. The child wished to go to him, to speak to him, but she was afraid. She crossed the kitchen slowly, hugging the dish; then she came slowly back, hesitating. She sidled into the kitchen; she crept round the table inch by inch, drawing nearer her father. At about a yard from his chair she stopped. He, from under his bent brows, could see her small feet in brown slippers, nearly kicked through at the toes, waiting and moving nervously near him. He pulled himself together, as a man does who watches the surgeon's lancet suspended over his wound. Would the child speak to him? Would she touch him with her small hands? He held his breath, and, it seemed, held his heart from beating. What he should do he did not know.

He waited in a daze of suspense. The child shifted from one foot to another. He could just see the edge of her white-frilled drawers. He wanted, above all things, to take her in his arms, to have something against which to hide his face. Yet he was afraid. Often, when all the world was hostile, he had found her full of love, he had hidden his face against her, she had gone to sleep in his arms, she had been like a piece of apple-blossom in his arms. If she should come to him now—his heart halted again in suspense—he knew not what he would do. It would open, perhaps, the tumour of his sickness. He was quivering too fast with suspense to know what he feared, or wanted, or hoped.

"Gwen!" called Vera, wondering why she did not return. "Gwen!"

"Yes," answered the child, and slowly Siegmund saw her feet lifted, hesitate, move, then turn away.

She had gone. His excitement sank rapidly, and the sickness returned stronger, more horrible and wearying than ever. For a moment it was so bad that he was afraid of losing consciousness. He recovered slightly, pulled himself up, and went upstairs. His fists were tightly clenched, his fingers closed over his thumbs, which were pressed bloodless. He lay down on the bed.

For two hours he lay in a dazed condition resembling sleep. At the end of that time the knowledge that he had to meet Helena was actively at work—an activity quite apart from his will or his consciousness, jogging and pulling him awake. At eight o'clock he sat up. A cramped pain in his thumbs made him wonder. He looked at them, and mechanically shut them again under his fingers into the position they sought after two hours of similar constraint. Siegmund opened his hands again, smiling.

"It is said to be the sign of a weak, deceitful character," he said to himself.

His head was peculiarly numbed; at the back it felt heavy, as if weighted with lead. He could think only one detached sentence at intervals. Between-whiles there was a blank, grey sleep or swoon.

"I have got to go and meet Helena at Wimbledon," he said to himself, and instantly he felt a peculiar joy, as if he had laughed somewhere. "But I must be getting ready. I can't disappoint her," said Siegmund.

The idea of Helena woke a craving for rest in him. If he should say to her, "Do not go away from me; come with me somewhere," then he might lie down somewhere beside her, and she might put her hands on his head. If she could hold his head in her hands—for she had fine, silken hands that adjusted themselves with a rare pressure, wrapping his weakness up in life—then his head would gradually grow healed, and he could rest. This was the one thing that remained for his restoration—that she should with long, unwearying gentleness put him to rest. He longed for it utterly—for the hands and the restfulness of Helena.

"But it is no good," he said, staring like a drunken man from sleep. "What time is it?"

It was ten minutes to nine. She would be in Wimbledon by 10.10. It was time he should be getting ready. Yet he remained sitting on the bed.

"I am forgetting again," he said. "But I do not want to go. What is the good? I have only to tie a mask on for the meeting. It is too much."

He waited and waited; his head dropped forward in a sort of sleep. Suddenly he started awake. The back of his head hurt severely.

"Goodness," he said, "it's getting quite dark!"

It was twenty minutes to ten. He went bewildered into the bathroom to wash in cold water and bring back his senses. His hands were sore, and his face blazed with sun inflammation. He made himself neat as usual. It was ten minutes to ten. He would be very late. It was practically dark, though these bright days were endless. He wondered whether the children were in bed. It was too late, however, to wonder.

Siegmund hurried downstairs and took his hat. He was walking down the path when the door was snatched open behind him, and Vera ran out crying:

"Are you going out? Where are you going?"

Siegmund stood still and looked at her.

"She is frightened," he said to himself, smiling ironically.

"I am only going a walk. I have to go to Wimbledon. I shall not be very long."

"Wimbledon, at this time!" said Vera sharply, full of suspicion.

"Yes, I am late. I shall be back in an hour."

He was was sorry for her. She knew he gave her an honourable promise.

"You need not keep us sitting up," she said.

He did not answer, but hurried to the station.

CHAPTER XXVI

HELENA, Louisa, and Olive climbed the steps to go to the South-Western platform. They were laden with dress-baskets, umbrellas, and little packages. Olive and Louisa, at least, were in high spirits. Olive stopped before the indicator.

"The next train for Waterloo," she announced, in her contralto voice, "is 10.30. It is now 10.12."

"We go by the 10.40; it is a better train," said Helena.

Olive turned to her with a heavy-arch manner.

"Very well, dear. There is a parting to be got through, I am told. We sympathise, dear, but we regret it. Starting for a holiday is always a prolonged agony. But I am strong to endure it."

"You look it. You look as if you could tackle a bull," cried Louisa, skittish.

"My dear Louisa," rang out Olive's contralto, "don't judge me by appearances. You're sure to be taken in. With me it's a case of

> " 'Oh, the gladness of her gladness when she's sad,
>   And the sadness of her sadness when she's glad!' "

She looked round to see the effect of this. Helena, expected to say something, chimed in sarcastically:

" 'They are nothing to her madness———' "

"When she's going for a holiday, dear," cried Olive.

"Oh, go on being mad," cried Louisa.

"What, do you like it? I thought you'd be thanking Heaven that sanity was given me in large doses."

"And holidays in small," laughed Louisa. "Good! No, I like your madness, if you call it such. You are always so serious."

" 'It's ill talking of halters in the house of the hanged,' dear," boomed Olive.

She looked from side to side. She felt triumphant. Helena smiled, acknowledging the sarcasm.

"But," said Louisa, smiling anxiously, "I don't quite see it. What's the point?"

"Well, to be explicit, dear," replied Olive, "it is hardly safe to accuse me of sadness and seriousness in *this* trio."

Louisa laughed and shook herself.

"Come to think of it, it isn't," she said.

Helena sighed, and walked down the platform. Her heart was beating thickly; she could hardly breathe. The station lamps hung low, so they made a ceiling of heat and dusty light. She suffocated under them. For a moment she beat with hysteria, feeling, as most of us feel when sick on a hot summer night, as if she must certainly go crazed, smothered under the grey, woolly blanket of heat. Siegmund was late. It was already twenty-five minutes past ten.

She went towards the booking-office. At that moment Siegmund came on to the platform.

"Here I am!" he said. "Where is Louisa?"

Helena pointed to the seat without answering. She was looking at Siegmund. He was distracted by the excitement of the moment, so she could not read him.

"Olive is there, too," she explained.

Siegmund stood still, straining his eyes to see the two women seated amidst pale wicker dress-baskets and dark rugs. The stranger made things more complex.

"Does she—your other friend—does she know?" he asked.

"She knows nothing," replied Helena in a low tone, as she led him forward to be introduced.

"How do you do?" replied Olive in most mellow contralto. "Behold the dauntless three, with their traps! You will see us forth on our perils?"

"I will, since I may not do more," replied Siegmund, smiling, continuing: "And how is Sister Louisa?"

"She is very well, thank you. It is *her* turn now," cried Louisa, vindictive, triumphant.

There was always a faint animosity in her bearing towards Siegmund. He understood, and smiled at her enmity, for the two were really good friends.

"It is your turn now," he repeated, smiling, and he turned away.

He and Helena walked down the platform.

"How did you find things at home?" he asked her.

"Oh, as usual," she replied indifferently. "And you?"

"Just the same," he answered. He thought for a moment or two, then added: "The children are happier without me."

"Oh, you mustn't say that kind of thing!" protested Helena miserably. "It's not true."

"It's all right, dear," he answered. "So long as they are happy, it's all right." After a pause he added: "But I feel pretty bad to-night."

Helena's hand tightened on his arm. He had reached the end of the platform. There he stood, looking up the line which ran dark under a haze of lights. The high red signal-lamps hung aloft in a scarlet swarm; farther off, like spangles shaking downwards from a burst sky-rocket, was a tangle of brilliant red and green signal-lamps settling. A train with the warm flare on its thick column of smoke came thundering upon the lovers. Dazed, they felt the yellow bar of carriage-windows brush in vibration across their faces. The ground and the air rocked. Then Siegmund turned his head to watch the red and the green lights in the rear of the train swiftly dwindle on the darkness. Still watching the distance where the train had vanished, he said:

"Dear, I want you to promise that, whatever happens to me, you will go on. Remember, dear, two wrongs don't make a right."

Helena swiftly, with a movement of terror, faced him, looking into his eyes. But he was in the shadow, she could not see him. The flat sound of his voice, lacking resonance—the dead, expressionless tone—made her lose her presence of mind. She stared at him blankly.

"What do you mean? What has happened? Something has happened to you. What has happened at home? What are you going to do?" she said sharply. She palpitated with terror. For the first time she felt powerless. Siegmund was beyond her grasp. She was afraid of him. He had shaken away her hold over him.

"There is nothing fresh the matter at home," he replied wearily. He was to be scourged with emotion again. "I swear it," he added. "And I have not made up my mind. But I can't think of life without you—and life must go on."

"And I swear," she said wrathfully, turning at bay, "that I won't live a day after you."

Siegmund dropped his head. The dead spring of his emotion swelled up scalding hot again. Then he said, almost inaudibly: "Ah, don't speak to me like that, dear. It is late to be angry. When I have seen your train out to-night there is nothing left."

Helena looked at him, dumb with dismay, stupid, angry.

They became aware of the porters shouting loudly that the Waterloo train was to leave from another platform.

"You'd better come," said Siegmund, and they hurried down towards Louisa and Olive.

"We've got to change platforms," cried Louisa, running forward and excitedly announcing the news.

"Yes," replied Helena, pale and impassive.

Siegmund picked up the luggage.

"I say," cried Olive, rushing to catch Helena and Louisa by the arm, "look—look—both of you—look at that hat!" A lady in front was wearing on her hat a wild and dishevelled array of peacock feathers. "It's the sight of a lifetime. I wouldn't have you miss it," added Olive in hoarse *sotto voce*.

"Indeed not!" cried Helena, turning in wild exasperation to look. "Get a good view of it, Olive. Let's have a good mental impression of it—one that will last."

"That's right, dear," said Olive, somewhat nonplussed by this outburst.

Siegmund had escaped with the heaviest two bags. They could see him ahead, climbing the steps. Olive readjusted herself from the wildly animated to the calmly ironical.

"After all, dear," she said, as they hurried in the tail of the crowd, "it's not half a bad idea to get a man on the job."

Louisa laughed aloud at this vulgar conception of Siegmund.

"Just now, at any rate," she rejoined.

As they reached the platform the train ran in before them. Helena watched anxiously for an empty carriage. There was not one.

"Perhaps it is as well," she thought. "We needn't talk. There will be three-quarters of an hour at Waterloo. If we were alone, Olive would make Siegmund talk."

She found a carriage with four people, and hastily took possession. Siegmund followed her with the bags. He swung these on the rack, and then quickly received the rugs, umbrellas, and packages from the other two. These he put on the seats or anywhere, while Helena stowed them. She was very busy for a moment or two; the racks were full. Other people entered; their luggage was troublesome to bestow.

When she turned round again she found Louisa and Olive seated, but Siegmund was outside on the platform, and the door was closed. He saw her face move as if she would cry to him. She restrained herself, and immediately called:

"You are coming? Oh, you are coming to Waterloo?"

He shook his head.

"I cannot come," he said.

She stood looking blankly at him for some moments, unable to reach the door because of the portmanteau thrust through with umbrellas and sticks, which stood on the floor between the knees of the passengers. She was helpless. Siegmund was repeating deliriously in his mind:

"Oh—go—go—go—when will she go?"

He could not bear her piteousness. Her presence made him feel insane.

"Would you like to come to the window?" a man asked of Helena kindly.

She smiled suddenly in his direction, without perceiving him. He pulled the portmanteau under his legs, and Helena edged past. She stood by the door, leaning forward with some of her old protective grace, her "Hawwa" spirit evident. Benign and shielding, she bent forward, looking at Siegmund. But her face was blank with helplessness, with misery of helplessness. She stood looking at Siegmund, saying nothing. His forehead was scorched and swollen, she noticed sorrowfully, and beneath one eye the skin was blistered. His eyes were bloodshot and glazed in a kind of apathy; they filled her with terror. He looked up at her because she wished it. For himself, he could not see her; he could only recoil from her. All he wished was to hide himself in the dark, alone. Yet she wanted him, and so far he yielded. But to go to Waterloo he could not yield.

The people in the carriage, made uneasy by this strange farewell, did not speak. There were a few taut moments of silence. No one seemed to have strength to interrupt these spaces of irresolute anguish. Finally, the guard's whistle went. Siegmund and Helena clasped hands. A warm flush of love and healthy grief came over Siegmund for the last time. The train began to move, drawing Helena's hand from his.

"Monday," she whispered—"Monday," meaning that on Monday she should receive a letter from him. He nodded, turned, hesitated, looked at her, turned and walked away. She remained at the window watching him depart.

"Now, dear, we are manless," said Olive in a whisper. But her attempt at a joke fell dead. Everybody was silent and uneasy.

CHAPTER XXVII

HE hurried down the platform, wincing at every stride, from the memory of Helena's last look of mute, heavy yearning. He gripped his fists till they trembled; his thumbs were again closed under his fingers. Like a picture on a cloth before him he still saw Helena's face, white, rounded, in feature quite mute and expressionless, just made terrible by the heavy eyes, pleading dumbly. He thought of her going on and on, still at the carriage window looking out; all through the night rushing west and west to the land of Isolde. Things began to haunt Siegmund like a delirium. He knew not where he was hurrying. Always in front of him, as on a cloth, was the face of Helena, while somewhere behind the cloth was Cornwall, a far-off lonely place where darkness came on intensely. Sometimes he saw a dim, small phantom in the darkness of Cornwall, very far off. Then the face of Helena, white, inanimate as a mask, with heavy eyes, came between again.

He was almost startled to find himself at home, in the porch of his house. The door opened. He remembered to have heard the quick thud of feet. It was Vera. She glanced at him, but said nothing. Instinctively she shrank from him. He passed without noticing her. She stood on the door-mat, fastening the door, striving to find something to say to him.

"You have been over an hour," she said, still more troubled when she found her voice shaking. She had no idea what alarmed her.

"Ay," returned Siegmund.

He went into the dining-room and dropped into his chair, with his head between his hands. Vera followed him nervously.

"Will you have anything to eat?" she asked.

He looked up at the table, as if the supper laid there were curious and incomprehensible. The delirious lifting of his eye-lids showed the whole of the dark pupils and the bloodshot white of his eyes. Vera held her breath with fear. He sank his head again and said nothing. Vera sat down and waited. The minutes ticked slowly off. Siegmund neither moved nor spoke. At last the clock struck midnight. She was weary with sleep, querulous with trouble.

"Aren't you going to bed?" she asked.

Siegmund heard her without paying any attention. He seemed only to half hear. Vera waited awhile, then repeated plaintively:

"Aren't you going to bed, Father?"

Siegmund lifted his head and looked at her. He loathed the idea of having to move. He looked at her confusedly.

"Yes, I'm going," he said, and his head dropped again. Vera knew he was not asleep. She dared not leave him till he was in his bedroom. Again she sat waiting.

"Father!" she cried at last.

He started up, gripping the arms of his chair, trembling.

"Yes, I'm going," he said.

He rose, and went unevenly upstairs. Vera followed him close behind.

"If he reels and falls backwards he will kill me," she thought, but he did not fall. From habit he went into the bathroom. While trying to brush his teeth he dropped the tooth-brush on to the floor.

"I'll pick it up in the morning," he said, continuing deliriously: "I must go to bed—I must go to bed—I am very tired." He stumbled over the door-mat into his own room.

Vera was standing behind the unclosed door of her room. She heard the sneck of his lock. She heard the water still running in the bathroom, trickling with the mysterious sound of water at dead of night. Screwing up her courage, she went and turned off the tap. Then she stood again in her own room, to be near the companionable breathing of her sleeping sister, listening. Siegmund undressed quickly. His one thought was to get into bed.

"One must sleep," he said as he dropped his clothes on the floor. He could not find the way to put on his sleeping-jacket, and that made him pant. Any little thing that roused or thwarted his mechanical action aggravated his sickness till his brain seemed to be bursting. He got things right at last, and was in bed.

Immediately he lapsed into a kind of unconsciousness. He would have called it sleep, but such it was not. All the time he could feel his brain working ceaselessly, like a machine running with unslackening rapidity. This went on, interrupted by little flickerings of consciousness, for three or four hours. Each time he had a glimmer of consciousness he wondered if he made any noise.

"What am I doing? What is the matter? Am I unconscious? Do I make any noise? Do I disturb them?" he wondered, and he tried to cast back to find the record of mechanical sense impression. He believed he could remember the sound of inarticulate murmuring in his throat. Immediately he remembered, he could feel his throat producing the sounds. This frightened him. Above all things, he was afraid of disturbing the family. He roused himself to listen. Everything was breathing in silence. As he listened to this silence he relapsed into his sort of sleep.

He was awakened finally by his own perspiration. He was terribly hot. The pillow, the bedclothes, his hair, all seemed to be steaming with hot vapour, whilst his body was bathed in sweat. It was coming light. Immediately he shut his eyes again and lay still. He was now conscious, and his brain was irritably active, but his body was a separate thing, a terrible, heavy, hot thing over which he had slight control.

Siegmund lay still, with his eyes closed, enduring the exquisite torture of the trickling of drops of sweat. First it would be one gathering and running its irregular, hesitating way into the hollow of his neck. His every nerve thrilled to it, yet he felt he could not move more than to stiffen his throat slightly. While yet the nerves in the track of this drop were quivering, raw with sensitiveness, another drop would start from off the side of his chest, and trickle downwards among the little muscles of his side, to drip on to the bed. It was like the running of a spider over his sensitive, moveless body. Why he did not wipe himself he did not know. He lay still and endured this horrible tickling, which seemed to bite deep into him, rather than make the effort to move, which he loathed to do. The drops ran off his forehead down his temples. Those he did not mind: he was blunt there. But they started again, in tiny, vicious spurts, down the sides of his chest, from under his armpits, down the inner sides of his thighs, till he seemed to have a myriad quivering tracks of a myriad running insects over his hot, wet, highly-sensitised body. His nerves were trembling, one and all, with outrage and vivid suspense. It became unbearable. He felt that, if he endured it another moment, he would cry out, or suffocate and burst.

He sat up suddenly, threw away the bedclothes, from which came a puff of hot steam, and began to rub his pyjamas against his sides and his legs. He rubbed madly for a few moments.

Then he sighed with relief. He sat on the side of the bed, moving from the hot dampness of the place where he had lain. For a moment he thought he would go to sleep. Then, in an instant his brain seemed to click awake. He was still as loath as ever to move, but his brain was no longer clouded in hot vapour: it was clear. He sat, bowing forward on the side of the bed, his sleeping-jacket open, the dawn stealing into the room, the morning air entering fresh through the wide-flung window-door. He felt a peculiar sense of guilt, of wrongness, in thus having jumped out of bed. It seemed to him as if he ought to have endured the heat of his body, and the infernal trickling of the drops of sweat. But at the thought of it he moved his hands gratefully over his sides, which now were dry, and soft, and smooth; slightly chilled on the surface perhaps, for he felt a sudden tremor of shivering from the warm contact of his hands.

Siegmund sat up straight: his body was re-animated. He felt the pillow and the groove where he had lain. It was quite wet and clammy. There was a scent of sweat on the bed, not really unpleasant, but he wanted something fresh and cool.

Siegmund sat in the doorway that gave on to the small veranda. The air was beautifully cool. He felt his chest again to make sure it was not clammy. It was smooth as silk. This pleased him very much. He looked out on the night again, and was startled. Somewhere the moon was shining duskily, in a hidden quarter of sky; but straight in front of him, in the north-west, silent lightning was fluttering. He waited breathlessly to see if it were true. Then, again, the pale lightning jumped up into the dome of the fading night. It was like a white bird stirring restlessly on its nest. The night was drenching thinner, greyer. The lightning, like a bird that should have flown before the arm of day, moved on its nest in the boughs of darkness, raised itself, flickered its pale wings rapidly, then sank again, loath to fly. Siegmund watched it with wonder and delight.

The day was pushing aside the boughs of darkness, hunting The poor moon would be caught when the net was flung. Siegmund went out on the balcony to look at it. There it was, like a poor white mouse, a half-moon, crouching on the mound of its course. It would run nimbly over to the western slope, then it would be caught in the net, and the sun would laugh, like a great yellow cat, as it stalked behind playing with its prey, flashing out its bright paws. The moon, before making its last run, lay crouched, palpitating. The sun crept forth, laughing to itself as it saw its prey could not escape. The lightning, however, leaped low off the nest like a bird decided to go, and flew away. Siegmund no longer saw it opening and shutting its wings in hesitation amid the disturbance of the dawn. Instead there came a flush, the white lightning gone. The brief pink butterflies of sunrise and sunset rose up from the mown fields of darkness, and fluttered low in a cloud. Even in the west they flew in a narrow, rosy swarm. They separated, thinned, rising higher. Some, flying up, became golden. Some flew rosy gold across the moon, the mouse-moon motionless with fear. Soon the pink butterflies had gone, leaving a scarlet stretch like a field of poppies in the fens. As a wind, the light of day blew in from the east, puff after puff filling with whiteness the space which had been the night. Siegmund sat watching the last morning blowing in across the mown darkness, till the whole field of the world was exposed, till the moon was like a dead mouse which floats on water.

When the few birds had called in the August morning, when the cocks had finished their crowing, when the minute sounds of the early day were astir, Siegmund shivered disconsolate. He felt tired again, yet he knew he could not sleep. The bed was repulsive to him. He sat in his chair at the open door, moving uneasily. What should have been sleep was an ache and a restlessness. He turned and twisted in his chair.

"Where is Helena?" he asked himself, and he looked out on the morning.

Everything out of doors was unreal, like a show, like a peep-show. Helena was an actress somewhere in the brightness of this view. He alone was out of the piece. He sighed petulantly, pressing back his shoulders as if they ached. His arms, too, ached with irritation, while his head seemed to be hissing with angry irritability. For a long time he sat with clenched teeth, merely holding himself in check. In his present state of irritability everything that occurred to his mind stirred him with dislike or disgust. Helena, music, the pleasant company of friends, the sunshine of the country, each, as it offered itself to his thoughts, was met by an angry contempt, was rejected scornfully. As nothing could please or distract him, the only thing that remained was to support the discord. He felt as if he were a limb out of joint from the body of life: there occurred to his imagination a disjointed finger, swollen and discoloured, racked with pains. The question was, How should he reset himself into joint? The body of life for him meant Beatrice, his children, Helena, the Comic Opera, his friends of the orchestra. How could he set himself again into joint with these? It was impossible. Towards his family he would henceforward have to bear himself with humility. That was a cynicism. He would have to leave Helena, which he could not do. He would have to play strenuously, night after night, the music of "The Saucy Little Switzer", which was absurd. In fine, it was all absurd and impossible. Very well, then, that being so, what remained possible? Why, to depart. "If thine hand offend thee, cut it off." He could cut himself off from life. It was plain and straightforward.

But Beatrice, his young children, without him! He was bound by an agreement which there was no discrediting to provide for them. Very well, he must provide for them. And then what? Humiliation at home, Helena forsaken, musical comedy night after night. That was insufferable—impossible! Like a man tangled up in a rope, he was not strong enough to free himself. He could not break with Helena and return to a degrading life at home; he could not leave his children and go to Helena.

Very well, it was impossible! Then there remained only one door which he could open in this prison corridor of life. Siegmund looked round the room. He could get his razor, or he could hang himself. He had thought of the two ways before. Yet now he was unprovided. His portmanteau stood at the foot of the bed, its straps flung loose. A portmanteau strap would do. Then it should be a portmanteau strap!

"Very well!" said Siegmund, "it is finally settled. I had better write to Helena, and tell her, and say to her she must go on. I'd better tell her."

He sat for a long time with his notebook and a pencil, but he wrote nothing. At last he gave up.

"Perhaps it is just as well," he said to himself. "She said she would come with me—perhaps that is just as well. She will go to the sea. When she knows, the sea will take her. She must know."

He took a card, bearing her name and her Cornwall address, from his pocket-book, and laid it on the dressing-table.

"She will come with me," he said to himself, and his heart rose with elation.

"That is a cowardice," he added, looking doubtfully at the card, as if wondering whether to destroy it.

"It is in the hands of God. Beatrice may or may not send word to her at Tintagel. It is in the hands of God," he concluded.

Then he sat down again.

" 'But for that fear of something after death,' " he quoted to himself.

"It is not fear," he said. "The act itself will be horrible and fearsome, but the after-death—it's no more than struggling awake when you're sick with a fright of dreams. 'We are such stuff as dreams are made of.' "

Siegmund sat thinking of the after-death, which to him seemed so wonderfully comforting, full of rest, and reassurance, and renewal. He experienced no mystical ecstasies. He was sure of a wonderful kindness in death, a kindness which really reached right through life, though here he could not avail himself of it. Siegmund had always inwardly held faith that the heart of life beat kindly towards him. When he was cynical and sulky he knew that in reality it was only a waywardness of his.

The heart of life is implacable in its kindness. It may not be moved to fluttering of pity; it swings on uninterrupted by cries of anguish or of hate.

Siegmund was thankful for this unfaltering sternness of life. There was no futile hesitation between doom and pity. Therefore, he could submit and have faith. If each man by his crying could swerve the slow, sheer universe, what a doom of guilt he might gain. If Life could swerve from its orbit for pity, what terror of vacillation; and who would wish to bear the responsibility of the deflection?

Siegmund thanked God that life was pitiless, strong enough to take his treasures out of his hands, and to thrust him out of the room; otherwise, how could he go with any faith to death; otherwise, he would have felt the helpless disillusion of a youth who finds his infallible parents weaker than himself.

"I know the heart of life is kind," said Siegmund, "because I feel it. Otherwise I would live in defiance. But Life is greater than me or anybody. We suffer, and we don't know why, often. Life doesn't explain. But I can keep faith in it, as a dog has faith in his master. After all, Life is as kind to me as I am to my dog. I have, proportionally, as much zest. And my purpose towards my dog is good. I need not despair of Life."

It occurred to Siegmund that he was meriting the old gibe of the atheists. He was shirking the responsibility of himself, turning it over to an imaginary god.

"Well," he said, "I can't help it. I do not feel altogether self-responsible."

The morning had waxed during these investigations. Siegmund had been vaguely aware of the rousing of the house. He was finally startled into a consciousness of the immediate present by the calling of Vera at his door.

"There are two letters for you, Father."

He looked about him in bewilderment; the hours had passed in a trance, and he had no idea of his time or place.

"Oh, all right," he said, too much dazed to know what it meant. He heard his daughter going downstairs. Then swiftly returned over him the throbbing ache of his head and his arms, the discordant jarring of his body.

"What made her bring me the letters?" he asked himself. It was a very unusual attention. His heart replied, very sullen and shameful: "She wanted to know; she wanted to make sure I was all right."

Siegmund forgot all his speculations on a divine benevolence. The discord of his immediate situation overcame every harmony. He did not fetch in the letters.

"Is it so late?" he said. "Is there no more time for me?"

He went to look at his watch. It was a quarter to nine. As he walked across the room he trembled, and a sickness made his bones feel rotten. He sat down on the bed.

"What am I going to do?" he asked himself.

By this time he was shuddering rapidly. A peculiar feeling, as if his belly were turned into nothingness, made him want to press his fists into his abdomen. He remained shuddering drunkenly, like a drunken man who is sick, incapable of thought or action.

A second knock came at the door. He started with a jolt.

"Here is your shaving-water," said Beatrice in cold tones. 'It's half-past nine."

"All right," said Siegmund, rising from the bed, bewildered.

"And what time shall you expect dinner?" asked Beatrice. She was still contemptuous.

"Any time. I'm not going out," he answered.

He was surprised to hear the ordinary cool tone of his own

voice, for he was shuddering uncontrollably, and was almost sobbing. In a shaking, bewildered, disordered condition he set about fulfilling his purpose. He was hardly conscious of anything he did; try as he would, he could not keep his hands steady in the violent spasms of shuddering, nor could he call his mind to think. He was one shuddering turmoil. Yet he performed his purpose methodically and exactly. In every particular he was thorough, as if he were the servant of some stern will. It was a mesmeric performance, in which the agent trembled with convulsive sickness.

CHAPTER XXVIII

SIEGMUND'S lying late in bed made Beatrice very angry. The later it became, the more wrathful she grew. At half-past nine she had taken up his shaving-water. Then she proceeded to tidy the dining-room, leaving the breakfast spread in the kitchen.

Vera and Frank were gone up to town; they would both be home for dinner at two o'clock. Marjory was despatched on an errand, taking Gwen with her. The children had no need to return home immediately, therefore it was highly probable they would play in the field or in the lane for an hour or two. Beatrice was alone downstairs. It was a hot, still morning, when everything outdoors shone brightly, and all indoors was dusked with coolness and colour. But Beatrice was angry. She moved rapidly and determinedly about the dining-room, thrusting old newspapers and magazines between the cupboard and the wall, throwing the litter in the grate, which was clear, Friday having been charwoman's day, passing swiftly, lightly over the front of the furniture with the duster. It was Saturday, when she did not spend much time over the work. In the afternoon she was going out with Vera. That was not, however, what occupied her mind as she brushed aside her work. She had determined to have a settlement with Siegmund, as to how matters should continue. She was going to have no more of the past three years' life; things had come to a crisis, and there must be an alteration. Beatrice was going to do battle, therefore she flew at her work, thus stirring herself up to a proper heat of blood. All the time, as she thrust things out of sight or straightened a cover, she listened for Siegmund to come downstairs.

He did not come, so her anger waxed.

"He can lie skulking in bed!" she said to herself. "Here I've been up since seven, broiling at it. I should think he's pitying himself. He ought to have something else to do. He ought to have to go out to work every morning, like another man, as his son has to do. He has had too little work. He has had too much his own way. But it's come to a stop now. I'll servant-housekeeper him no longer."

Beatrice went to clean the step of the front door. She clanged the bucket loudly, every minute becoming more and more angry. That piece of work finished, she went into the kitchen. It was twenty past ten. Her wrath was at ignition point. She cleared all the things from the table and washed them up. As she was so doing, her anger, having reached full intensity without bursting into flame, began to dissipate in uneasiness. She tried to imagine what Siegmund would do and say to her. As she was wiping a cup, she dropped it, and the smash so unnerved her that her hands trembled almost too much to finish drying the things and putting them away. At last it was done. Her next piece of work was to make the beds. She took her pail and went upstairs. Her heart was beating so heavily in her throat that she had to stop on the landing to recover breath. She dreaded the combat with him. Suddenly controlling herself, she said loudly at Siegmund's door, her voice coldly hostile:

"Aren't you going to get up?"

There was not the faintest sound in the house. Beatrice stood in the gloom of the landing, her heart thudding in her ears.

"It's after half-past ten—aren't you going to get up?" she called.

She waited again. Two letters lay unopened on a small table. Suddenly she put down her pail and went into the bathroom. The pot of shaving-water stood untouched on the shelf, just as she had left it. She returned and knocked swiftly at her husband's door, not speaking. She waited, then she knocked again, loudly, a long time. Something in the sound of her knocking made her afraid to try again. The noise was dull and thudding: it did not resound through the house with a natural ring, so she thought. She ran downstairs in terror, fled out into the front garden, and there looked up at his room. The window-door was open—everything seemed quiet.

Beatrice stood vacillating. She picked up a few tiny pebbles and flung them in a handful at his door. Some spattered on the panes sharply; some dropped dully in the room. One clinked on the wash-hand bowl. There was no response. Beatrice was terribly excited. She ran, with her black eyes blazing, and wisps of her black hair flying about her thin temples, out on to the road. By a mercy she saw the window-cleaner just pushing his ladder out of the passage of a house a little farther down the road. She hurried to him.

"Will you come and see if there's anything wrong with my husband?" she asked wildly.

"Why, mum?" answered the window-cleaner, who knew her, and was humbly familiar. "Is he taken bad or something? Yes, I'll come."

He was a tall thin man with a brown beard. His clothes were all so loose, his trousers so baggy, that he gave one the impression his limbs must be bone, and his body a skeleton. He pushed at his ladders with a will.

"Where is he, Mum?" he asked officiously, as they slowed down at the side passage.

"He's in his bedroom, and I can't get an answer from him."

"Then I s'll want a ladder," said the window-cleaner, proceeding to lift one off his trolley. He was in a very great bustle. He knew which was Siegmund's room: he had often seen Siegmund rise from some music he was studying and leave the drawing-room when the window-cleaning began, and afterwards he had found him in the small front bedroom. He also knew there were matrimonial troubles: Beatrice was not reserved.

"Is it the least of the front rooms he's in?" asked the window-cleaner.

"Yes, over the porch," replied Beatrice.

The man bustled with his ladder.

"It's easy enough," he said. "The door's open, and we're soon on the balcony."

He set the ladder securely. Beatrice cursed him for a slow, officious fool. He tested the ladder, to see it was safe, then he cautiously clambered up. At the top he stood leaning sideways, bending over the ladder to peer into the room. He could see all sorts of things, for he was frightened.

"I say there!" he called loudly.

Beatrice stood below in horrible suspense.

"Go in!" she cried. "Go in! Is he there?"

The man stepped very cautiously with one foot on to the balcony, and peered forward. But the glass door reflected into his eyes. He followed slowly with the other foot, and crept forward, ready at any moment to take flight.

"Hie, hie!" he suddenly cried in terror, and he drew back.

Beatrice was opening her mouth to scream, when the window-cleaner exclaimed weakly, as if dubious:

"I believe 'e's 'anged 'imself from the door-'ooks!"

"No!" cried Beatrice. "No, no, no!"

"I believe 'e 'as!" repeated the man.

"Go in and see if he's dead!" cried Beatrice.

The man remained in the doorway, peering fixedly.

"I believe he is," he said doubtfully.

"No—go and see!" screamed Beatrice.

The man went into the room, trembling, hesitating. He approached the body as if fascinated. Shivering, he took it round the loins and tried to lift it down. It was too heavy.

"I know!" he said to himself, once more bustling now he had something to do. He took his clasp-knife from his pocket, jammed the body between himself and the door so that it should not drop, and began to saw his way through the leathern strap. It gave. He started, and clutched the body, dropping his knife. Beatrice, below in the garden, hearing the scuffle and the clatter, began to scream in hysteria. The man hauled the body of Siegmund, with much difficulty, on to the bed, and with trembling fingers tried to unloose the buckle in which the strap ran. It was bedded in Siegmund's neck. The window-cleaner tugged at it frantically, till he got it loose. Then he looked at Siegmund. The dead man lay on the bed with swollen, discoloured face, with his sleeping-jacket pushed up in a bunch under his armpits, leaving his side naked. Beatrice was screaming below. The window-cleaner, quite unnerved, ran from the room and scrambled down the ladder. Siegmund lay heaped on the bed, his sleeping-suit twisted and bunched up about him, his face hardly recognisable.

CHAPTER XXIX

HELENA was dozing down in the cove at Tintagel. She and Louisa and Olive lay on the cool sands in the shadow, and steeped themselves in rest, in a cool, sea-fragrant tranquillity.

The journey down had been very tedious. After waiting for half an hour in the midnight turmoil of an August Friday in Waterloo station, they had seized an empty carriage, only to be followed by five north-countrymen, all of whom were affected by whisky. Olive, Helena, Louisa, occupied three corners of the carriage. The men were distributed between them. The three women were not alarmed. Their tipsy travelling companions promised to be tiresome, but they had a frank honesty of manner that placed them beyond suspicion. The train drew out westward. Helena began to count the miles that separated her from Siegmund. The north-countrymen began to be jolly: they talked loudly in their uncouth English; they sang the music-hall songs of the day; they furtively drank whisky. Through all this they were polite to the girls. As much could hardly be said in return of Olive and Louisa. They leaned forward whispering one to another. They sat back in their seats laughing, hiding their laughter by turning their backs on the men, who were a trifle disconcerted by this amusement.

The train spun on and on. Little homely clusters of lamps, suggesting the quiet of country life, turned slowly round through the darkness. The men dropped into a doze. Olive put a handkerchief over her face and went to sleep. Louisa gradually nodded and jerked into slumber. Helena sat weariedly and watched the rolling of the sleeping travellers and the dull blank of the night sheering off outside. Neither the men nor the women looked well asleep. They lurched and nodded stupidly. She thought of Bazarof in "Fathers and Sons", endorsing his opinion on the appearance of sleepers: all but Siegmund. Was Siegmund asleep? She imagined him breathing regularly on the pillows; she could see the under arch of his eyebrows, the fine shape of his nostrils, the curve of his lips, as she bent in fancy over his face.

The dawn came slowly. It was rather cold. Olive wrapped herself in rugs and went to sleep again. Helena shivered, and stared out of the window. There appeared a wanness in the night, and Helena felt inexpressibly dreary. A rosiness spread out far away. It was like a flock of flamingoes hovering over a dark lake. The world vibrated as the sun came up.

Helena waked the tipsy men at Exeter, having heard them say that there they must change. Then she walked the platform, very jaded. The train rushed on again. It was a most, most wearisome journey. The fields were very flowery, the morning was very bright, but what were these to her? She wanted dimness, sleep, forgetfulness. At eight o'clock, breakfast-time, the "dauntless three" were driving in a waggonette amid blazing, breathless sunshine, over country naked of shelter, ungracious and harsh.

"Why am I doing this?" Helena asked herself.

The three friends, washed, dressed, and breakfasted. It was too hot to rest in the house, so they trudged to the coast, silently, each feeling in an ill humour.

When Helena was really rested, she took great pleasure in Tintagel. In the first place, she found that the cove was exactly, almost identically the same as the Walhalla scene in "Walküre"; in the second place, "Tristan" was here, in the tragic country filled with the flowers of a late Cornish summer, an everlasting reality; in the third place, it was a sea of marvellous, portentous sunsets, of sweet morning baths, of pools blossomed with life, of terrible suave swishing of foam which suggested the Anadyomene. In sun it was the enchanted land of divided lovers. Helena for ever hummed fragments of "Tristan". As she stood on the rocks she sang, in her little, half-articulate way, bits of Isolde's love, bits of Tristan's anguish, to Siegmund.

She had not received her letter on Sunday. That had not very much disquieted her, though she was disappointed. On Monday she was miserable because of Siegmund's silence, but there was so much of enchantment in Tintagel, and Olive and Louisa were in such high spirits, that she forgot most whiles.

On Monday night, towards two o'clock, there came a violent storm of thunder and lightning. Louisa started up in bed at the first clap, waking Helena. The room palpitated with white light for two seconds; the mirror on the dressing-table glared supernaturally. Louisa clutched her friend. All was dark again, the thunder clapping directly.

"There, wasn't that lovely!" cried Louisa, speaking of the lightning. "Oo, wasn't it magnificent!—glorious!"

The door clicked and opened: Olive entered in her long white nightgown. She hurried to the bed.

"I say, dear!" she exclaimed, "may I come into the fold? I prefer the shelter of your company, dear, during this little lot."

"Don't you like it?" cried Louisa. "I think it's *lovely—lovely!*"

There came another slash of lightning. The night seemed to open and shut. It was a pallid vision of a ghost-world between the clanging shutters of darkness. Louisa and Olive clung to each other spasmodically.

"There!" exclaimed the former, breathless. "That was fine! Helena, did you see that?"

She clasped ecstatically the hand of her friend, who was lying down. Helena's answer was extinguished by the burst of thunder.

"There's no accounting for tastes," said Olive, taking a place in the bed. "I can't say I'm struck on lightning. What about you, Helena?"

"I'm not struck yet," replied Helena, with a sarcastic attempt at a jest.

"Thank you, dear," said Olive; "you do me the honour of catching hold."

Helena laughed ironically.

"Catching what?" asked Louisa, mystified.

"Why, dear," answered Olive, heavily condescending to explain, "I offered Helena the handle of a pun, and she took it. What a flash! You know, it's not that I'm afraid. . . ."

The rest of her speech was overwhelmed in thunder.

Helena lay on the edge of the bed, listening to the ecstatics of one friend and to the impertinences of the other. In spite of her ironical feeling, the thunder impressed her with a sense of fatality. The night opened, revealing a ghostly landscape, instantly to shut again with blackness. Then the thunder crashed. Helena felt as if some secret were being disclosed too swiftly and violently for her to understand. The thunder exclaimed horribly on the matter. She was sure something had happened.

Gradually the storm drew away. The rain came down with a rush, persisted with a bruising sound upon the earth and the leaves.

"What a deluge!" exclaimed Louisa.

No one answered her. Olive was falling asleep, and Helena was in no mood to reply. Louisa, disconsolate, lay looking at the black window, nursing a grievance, until she, too, drifted into sleep. Helena was awake; the storm had left her with a settled sense of calamity. She felt bruised. The sound of the heavy rain bruising the ground outside represented her feeling; she could not get rid of the bruised sense of disaster.

She lay wondering what it was, why Siegmund had not written, what could have happened to him. She imagined all of them terrible, and endued with grandeur, for she had kinship with Hedda Gabler.

"But no," she said to herself, "it is impossible anything should have happened to him—I should have known. I should have known the moment his spirit left his body; he would have come to me. But I slept without dreams last night, and to-day I am sure there has been no crisis. It is impossible it should have happened to him: I should have known."

She was very certain that in event of Siegmund's death, she would have received intelligence. She began to consider all the causes which might arise to prevent his writing immediately to her.

"Nevertheless," she said at last, "if I don't hear to-morrow I will go and see."

She had written to him on Monday. If she should receive no answer by Wednesday morning she would return to London. As she was deciding this she went to sleep.

The next day passed without news. Helena was in a state of distress. Her wistfulness touched the other two women very keenly. Louisa waited upon her, was very tender and solicitous. Olive, who was becoming painful by reason of her unsatisfied curiosity, had to be told in part of the state of affairs.

Helena looked up a train. She was quite sure by this time that something fatal awaited her.

The next morning she bade her friends a temporary good-bye, saying she would return in the evening. Immediately the train had gone, Louisa rushed into the little waiting-room of the station and wept. Olive shed tears for sympathy and self-pity. She pitied herself that she should be let in for so dismal a holiday. Louisa suddenly stopped crying and sat up:

"Oh, I know I'm a pig, dear, am I not?" she exclaimed. "Spoiling your holiday. But I couldn't help it, dear, indeed I could not."

"My dear Lou!" cried Olive in tragic contralto, "Don't refrain for my sake. The bargain's made; we can't help what's in the bundle."

The two unhappy women trudged the long miles back from the station to their lodging. Helena sat in the swinging express revolving the same thought like a prayer-wheel. It would be difficult to think of anything more trying than thus sitting motionless in the train, which itself is throbbing and bursting its heart with anxiety, while one waits hour after hour for the blow which falls nearer as the distance lessens. All the time Helena's heart and her consciousness were with Siegmund in London, for she believed he was ill and needed her.

"Promise me," she had said, "if ever I were sick and wanted you, you would come to me."

"I would come to you from hell!" Siegmund had replied.

"And if you were ill—you would let me come to you?" she had added.

"I promise," he answered.

Now Helena believed he was ill, perhaps very ill, perhaps she only could be of any avail. The miles of distance were like hot bars of iron across her breast, and against them it was impossible to strive. The train did what it could.

That day remains as a smear in the record of Helena's life. In it there is no spacing of hours, no lettering of experience, merely a smear of suspense.

Towards six o'clock she alighted, at Surbiton station, deciding that this would be the quickest way of getting to Wimbledon. She paced the platform slowly, as if resigned, but her heart was crying out at the great injustice of delay. Presently the local train came in. She had planned to buy a local paper at Wimbledon, and if from that source she could learn nothing, she would go on to his house and inquire. She had prearranged everything minutely.

After turning the newspaper several times she found what she sought.

"The funeral took place, at two o'clock to-day at Kingston Cemetery, of ——. Deceased was a professor of music, and had just returned from a holiday on the South Coast. . . ."

The paragraph, in a bald twelve lines, told her everything.

"Jury returned a verdict of suicide during temporary insanity. Sympathy was expressed for the widow and children."

Helena stood still on the station for some time, looking at

the print. Then she dropped the paper and wandered into the town, not knowing where she was going.

"That was what I got," she said, months afterwards; "and it was like a brick, it was like a brick."

She wandered on and on, until suddenly she found herself in the grassy lane with only a wire fence bounding her from the open fields on either side, beyond which fields, on the left, she could see Siegmund's house standing florid by the road, catching the western sunlight. Then she stopped, realising where she had come. For some time she stood looking at the house. It was no use her going there; it was of no use her going anywhere; the whole wide world was opened, but in it she had no destination, and there was no direction for her to take. As if marooned in the world, she stood desolate, looking from the house of Siegmund over the fields and the hills. Siegmund was gone; why had he not taken her with him?

The evening was drawing on; it was nearly half-past seven when Helena looked at her watch, remembering Louisa, who would be waiting for her to return to Cornwall.

"I must either go to her, or wire to her. She will be in a fever of suspense," said Helena to herself, and straightway she hurried to catch a tramcar to return to the station. She arrived there at a quarter to eight; there was no train down to Tintagel that night. Therefore she wired the news:

"Siegmund dead. No train to-night. Am going home."

This done, she took her ticket and sat down to wait. By the strength of her will everything she did was reasonable and accurate. But her mind was chaotic.

"It was like a brick," she reiterated, and that brutal simile was the only one she could find, months afterwards, to describe her condition. She felt as if something had crashed into her brain, stunning and maiming her.

As she knocked at the door of home she was apparently quite calm. Her mother opened to her.

"What, are you alone?" cried Mrs. Verden.

"Yes. Louisa did not come up," replied Helena, passing into the dining-room. As if by instinct she glanced on the mantel-piece to see if there was a letter. There was a newspaper cutting. She went forward and took it. It was from one of the London papers.

"Inquest was held to-day upon the body of ——."

Helena read it, read it again, folded it up and put in in her purse. Her mother stood watching her, consumed with distress and anxiety.

"How did you get to know?" she asked.

"I went to Wimbledon and bought a local paper," replied the daughter, in her muted, toneless voice.

"Did you go to the house?" asked the mother sharply.

"No," replied Helena.

"I was wondering whether to send you that paper," said her mother hesitatingly.

Helena did not answer her. She wandered about the house mechanically, looking for something. Her mother followed her, trying very gently to help her.

For some time Helena sat at table in the dining-room staring before her. Her parents moved restlessly in silence, trying not to irritate her by watching her, praying for something to change the fixity of her look. They acknowledged themselves helpless; like children, they felt powerless and forlorn, and were very quiet.

"Won't you go to rest, Nellie?" asked the father at last. He was an unobtrusive, obscure man, whose sympathy was very delicate, whose ordinary attitude was one of gentle irony.

"Won't you go to rest, Nellie?" he repeated.

Helena shivered slightly.

"Do, my dear," her mother pleaded. "Let me take you to bed."

Helena rose. She had a great horror of being fussed or petted, but this night she went dully upstairs, and let her mother help her to undress. When she was in bed the mother stood for some moments looking at her, yearning to beseech her daughter to pray to God; but she dared not. Helena moved with a wild impatience under her mother's gaze.

"Shall I leave you the candle?" said Mrs. Verden.

"No, blow it out," replied the daughter. The mother did so, and immediately left the room, going downstairs to her husband. As she entered the dining-room he glanced up timidly at her. She was a tall, erect woman. Her brown eyes, usually so swift and searching, were haggard with tears that did not fall. He bowed down, obliterating himself. His hands were tightly clasped.

"Will she be all right if you leave her?" he asked.

"We must listen," replied the mother abruptly.

The parents sat silent in their customary places. Presently Mrs. Verden cleared the supper table, sweeping together a few crumbs from the floor in the place where Helena had sat, carefully putting her pieces of broken bread under the loaf to keep moist. Then she sat down again. One could see she was keenly alert to every sound. The father had his hand to his head; he was thinking and praying.

Mrs. Verden suddenly rose, took a box of matches from the mantelpiece, and hurrying her stately, heavy tread, went upstairs. Her husband followed in much trepidation, hovering near the door of his daughter's room. The mother tremblingly lit the candle. Helena's aspect distressed and alarmed her. The girl's face was masked as if in sleep, but occasionally it was crossed by a vivid expression of fear or horror. Her wide eyes showed the active insanity of her brain. From time to time she uttered strange, inarticulate sounds. Her mother held her hands and soothed her. Although she was hardly aware of the mother's presence, Helena was more tranquil. The father went downstairs and turned out the light. He brought his wife a large shawl, which he put on the bed-rail, and silently left the room. Then he went and kneeled down by his own bedside, and prayed.

Mrs. Verden watched her daughter's delirium, and all the time, in a kind of mental chant, invoked the help of God. Once or twice the girl came to herself, drew away her hand on recognising the situation, and turned from her mother, who patiently waited until, upon relapse, she could soothe her daughter again. Helena was glad of her mother's presence, but she could not bear to be looked at.

Towards morning the girl fell naturally asleep. The mother regarded her closely, lightly touched her forehead with her lips, and went away, having blown out the candle. She found her husband kneeling in his nightshirt by the bed. He muttered a few swift syllables, and looked up as she entered.

"She is asleep," whispered the wife hoarsely.

"Is it a—a natural sleep?" hesitated the husband.

"Yes. I think it is. I think she will be all right."

"Thank God!" whispered the father, almost inaudibly.

He held his wife's hand as she lay by his side. He was the comforter. She felt as if now she might cry and take comfort and sleep. He, the quiet, obliterated man, held her hand, taking the responsibility upon himself.

CHAPTER XXX

BEATRICE was careful not to let the blow of Siegmund's death fall with full impact upon her. As it were, she dodged it. She was afraid to meet the accusation of the dead Siegmund, with the sacred jury of memories. When the event summoned her to stand before the bench of her own soul's understanding, she fled, leaving the verdict upon herself eternally suspended.

When the neighbours had come, alarmed by her screaming, she had allowed herself to be taken away from her own house into the home of a neighbour. There the children were brought to her. There she wept, and stared wildly about, as if by instinct seeking to cover her mind with confusion. The good neighbour controlled matters in Siegmund's house, sending for the police, helping to lay out the dead body. Before Vera and Frank came home, and before Beatrice returned to her own place, the bedroom of Siegmund was locked.

Beatrice avoided seeing the body of her husband; she gave him one swift glance, blinded by excitement; she never saw him after his death. She was equally careful to avoid thinking of him. Whenever her thoughts wandered towards a consideration of how he must have felt, what his inner life must have been, during the past six years, she felt herself dilate with terror, and she hastened to invoke protection.

"The children!" she said to herself—"the children. I must live for the children; I must think for the children."

This she did, and with much success. All her tears and her wildness rose from terror and dismay rather than from grief. She managed to fend back a grief that would probably have broken her. Vera was too practical-minded, she had too severe a notion of what ought to be and what ought not, ever to put herself in her father's place and try to understand him. She concerned herself with judging him sorrowfully, exonerating him in part because Helena, that other, was so much more to blame. Frank, as a sentimentalist, wept over the situation, not over the personæ. The children were acutely distressed by the harassing behaviour of the elders, and longed for a restoration of equanimity. By common consent no word was spoken of Siegmund. As soon as possible after the funeral Beatrice moved from South London to Harrow. The memory of Siegmund began to fade rapidly.

Beatrice had had all her life a fancy for a more open, public form of living than that of a domestic circle. She liked strangers about the house; they stimulated her agreeably. Therefore, nine months after the death of her husband, she determined to carry out the scheme of her heart, and take in boarders. She came of a well-to-do family, with whom she had been in disgrace owing to her early romantic but degrading marriage with a young lad who had neither income nor profession. In the tragic, but also sordid, event of his death, the Waltons returned again to the aid of Beatrice. They came hesitatingly, and kept their gloves on. They inquired what she intended to do. She spoke highly and hopefully of her future boarding-house. They found her a couple of hundred pounds, glad to salve their consciences so cheaply. Siegmund's father, a winsome old man with a heart of young gold, was always ready further to diminish his diminished income for the sake of his grandchildren. So Beatrice was set up in a fairly large house in Highgate, was equipped with two maids, and gentlemen were invited to come and board in her house. It was a huge adventure, wherein Beatrice was delighted. Vera was excited and interested; Frank was excited, but doubtful and grudging; the children were excited, elated, wondering. The world was big with promise.

Three gentlemen came, before a month was out, to Beatrice's establishment. She hoped shortly to get a fourth or a fifth. Her plan was to play hostess, and thus bestow on her boarders the inestimable blessing of family life. Breakfast was at eight-thirty, and everyone attended. Vera sat opposite Beatrice, Frank sat on the maternal right hand; Mr. MacWhirter, who was *superior*, sat on the left hand; next him sat Mr. Allport, whose opposite was Mr. Holiday. All were young men of less than thirty years. Mr. MacWhirter was tall, fair, and stoutish; he was very quietly spoken, was humorous and amiable, yet extraordinarily learned. He never, by any chance, gave himself away, maintaining always an absolute reserve amid all his amiability. Therefore Frank would have done anything to win his esteem, while Beatrice was deferential to him. Mr. Allport was tall and broad, and thin as a door; he had also a remarkably small chin. He was naïve, inclined to suffer in the first pangs of disillusionment; nevertheless, he was waywardly humorous, sometimes wistful, sometimes petulant, always gallant. Therefore Vera liked him, whilst Beatrice mothered him. Mr. Holiday was short, very stout, very ruddy, with black hair. He had a disagreeable voice, was vulgar in the grain, but officiously helpful if appeal were made to him. Therefore Frank hated him. Vera liked his handsome, lusty appearance, but resented bitterly his behaviour. Beatrice was proud of the superior and skilful way in which she handled him, clipping him into shape without hurting him.

One evening in July, eleven months after the burial of Sieg-mund, Beatrice went into the dining-room and found Mr. Allport sitting with his elbow on the window-sill, looking out on the garden. It was half-past seven. The red rents between the foliage of the trees showed the sun was setting; a fragrance of evening-scented stocks filtered into the room through the open window; towards the south the moon was budding out of the twilight.

"What, you here all alone!" exclaimed Beatrice, who had just come from putting the children to bed. "I thought you had gone out."

"No—o! What's the use," replied Mr. Allport, turning to look at his landlady, "of going out? There's nowhere to go."

"Oh, come! There's the Heath, and the City—and you must join a tennis club. Now I know just the thing—the club to which Vera belongs."

"Ah, yes! You go down to the City—but there's nothing there—what I mean to say—you want a pal—and even then—well"—he drawled the word—"we-ell, it's merely escaping from yourself—killing time."

"Oh, don't say that!" exclaimed Beatrice. "You want to enjoy life."

"Just so! Ah, just so!" exclaimed Mr. Allport. "But all the same—it's like this—you only get up to the same thing to-morrow. What I mean to say—what's the good, after all? It's merely living because you've got to."

"You are too pessimistic altogether for a young man. I look at it differently myself; yet I'll be bound I have more cause for grumbling. What's the trouble now?"

"We-ell—you can't lay your finger on a thing like that! What I mean to say—it's nothing very definite. But, after all— what is there to do but to hop out of life as quickly as possible? That's the best way."

Beatrice became suddenly grave.

"You talk in that way, Mr. Allport," she said. "You don't think of the others."

"I don't know," he drawled. "What does it matter? Look here—who'd care? What I mean to say—for long?"

"That's all very easy, but it's cowardly," replied Beatrice gravely.

"Nevertheless," said Mr. Allport, "it's true—isn't it?"

"It is not—and I *should* know," replied Beatrice, drawing a cloak of reserve ostentatiously over her face. Mr. Allport looked at her and waited. Beatrice relaxed toward the pessimistic young man.

"Yes," she said, "I call it very cowardly to want to get out of your difficulties in that way. Think what you inflict on other people. You men, you're all selfish. The burden is always left for the women."

"Ah, but then," said Mr. Allport very softly and sympathetically, looking at Beatrice's black dress, "I've no one depending on *me*."

"No—you haven't—but you've a mother and sister. The women always have to bear the brunt."

Mr. Allport looked at Beatrice, and found her very pathetic.

"Yes, they do rather," he replied sadly, tentatively waiting.

"My husband——" began Beatrice. The young man waited. "My husband was one of your sort: he ran after trouble, and when he'd found it—he couldn't carry it off—and left it—to me."

Mr. Allport looked at her very sympathetically.

"You don't mean it!" he exclaimed softly. "Surely he didn't——?"

Beatrice nodded, and turned aside her face.

"Yes," she said. "I know what it is to bear that kind of thing—and it's no light thing, I can assure you."

There was a suspicion of tears in her voice.

"And when was this, then—that he——?" asked Mr. Allport, almost with reverence.

"Only last year," replied Beatrice.

Mr. Allport made a sound expressing astonishment and dismay. Little by little Beatrice told him so much: Her husband had got entangled with another woman. She herself had put up with it for a long time. At last she had brought matters to a crisis, declaring what she should do. He had killed himself—hanged himself—and left her penniless. Her people, who were very wealthy, had done for her as much as she would allow them. She and Frank and Vera had done the rest. She did not mind for herself; it was for Frank and Vera, who should be now enjoying their careless youth, that her heart was heavy.

There was silence for a time. Mr. Allport murmured his sympathy, and sat overwhelmed with respect for this little woman who was unbroken by tragedy. The bell rang in the kitchen. Vera entered.

"Oh, what a nice smell! Sitting in the dark, Mother?"

"I was just trying to cheer up Mr. Allport; he is very despondent."

"Pray do not overlook me," said Mr. Allport, rising and bowing.

"Well! I did not see you! Fancy your sitting in the twilight chatting with the mater. You must have been an unscrupulous bore, maman."

"On the contrary," replied Mr. Allport, "Mrs. MacNair has been so good as to bear with me making a fool of myself."

"In what way?" asked Vera sharply.

"Mr. Allport is so despondent. I think he must be in love," said Beatrice playfully.

"Unfortunately, I am not—or at least I am not yet aware of it," said Mr. Allport, bowing slightly to Vera.

She advanced and stood in the bay of the window, her skirt touching the young man's knees. She was tall and graceful. With her hands clasped behind her back she stood looking up at the moon, now white upon the richly darkening sky.

"Don't look at the moon, Miss MacNair, it's all rind," said Mr. Allport in melancholy mockery. "Somebody's bitten all the meat out of our slice of moon, and left us nothing but peel."

"It certainly does look like a piece of melon-shell—one portion," replied Vera.

"Never mind, Miss MacNair," he said. "Whoever got the slice found it raw, I think."

"Oh, I don't know," she said. "But isn't it a beautiful evening? I will just go and see if I can catch the primroses opening."

"What! primroses?" he exclaimed.

"Evening primroses—there are some."

"Are there?" he said in surprise. Vera smiled to herself.

"Yes, come and look," she said.

The young man rose with alacrity.

Mr. Holiday came into the dining-room whilst they were down the garden.

"What, nobody in!" they heard him exclaim.

"There is Holiday," murmured Mr. Allport resentfully.

Vera did not answer. Holiday came to the open window, attracted by the fragrance.

"Ho! that's where you are!" he cried in his nasal tenor, which annoyed Vera's trained ear. She wished she had not been wearing a white dress to betray herself.

"What have you got?" he asked.

"Nothing in particular," replied Mr. Allport.

Mr. Holiday sniggered.

"Oh, well, if it's nothing particular and private——" said Mr. Holiday, and with that he leaped over the window-sill and went to join them.

"Curst fool!" muttered Mr. Allport. "I beg your pardon," he added swiftly to Vera.

"Have you ever noticed, Mr. Holiday," asked Vera, as if very friendly, "how awfully tantalising these flowers are? They won't open while you're looking."

"No," sniggered he, "I don't blame 'em. Why should they give themselves away any more than you do? You won't open while you're watched." He nudged Allport facetiously with his elbow.

After supper, which was late and badly served, the young men were in poor spirits. Mr. MacWhirter retired to read. Mr. Holiday sat picking his teeth; Mr. Allport begged Vera to play the piano.

"Oh, the piano is not my instrument; mine was the violin, but I do not play now," she replied.

"But you will begin again," pleaded Mr. Allport.

"No, never!" she said decisively. Allport looked at her closely. The family tragedy had something to do with her decision, he was sure. He watched her interestedly.

"Mother used to play——" she began.

"Vera!" said Beatrice reproachfully.

"Let us have a song," suggested Mr. Holiday.

"Mr. Holiday wishes to sing, Mother," said Vera, going to the music-rack.

"Nay—I—it's not me," Holiday began.

" 'The Village Blacksmith'," said Vera, pulling out the piece. Holiday advanced. Vera glanced at her mother.

"But I have not touched the piano for—for years, I am sure," protested Beatrice.

"You can play beautifully," said Vera.

Beatrice accompanied the song. Holiday sang atrociously. Allport glared at him. Vera remained very calm.

At the end Beatrice was overcome by the touch of the piano. She went out abruptly.

"Mother has suddenly remembered that to-morrow's jellies are not made," laughed Vera.

Allport looked at her, and was sad.

When Beatrice returned, Holiday insisted she should play again. She would have found it more difficult to refuse than to comply.

Vera retired early, soon to be followed by Allport and Holiday. At half-past ten Mr. MacWhirter came in with his ancient volume. Beatrice was studying a cookery-book.

"You, too, at the midnight lamp!" exclaimed MacWhirter politely.

"Ah, I am only looking for a pudding for to-morrow," Beatrice replied.

"We shall feel hopelessly in debt if you look after us so well," smiled the young man ironically.

"I must look after you," said Beatrice.

"You do—wonderfully. I feel that we owe you large debts of gratitude." The meals were generally late, and something was always wrong.

"Because I scan a list of puddings?" smiled Beatrice uneasily.

"For the puddings themselves, and all your good things. The piano, for instance. That was very nice indeed." He bowed to her.

"Did it disturb you? But one does not hear very well in the study."

"I opened the door," said MacWhirter, bowing again.

"It is not fair," said Beatrice. "I am clumsy now—clumsy. I once could play."

"You play excellently. Why that 'once could'?" said MacWhirter.

"Ah, you are amiable. My old master would have said differently," she replied.

"We," said MacWhirter, "are humble amateurs, and to us you are more than excellent."

"Good old Monsieur Fannière, how he would scold me! He said I would not take my talent out of the napkin. He would quote me the New Testament. I always think Scripture false in French, do not you?"

"Er—my acquaintance with modern languages is not extensive, I regret to say."

"No? I was brought up at a convent school near Rouen."

"Ah—that would be very interesting."

"Yes, but I was there six years, and the interest wears off everything."

"Alas!" assented MacWhirter, smiling.

"Those times were very different from these," said Beatrice.

"I should think so," said MacWhirter, waxing grave and sympathetic.

CHAPTER XXXI

In the same month of July, not yet a year after Siegmund's death, Helena sat on the top of the tramcar with Cecil Byrne. She was dressed in blue linen, for the day had been hot. Byrne was holding up to her a yellow-backed copy of "Einsame Menschen", and she was humming the air of the Russian folksong printed on the front page, frowning, nodding with her head, and beating time with her hand to get the rhythm of the song. She turned suddenly to him, and shook her head, laughing.

"I can't get it—it's no use. I think it's the swinging of the car prevents me getting the time," she said.

"These little outside things always come a victory over you," he laughed.

"Do they?" she replied, smiling, bending her head against the wind. It was six o'clock in the evening. The sky was quite overcast, after a dim, warm day. The tramcar was leaping along southwards. Out of the corners of his eyes Byrne watched the crisp morsels of hair shaken on her neck by the wind.

"Do you know," she said, "it feels rather like rain."

"Then," said he calmly, but turning away to watch the people below on the pavement, "you certainly ought not to be out."

"I ought not," she said, "for I'm totally unprovided."

Neither, however, had the slightest intention of turning back.

Presently they descended from the car, and took a road leading uphill off the highway. Trees hung over one side, whilst on the other side stood a few villas with lawns upraised. Upon one of these lawns two great sheep-dogs rushed and stood at the brink of the grassy declivity, at some height above the road, barking and urging boisterously. Helena and Byrne stood still to watch them. One dog was grey, as is usual, the other pale fawn. They raved extravagantly at the two pedestrians. Helena laughed at them.

"They are——" she began, in her slow manner.

"Villa sheep-dogs baying us wolves," he continued.

"No," she said, "they remind me of Fasner and Fasolt."

"Fasolt? They *are* like that. I wonder if they really dislike us."

"It appears so," she laughed.

"Dogs generally chum up to me," he said.

Helena began suddenly to laugh. He looked at her inquiringly.

"I remember," she said, still laughing, "at Knockholt—you—a half-grown lamb—a dog—in procession." She marked the position of the three with her finger.

"What an ass I must have looked!" he said.

"Sort of silent Pied Piper," she laughed.

"Dogs do follow me like that, though," he said.

"They did Siegmund," she said.

"Ah!" he exclaimed.

"I remember they had for a long time a little brown dog that followed him home."

"Ah!" he exclaimed.

"I remember, too," she said, "a little black-and-white kitten that followed me. Mater *would not* have it in—she would not. And I remember finding it, a few days after, dead in the road. I don't think I ever quite forgave my mater that."

"More sorrow over one kitten brought to destruction than over all the sufferings of men," he said.

She glanced at him and laughed. He was smiling ironically.

"For the latter, you see," she replied, "I am not responsible."
As they neared the top of the hill a few spots of rain
fell.

"You know," said Helena, "if it begins it will continue all
night. Look at that!"

She pointed to the great dark reservoir of cloud ahead.

"Had we better go back?" he asked.

"Well, we will go on and find a thick tree; then we can
shelter till we see how it turns out. We are not far from the
cars here."

They walked on and on. The raindrops fell more thickly,
then thinned away.

"It is exactly a year to-day," she said, as they walked on the
round shoulder of the down with an oak-wood on the left hand.
"Exactly!'

"What anniversary is it, then?" he inquired.

"Exactly a year to-day, Siegmund and I walked here—by the
day, Thursday. We went through the larch-wood. Have you
ever been through the larch-wood?"

"No."

"We will go, then," she said.

"History repeats itself," he remarked.

"How?" she asked calmly.

He was pulling at the heads of the cocksfoot grass as he
walked.

"I see no repetition," she added.

"No," he exclaimed bitingly; "you are right!"

They went on in silence. As they drew near a farm they
saw the men unloading a last wagon of hay on to a very
brown stack. He sniffed the air. Though he was angry, he
spoke.

"They got that hay rather damp," he said. "Can't you smell
it—like hot tobacco and sandal-wood?"

"What, is that the stack?" she asked.

"Yes, it's always like that when it's picked damp."

The conversation was restarted, but did not flourish. When
they turned on to a narrow path by the side of the field he
went ahead. Leaning over the hedge, he pulled three sprigs of
honeysuckle, yellow as butter, full of scent; then he waited for
her. She was hanging her head, looking in the hedge-bottom.
He presented her with the flowers without speaking. She bent
forward, inhaled the rich fragrance, and looked up at him over

the blossoms with her beautiful, beseeching blue eyes. He smiled gently to her.

"Isn't it nice?" he said. "Aren't they fine bits?"

She took them without answering, and put one piece carefully in her dress. It was quite against her rule to wear a flower. He took his place by her side.

"I always like the gold-green of cut fields," he said. "They seem to give off sunshine even when the sky's greyer than a tabby cat."

She laughed, instinctively putting out her hand towards the glowing field on her right.

They entered the larch-wood. There the chill wind was changed into sound. Like a restless insect he hovered about her, like a butterfly whose antennæ flicker and twitch sensitively as they gather intelligence, touching the aura, as it were, of the female. He was exceedingly delicate in his handling of her.

The path was cut windingly through the lofty, dark, and closely serried trees, which vibrated like chords under the soft bow of the wind. Now and again he would look down passages between the trees—narrow pillared corridors, dusky as if webbed across with mist. All round was a twilight, thickly populous with slender, silent trunks. Helena stood still, gazing up at the tree-tops where the bow of the wind was drawn, causing slight, perceptible quivering. Byrne walked on without her. At a bend in the path he stood, with his hand on the roundness of a larch-trunk, looking back at her, a blue fleck in the brownness of congregated trees. She moved very slowly down the path.

"I might as well not exist, for all she is aware of me," he said to himself bitterly. Nevertheless, when she drew near he said brightly:

"Have you noticed how the thousands of dry twigs between the trunks make a brown mist, a brume?"

She looked at him suddenly as if interrupted.

"H'm? Yes, I see what you mean."

She smiled at him, because of his bright boyish tone and manner.

"That's the larch fog," he laughed.

"Yes," she said, "you see it in pictures. I had not noticed it before."

He shook the tree on which his hand was laid.

"It laughs through its teeth," he said, smiling, playing with everything he touched.

As they went along she caught swiftly at her hat; then she stooped, picking up a hat-pin of twined silver. She laughed to herself as if pleased by a coincidence.

"Last year," she said, "the larch-fingers stole both my pins—the same ones."

He looked at her, wondering how much he was filling the place of a ghost with warmth. He thought of Siegmund, and seemed to see him swinging down the steep bank out of the wood exactly as he himself was doing at the moment, with Helena stepping carefully behind. He always felt a deep sympathy and kinship with Siegmund; sometimes he thought he hated Helena.

They had emerged at the head of a shallow valley—one of those wide hollows in the North Downs that are like a great length of tapestry held loosely by four people. It was raining. Byrne looked at the dark blue dots rapidly appearing on the sleeves of Helena's dress. They walked on a little way. The rain increased. Helena looked about for shelter.

"Here," said Byrne—"here is our tent—a black tartar's—ready pitched."

He stooped under the low boughs of a very large yew tree that stood just back from the path. She crept after him. It was really a very good shelter. Byrne sat on the ledge of a root, Helena beside him. He looked under the flap of the black branches down the valley. The grey rain was falling steadily; the dark hollow under the tree was immersed in the monotonous sound of it. In the open, where the bright young corn shone intense with wet green, was a fold of sheep. Exposed in a large pen on the hillside, they were moving restlessly; now and again came the "tong-ting-tong" of a sheep-bell. First the grey creatures huddled in the high corner, then one of them descended and took shelter by the growing corn lowest down. The rest followed, bleating and pushing each other in their anxiety to reach the place of desire, which was no whit better than where they stood before.

"That's like us all," said Byrne whimsically. "We're all penned out on a wet evening, but we think, if only we could get where someone else is, it would be deliciously cosy."

Helena laughed swiftly, as she always did when he became whimsical and fretful. He sat with his head bent down, smiling with his lips, but his eyes melancholy. She put her hand out to him. He took it without apparently observing it, folding his own hand over it, and unconsciously increasing the pressure.

"You are cold," he said.

"Only my hands, and they usually are," she replied gently.

"And mine are generally warm."

"I know that," she said. "It's almost the only warmth I get now—your hands. They really are wonderfully warm and close-touching."

"As good as a baked potato," he said.

She pressed his hand, scolding him for his mockery.

"So many calories per week—isn't that how we manage it?" he asked. "On credit?"

She put her other hand on his, as if beseeching him to forgo his irony, which hurt her. They sat silent for some time. The sheep broke their cluster, and began to straggle back to the upper side of the pen.

"Tong-tong, tong," went the forlorn bell. The rain waxed louder.

Byrne was thinking of the previous week. He had gone to Helena's home to read German with her as usual. She wanted to understand Wagner in his own language.

In each of the arm-chairs, reposing across the arms, was a violin-case. He had sat down on the edge of one seat in front of the sacred fiddle. Helena had come quickly and removed the violin.

"I shan't knock it—it is all right," he had said, protesting.

This was Siegmund's violin, which Helena had managed to purchase, and Byrne was always ready to yield its precedence.

"It was all right," he repeated.

"But you were not," she had replied gently.

Since that time his heart had beat quick with excitement. Now he sat in a little storm of agitation, of which nothing was betrayed by his gloomy, pondering expression, but some of which was communicated to Helena by the increasing pressure of his hand, which adjusted itself delicately in a stronger and stronger stress over her fingers and palm. By some movement he became aware that her hand was uncomfortable. He relaxed. She sighed, as if restless and dissatisfied. She wondered what he was thinking of. He smiled quietly.

"The Babes in the Wood," he teased.

Helena laughed, with a sound of tears. In the tree overhead

some bird began to sing, in spite of the rain, a broken evening song.

"That little beggar sees it's a hopeless case, so he reminds us of heaven. But if he's going to cover us with yew-leaves, he's set himself a job."

Helena laughed again, and shivered. He put his arm round her, drawing her nearer his warmth. After this new and daring move neither spoke for a while.

"The rain continues," he said.

"And will do," she added, laughing.

"Quite content," he said.

The bird overhead chirruped loudly again.

" 'Strew on us roses, roses,' " quoted Byrne, adding after a while, in wistful mockery: " 'And never a sprig of yew'—eh?"

Helena made a small sound of tenderness and comfort for him, and weariness for herself. She let herself sink a little closer against him.

"Shall it not be so—no yew?" he murmured.

He put his left hand, with which he had been breaking larch-twigs, on her chilled wrist. Noticing that his fingers were dirty, he held them up.

"I shall make marks on you," he said.

"They will come off," she replied.

"Yes, we come clean after everything. Time scrubs all sorts of scars off us."

"Some scars don't seem to go," she smiled.

And she held out her other arm, which had been pressed warm against his side. There, just above the wrist, was the red sun-inflammation from last year. Byrne regarded it gravely.

"But it's wearing off—even that," he said wistfully.

Helena put her arms round him under his coat. She was cold. He felt a hot wave of joy suffuse him. Almost immediately she released him, and took off her hat.

"That is better," he said.

"I was afraid of the pins," said she.

"I've been dodging them for the last hour," he said, laughing, as she put her arms under his coat again for warmth.

She laughed, and, making a small, moaning noise, as if of weariness and helplessness, she sank her head on his chest. He put down his cheek against hers.

"I want rest and warmth," she said, in her dull tones.

"All right!" he murmured.

THE POLYTECHNIC OF WALES
LIBRARY
TREFOREST

Library Services

University of
South Wales
Prifysgol
De Cymru